PRAISE FOR

FINDING MIGHTY

Children's Choice Book Award finalist
Junior Library Guild selection
ILA Children's Choices Reading List

"Fast-paced and intricately plotted, Chari's mystery is a rare achievement."—*Booklist*

"This novel contains all the right elements for an intriguing adventure."—*School Library Journal*

"A quick, agreeable caper."—*Kirkus Reviews*

"Notes of blended cultural identity and of being American ring subtly through this finely crafted middle-grade mystery."
—Uma Krishnaswami, writer and faculty member, Vermont College of Fine Arts

"Well worth every young mystery reader's time."—Timothy Capehart, librarian and author of *Shadowangel*

SHEELA CHARI

AMULET BOOKS • NEW YORK

FINDING
MIGHTY

PUBLISHER'S NOTE: This is a work of fiction. Names, characters, places, and incidents are either the product of the author's imagination or used fictitiously, and any resemblance to actual persons, living or dead, business establishments, events, or locales is entirely coincidental.

The Library of Congress has cataloged the hardcover edition as follows:
Names: Chari, Sheela.
Title: Finding Mighty / Sheela Chari.
Description: New York : Amulet Books, 2017. | Summary: "Along the train lines north of New York City, twelve-year-old neighbors Myla and Peter search for the link between Myla's necklace and the disappearance of Peter's brother, Randall. Thrown into a world of parkour, graffiti, and diamond-smuggling, Myla and Peter encounter a band of thugs who are after the same thing as Randall. Can Myla and Peter find Randall before it's too late, and their shared family secrets threaten to destroy them all?"—Provided by publisher.
Identifiers: LCCN 2016042022 (print) | LCCN 2016052878 (ebook) | ISBN 9781419722967 (hardback) | ISBN 9781683350613 (ebook)
Subjects: | CYAC: Mystery and detective stories. | Family life—New York (State)—Fiction. | Graffiti—Fiction. | Parkour—Fiction. | East Indian Americans—Fiction. | Racially mixed people—Fiction. | Dobbs Ferry (N.Y.)–Fiction. | BISAC: JUVENILE FICTION / Family / General (see also headings under Social Issues). | JUVENILE FICTION / Lifestyles / City & Town Life. | JUVENILE FICTION / Art & Architecture.
Classification: LCC PZ7.C37368 Fin 2017 (print) | LCC PZ7.C37368 (ebook) | DDC [Fic]—dc23
LC record available at https://lccn.loc.gov/2016042022

Paperback ISBN 978-1-4197-3479-3

Book design by Pamela Notarantonio

Printed and bound in U.S.A.
10 9 8 7 6 5 4 3 2 1

ABRAMS The Art of Books
195 Broadway, New York, NY 10007
abramsbooks.com

for Keerthana and Meera

for siblings everywhere

Prologue MYLA

BACK WHEN I WAS FIVE, I MET PETER FOR THE FIRST time. We were at Margaret's house for dinner, long before she moved to Vermont. There were other kids there, like Peter's brother and mine, but Peter was the only one who didn't talk. He kept close to his mom, who had the longest black hair I ever saw, with butterfly clips in it, and I wondered if she was Indian like us.

Peter sat next to me at the table. He was thin, and his hair was curly and dark as black licorice. Sometimes his mom gave him stuff on his plate like potatoes or a bread roll, but mostly Peter sat without eating.

After they left, everyone shook their heads like they were sorry.

Sorry for what? I wondered. There wasn't much I was sorry about, not at the age of five.

Then I heard the story of what happened to Peter's dad. I don't think I was meant to hear, but the adults got to talking and didn't pay attention to what the kids were listening to. Years later when I saw Peter again, I'd forgotten Margaret's party. I'd forgotten thinking his hair was like black licorice. But I didn't forget what happened to his dad. There are some things you never forget.

Maybe it was a coincidence, Peter moving to Dobbs Ferry. Maybe Margaret was the common thread. Or maybe, as Peter says, it was all a kind of magic. For him, it started with the duffel bag. For me, it was the necklace. Actually, it started further back with Rose, and what she did to hide her secret. But I'd have to imagine that part. Instead it's better to tell what we do know, the part that happened to us.

1 MYLA

AT THE END OF AUGUST BEFORE SIXTH GRADE started, Cheetah broke my bed. My best friend, Ana, and I were in the kitchen eating ice cream when we heard a loud crash. We ran upstairs, our cones dripping chocolate mint, and found my nine-year-old brother sprawled on the caved-in mattress, a big, stupid grin on his face. "Sorry," he said, but he wasn't.

Mom said, "It was just waiting to happen."

If you saw my bed, you'd understand why. When I was young, I was afraid to sleep on a real one. So I slept on a mattress on the floor. I liked that fine, until two years ago when I woke up eye to eye with a long, black spider on my pillow. Then I was done with sleeping on the floor. I took a sheet of plywood from the garage, plus some leftover cinder blocks, and I built myself a low bed. I even made a headboard and painted it white with the spray paint we used on our fence.

Dad said proudly, "Myla, my engineer." That's because he's a math teacher, and math people are into building things.

Mom was different. "What if it breaks?" But it didn't. It held up for two years, until my dorky brother jumped on it and snapped the plywood in two. So now Mom was adamant. "It's time you had a real bed, Myla. I didn't go back to work so my children could sleep on cinder blocks."

I don't know what the big deal was. But nothing could

change her mind, so on Sunday we headed to a furniture store in Yonkers where we bought our dining table last year. I invited Ana because we were going to Spice afterward, and the tandoori pizza there was so good, it was worth buying a bed I didn't want.

In the car, Ana leafed through a magazine she'd brought. "Look at this cool bed. It has curtains hanging over it from the ceiling."

"It's ugly," Cheetah said. "Plus it's too tall for Myla. She'd be scared."

"No, I wouldn't." I gave him a shove. Cheetah was always saying the wrong thing.

"And it isn't ugly," Ana said. "It's beautiful." She tucked her pale hair behind her ears. Ana is Norwegian on both sides—her grandparents are from Norway—but her parents grew up in Seattle. Which makes her American like me.

"I still don't get why you were jumping on my bed," I said. My brother was always destroying my stuff, like opening my Harry Potter books too wide until the spines broke, or using up all the ink in my Sharpies. I poked him but he still didn't answer. For a minute, I thought he was hiding something. But what? Everything he did was an open book. Not like me.

I pulled out my journal from my backpack. It was small, and I used it to record things. Sometimes I write down what's going on, like, "Cheetah's jump breaks my bed." Or I jot down what I see, like a billboard or a piece of graffiti. Once I drew High Bridge, because even though I'm scared of bridges, I liked the way the arches came down to meet the highway, like the legs of gigantic Transformer robots.

Ana records things, too—but she doesn't keep a journal—she uses her phone to take pictures. She doesn't care about signs or bridges or words. She takes pictures of horses. She's crazy about them. She goes riding on Saturdays at a stable on the other side of the Hudson River, and that's where she takes lots of pictures. She says she wants to be a trainer someday, or a professional horse photographer. I don't know yet what I want to be. I know it has to do with words, and building things with my hands.

"*Mighty*," my brother read from a highway wall, as we took the exit to St. Vincent Ave. So I wrote it down in round letters, even if I already have *Mighty* in my journal, because it's my favorite.

St. Vincent Ave is the ugliest and most beautiful street in the world. Dad says it starts in the Bronx and ends in the town of Yonkers. We go there to eat at Spice or to shop for furniture. The stores are close together, with rolling metal gates that pull down when it's time to close. Between windows, the walls are marked with graffiti. Not the quick words you see on the highway, but large, oversize letters, or characters drawn like cartoons. Only they're not funny. They're serious, telling the story of something I don't know.

My mom disagrees. She's an urban designer, which means she helps to decide where buildings go and how people use them. So something like graffiti drives her crazy. She's glad we don't have much of it in Dobbs Ferry. But I wish we did. When we come to St. Vincent Ave, I end up with so many new words in my notebook.

Today we squeezed our Subaru into the last parking space. We were lucky, because the rest of St. Vincent Ave was closed off. All along the sidewalks, there were booths lined with people selling things. I could smell the smoky scent of barbecued corn and refried beans cooking nearby.

"It's a street fair!" Ana said, excited.

"Can we look around?" Cheetah begged. "Can-we-can-we?"

My parents agreed as long as we made our way to the furniture store. So we walked along St. Vincent Ave, Ana and me on one side, my parents and Cheetah on the other. At a table with hats and scarves, Ana took a picture of me in a tie-dyed cap with an orange flower on it, which looked ridiculous over my big, frizzy hair. I could see my shadow next to hers on the ground, hers lean and tall, mine short and round with hair sticking out from under the hat.

While Ana tried on the same cap, I drifted to the next table, where there was a man and an elderly woman selling jewelry. I wouldn't have noticed them except they were arguing, their voices low and tight, like they were yelling with the volume turned down.

"How can you wear that?" asked the man, his face craggy like the side of a cliff. "Remember the train station. It's not safe."

Wear what? Then I noticed a brightly colored necklace around the woman's neck.

"I had to wear *something*," she said. "And a person selling jewelry can't be wearing an apron. Besides, you've been obsessing over it like a fool for years. I have a mind to sell it away today."

The man almost leaped out of his chair. "Don't you dare, Ma! Put it away!"

For a moment, she didn't say anything as they glared at each other, like two burning coals in our backyard grill. I was fascinated by their game of chicken. Who would win?

The woman finally gave in. "Fine," she said. She undid the necklace and laid it on the table. "Now, why don't you run along and get me some lemonade?"

He let out his breath and ruffled his hair up so that it reminded me of a bird's nest. "I'll do that, Ma. But put it away, okay?" Then he stood up, and he was like a tall building blocking the sun. But then, anyone next to me seemed like a tall building. He peered at me for a moment, his eyes gray against his olive-toned face, and walked away.

The woman was watching me, too, as I stood at the edge of the table, next to a tray of earrings. "All completely handmade," she said, trying to sound friendly, and not like she'd been fighting with her son a few seconds ago. "They're made from healing crystals, great for health."

I nodded. While she spoke, I stared at the necklace on the table. I knew I shouldn't ask. She probably didn't mean what she said to her son. "Is that for sale?" I said.

She saw what I was looking at and glanced down the street. I guessed what she was doing. She was checking to see if her son was coming back. After a moment, she picked up the necklace, the one she had been wearing a minute ago, and held it out to me.

I took it from her. I wanted to know what the big story was, why the craggy-faced man was so angry in the first place. It was a pendant the size of a checker piece, on a leather string. At first, I thought it was just a flower, but then I saw something in the middle, a symbol bordered by purple-and-pink petals.

"I've seen this before," I said suddenly. "I know someone with the same necklace."

"Is that so?" asked the woman mildly. "It was popular for some time."

I remembered Margaret wearing hers when she and Allie lived next door. But what was so special about this necklace? I turned it over. In tiny letters, a single word was etched: *keeper*.

"Handmade enamel, silver plated on the back. It's an Indian peace sign. Indian like you. You're from India, aren't you?"

I nodded, though I hated being asked that. Like, Ana never gets asked if she's from Norway. So I added, "My parents were born there, but I've lived in Dobbs Ferry my whole life."

The woman brightened. "Oh, I used to live near Dobbs."

We talked about the construction going on with the Aqueduct Trail and the waterfront. I let her do most of the talking while I looked at the pendant. I was never good at figuring out what to wear. I wasn't pretty like Ana or stylish like my mom. But I could picture myself with this necklace. And maybe some of the girls stopping me in the hall at school to say they liked it. Even if that kind of thing never happened to me.

"How much?" I asked. I could still see the storm in her eyes left by her son. But would she do it? Would she sell me the necklace in spite of him?

Her face puckered. Then she said, "Seeing you're from Dobbs, I'll let you have it for five."

Five! Didn't she say handmade? It was a good price. "I only have four," I said.

"Huh. A girl with a budget," she said gravely. "You know what it is, right?"

What it is? Wasn't it just a necklace? "It says 'keeper' on it. Is that the name of the person who made it?" Maybe it was the name of her son. Though he didn't look like a Keeper to me.

She shook her head. "It's a finders necklace. You know, finders keepers? Every necklace has one of those two words on the back. It tells you what sort of person you are. This one says you're somebody who keeps things."

"Oh." That didn't seem like much to me.

By now, Ana had joined me, and she was wearing the tie-dyed cap. Behind her, I saw something else. The craggy-faced man was coming back.

The woman must have seen him, too, because she said, "You have a deal. Four it is."

"Wait up, Myla," Ana called as I hurried across the street, just as the man reached the table. I could feel his eyes on me, but what was he going to do? I'd bought the necklace, and now it was mine.

At the furniture store, Mom saw the necklace I was wearing. "Where did you get that?"

"A woman sold it to me for four dollars. Margaret has the same one. Do you remember?"

My parents did not.

"She said it's an Indian peace sign," I said. "Indian like us."

Dad looked more carefully. "I see," he said, pushing up his glasses. "It's an Om."

"What's an Om?" Ana asked.

"A two-letter word," Cheetah said.

Dad pointed to the pendant. "It's this symbol. I suppose you could call it a peace sign. But it's more than that." He explained how in yoga, the sound our mouth makes when we say Om is very important. I guess he knew because he'd been doing yoga for as long as I could remember.

"But it's not the only two-letter word," Cheetah went on. "There's 'ai,' which is a kind of sloth. And 'xu,' which was a coin used in Vietnam. And in Scrabble, you can—"

"Stop," I said. Cheetah was a spelling whiz, which meant we had to quit family game night because he always beat everyone at Scrabble. But that didn't stop him from *talking* about it.

"What about 'at'?" Ana asked. "And 'it'? There are lots of two-letter words."

"Yeah, but those are *common*," Cheetah said.

Ana laughed. "You're hilarious."

She was always saying that to my brother, even though I didn't think he was particularly funny. It was weird how they got along so easily, when I hardly spoke to Ana's little sister.

I fingered the cool back of my necklace. "Om," I said to myself, testing out the sound in my mouth. It felt rich. Like a piece of chocolate.

Inside the store, the salesman showed us a platform bed eighteen inches above the floor, six inches taller than my cinder blocks. Mom said that was "nothing," even though you'd think for an urban designer six inches was *everything*. Like falling into the space between the train and the platform. Six inches could mean the difference between life and death.

"Myla, you brought a *ruler*?" Ana asked, watching as I measured.

"She's scared of sleeping on a bed," Cheetah explained to the salesman.

I gave him a shove when my parents weren't watching. By now, I was tired of looking like a freak, so I said yes to the eighteen-inch-high bed. Then I went to the bathroom.

As I washed my hands, I studied my reflection with the necklace on. Would people finally notice me because of it? I've thought about it before, about being noticed, because I'm short and I have thin eyebrows and a thin nose, and I'm not the most smiley person. My hair is frizzy and isn't a true Indian black like my parents', more a dark brown with highlights you only see in the sun. That sounds interesting, but most people don't notice the highlights—or me.

Just then, the door to the bathroom opened. I thought it was Ana, but it wasn't her. Or even a girl. It was the craggy-faced man from the jewelry table.

"That necklace," he said, his voice like gravel. "I want it back."

2 PETER

AT THE BEGINNING OF SUMMER, MA BOUGHT Randall and me each a pair of Air Jordans. She got them off the street near St. Vincent Ave, and probably they were fakes, but when you put them on, you hoped they weren't. Like, maybe the dude was selling them cheap because he needed the cash. There was something sweet about the sound of the new rubber on the sidewalk, the way it squeaked when I stopped in my tracks. I wore my Jordans all summer, even when my feet got sweaty and the shadows of Michael Jordan on the sides cracked. I wore them because Randall did, and it was one way of telling the world we were brothers—though Randall probably didn't see it that way.

The Saturday night before he disappeared, Randall slipped his Jordans on and went out the fire escape to meet with his crew. But when I tried to follow him like I always did, he stopped me.

"I can't have you tripping on your face and getting hurt," he said, standing on the fire escape, while I was at the window.

"I don't do that," I said, insulted.

"Your feet are too big. That makes you a clown. Stay home, clown."

"But you need me. How else will you climb back up?"

"I've got my brothers," he said.

When he said that, it stabbed me inside my chest. "I'm your brother."

"You're a clown."

I tried to think of something to say that would stop him from leaving without me. "What's in the duffel bag?" I asked. I was talking about the blue canvas bag Randall kept locked and hidden under his bed, which he went through at night when he thought I was asleep. I knew the duffel bag had belonged to our pop. And our pop was dead.

"None of your business," Randall said. "Go back to sleep, Petey." Then he leaped down to the sidewalk below.

I watched him. Then I thought, why do I always have to listen to him? So I didn't. I went out the window the way he did. The metal rungs of the fire escape were bumpy with rust under my hands. At the end of the steps, I jumped. I hit the ground hard, like I always did, scuffing up my knees. But so far I'd never broken my legs.

Ten minutes later, Randall reached the train station, with me twenty paces away. I hid behind a trash can. Up ahead I saw all the guys—Skinny, MaxD, Nike, and the two Points, dressed in dark clothes with scarves around their faces. There was no moon, and barely any light except from the platform. The guys had a small convo and got to it. I heard the sound of spraying.

Over the summer, I'd watched Randall paint. First he was *Speed*. Then he was *Mighty*, the name everyone now called him. He always used orange, and his letters filled up the sides of empty parking lots, bus yards, and the Saw Mill Parkway. But now at the end of a long, hot summer, his crew had finally hit the train station. I heard Randall say it was where they could reach the most people. But I didn't get who they wanted to reach, or what they were trying to say.

Whenever Randall went out with his crew, the next morning he acted like nothing happened. The spray paint was gone, the duffel bag out of sight, and he was a just a regular kid. But this night it all came to an end. Maybe they didn't have an ear for it, but from where I crouched behind the trash can, I heard it loud and clear.

The platform walls were no good for them, not big enough or bad enough. Which was why the crew had jumped down next to the tracks, near the third rail with all those warning signs blazing everywhere about DANGER and DEATH BY ELECTROCUTION. If that wasn't enough to give you the creeps, now there was the Train of Death rounding the bend.

Randall was spraying big strokes of orange when I first started yelling. Soon as I did, Skinny, MaxD, Nike, and the two Points looked up. They saw me jumping up and down, and then they themselves heard the Train of Death. That got them going, and they leaped over the third rail, hoisting themselves onto the platform next to me. But what was Randall the crazy fool doing?

My brother was putting the finishing touches on a new tag: *Om*. It was a word I'd never seen. Randall glanced at us, then at a rat that ran past him, wobbling along the third rail like it was running for its life. Randall must have heard the train, but he looked and looked at the rat like all the answers lay in that stupid rodent. Meanwhile, we could see the lights of the train.

What in the world was Randall waiting for?

"Jump the rail, man," everyone was yelling at him.

Randall's face was a sea of concentration, and I could feel myself straining, as if I was willing him with every bone in my body to jump. Then I caught my breath as he did. Not over the third rail, but *on top of it*, both feet planted at the same time, balancing on the rubber soles of his Air Jordans. Then he leaped again, flying through the air and landing squarely on the platform, fully extended while the train rushed by behind him.

What had my brother done? He had landed on the third rail and lived to tell about it.

The crew piled on him, rocked him back and forth, messed his hair, laughing and cursing.

MaxD said, "Mighty, you lifted that tag from somewhere."

Nike said, "Aw, give it a rest, Max."

MaxD shifted his weight. "In fact, I *know* you lifted that tag."

Nike stared MaxD down. "Did you hear me? Give it a rest. Didn't you see Mighty fly?"

"It was the fakes that made him fly," one of the Points said.

And that's when my brother punched me, even though I hadn't said a word. "Don't ever follow me again," he said. But his punch didn't hurt. He looked downright sad, like somebody died.

Randall wouldn't talk on the way home. On the fire escape, I felt his strong, slippery grasp as I pulled him up and he crashed into me on the metal landing. He frowned. "With your clown feet, there's no way you'd clear that rail."

"What are you talking about? I wasn't down there with you."

"Still," he said darkly.

"You didn't clear that rail. You stood on it. You and the rat. How'd you do it? Tell me."

I waited for him to explain the magic. I had on the same Jordans.

"Everyone knows rubber soles can do that, even fakes, so long as you don't ground yourself. But don't you try it, Petey. Don't you *ever* go down with that crew." Then he looked me square in the eye and said, "Promise?"

Randall never made me promise anything. Promises weren't what we did. But I promised anyway. There was no chance I was going anywhere with those losers. I didn't need them. But I knew Randall needed me, no matter what he thought. Crew or no crew.

The next morning, Randall was gone. So were his clothes, wallet, and 120 bucks from the candy jar in the kitchen. On Ma's bed he'd left a note: Don't find me. The only thing that wasn't gone was the duffel bag. That he left under my bed, and I don't know why. Maybe as a secret message to me.

When Ma read her note, she stormed out from her bedroom. "When did you last see him?" she demanded. That's when I broke down. Swearing, she dragged me to the train station, where we stood with the other commuters, staring at the two letters my brother had left on the wall: *Om*. Only now across the blazing orange of Randall's tag, someone had added, in black paint, three straight lines going up and down like an angry bear slash.

Ma's eyes flashed with fear. But I couldn't tell who she was afraid for, my brother or us. She looked around like somebody might be watching. "Come on, Petey," she whispered. "Come quick."

"What about Randall?" I whimpered.

She looked at me. "He'll be back, don't worry. Unless . . ." She stopped.

"What, Ma?" I whispered. "Will the cops catch him?"

She shook her head, as if she was thinking of something much worse. We hurried away, and I wondered who could be worse than the cops.

Now it was Saturday again. A whole week had gone by, and we hadn't talked about the black lines, and I hadn't told Ma about the duffel bag. I hadn't told her about Randall's shoes either, about those rubber soles saving him from dying on the third rail. I didn't think she'd understand that kind of magic. But I did. I knew that magic was powerful and true. It made me suppose, no matter who was after us, that if I kept wearing my Jordans, Randall would come back, like we were two magnets being pulled together by the charge of our shoes. Of course, what I didn't know was which direction the magic would go. Shoes don't tell you where they're taking you. But they have a path, and you have to follow it. I just hoped that path would lead me to him.

3 MYLA

IN ALL THE MOVIES I'VE SEEN, AS SOON AS YOU hand it over to the strange man, whatever it is, you're toast. That's when your body gets thrown off the bridge. So I said the first thing that came to me: "I don't know what you're talking about." *Good one. Never mind the necklace hanging around your neck.*

"Let's not play games." The man rubbed his craggy chin. "You've heard of the Fencers?"

Fencers? The only ones I knew were on the girls' fencing team at Mercy College. They wore masks and used long, bendy swords. But somehow I didn't think that's what he meant.

He went on. "Well, they're a mean crew. You don't want them thinking you got this necklace. You don't want to be that kid."

He was right on one count. I didn't want a "mean crew," with bendy swords or otherwise, thinking about me. But what he said didn't ring true. I remembered how angry he'd been with his mom. He was the one who wanted the necklace, not the Fencers, whoever they were. "It's just a finders necklace," I blurted.

He looked surprised. "I don't know what my mama told you, but she had no right selling it." He took a step toward me, and he was a mixture of sweat and that hard smell men have who work outside all day, which my dad the math teacher didn't. And okay, that's when I lost it. I could see faint spots, and worse, tears welled in my eyes. The last thing I wanted was to cry in front of him.

Just then, the bathroom door opened again. My heart leaped. But it wasn't my mom or Ana. It was a woman carrying a small, white dog. The dog started barking and the man fell back in surprise. That was all I needed. I bolted past him.

At the front, my parents were checking the receipt while Cheetah and Ana were looking at her phone. Ana looked up at me. "What took you so long?"

"Yeah," Cheetah said. "We thought someone was bothering you."

"What?" Ana said. "No, we didn't."

"There was a line." I grabbed Ana's arm. "We'll meet you at Spice," I said over my shoulder.

"Wait," Cheetah called after us, but I didn't stop.

Outside, I dragged Ana down the sidewalk. "What's going on?" she yelled.

Without stopping, I told her what had happened in the bathroom.

"Oh my God, what if he's still after you? Maybe we should return the necklace."

"Of course not!" I tucked the pendant inside my shirt. There was no way I was going back.

By then we came to a footbridge that went over the train station. Spice was on the other side. Halfway across, Ana stopped me. I was going to say let's not stop, but then I saw what she was pointing at. There it was in bright orange, standing out from the mess of other graffiti along the train tracks.

"No way," I said.

"It's like Om is following you," Ana said. She clicked a picture of it with her phone.

Only this time it wasn't a symbol. It was the word *Om* spray-painted on the station wall. Not only that—there were three black lines painted over it, like someone was cancelling it out. For some reason this made me think of Craggy Face. I turned around, half expecting him to be there. Instead, someone else was on the footbridge. It was a boy with dark curly hair who looked kind of Indian but not. Our eyes met before I turned away.

"Let's go," I said uneasily to Ana. "We've been here too long."

At Spice, my family joined us and we ordered our usual tandoori pizza. Every time the front door opened, I tensed, thinking it was Craggy, but so far, nothing.

"Myla, you've barely touched your plate," Mom said.

I'd eaten the paneer cheese off my pizza slices, but I was too nervous to eat anything else.

"All that running ahead of us made her tired," Dad said, winking at me.

"Right." What else was I supposed to say? I stood up. "I'm getting some napkins."

As I was pulling them out from the dispenser, the door

opened. My stomach clenched but it wasn't Craggy. It was the curly-haired boy from the footbridge.

"I'm here for takeout," he said to the man behind the counter. "Last name Wilson."

I expected him to be surprised to see me, too, but he didn't notice me at all. Instead he kept looking out the window. Curious, I watched him. His hair was a mass of dark curls, black like the licorice Ana gets from her grandparents at Christmas. I frowned. I felt I'd had that thought before.

The man brought out his order. "One tandoori pizza with a side order of naan bread."

"Thanks," the boy said, leaving some bills on the counter and hurrying out the door.

"Hey," the man called after him. He looked at me. "He forgot his naan."

"I'll take it to him," I said suddenly. But when I opened the door, the boy was turning down a street. I hesitated. I had better things to do than chase after a strange boy with a bag of naan. Still, he'd made me curious. Was he Indian? Why hadn't he noticed me? And why was he in such a hurry?

I got to the corner. Halfway down the alley, I saw him, surrounded by a group of teenage guys. One of them pushed him against the wall, almost toppling the pizza box. I saw something black across the teenage guy's arm like a spider. It was a tattoo. "Where's Mighty?" he hissed.

The curly-haired boy cowered behind his box. "I told you, I don't know."

The tattooed guy leaned in. "I guess that's why I wear rings." He made his hand into a fist.

Why he wore rings? My brain tried to understand, and then I saw it. The studded fist pulled back and shot forward and the boy fell back. Then he was spilling bright red from his mouth.

I felt myself go weak in the knees. One of them said something and they all saw me, the short Indian girl at the end of the street. I trembled. What would happen now? Would the guy with the tattoo come after me? But before I could say anything, they ran off like cockroaches in all directions, leaving the curly-haired boy behind. He stood in the middle of the alley staring at me, his mouth bleeding as he grasped the pizza box in his hands.

I held up the bag. "You forgot your naan," I said stupidly. But it wasn't like I could ask, who were those guys that wanted to beat the daylights out of you?

He ran up and snatched the bag. "Mind your own business!" he cried, and he was gone.

Back at the restaurant, I slid into the table, pale and trembling, but no one seemed to notice. Cheetah and Ana were doing a word search on the back of a menu.

"Where's the napkins?" Cheetah wanted to know. "I got sauce on my shirt."

"Get them yourself," I growled. It was all I could do to stop from shaking. Was the boy seriously hurt? Would he be okay? At the same time, I felt a wild elation. Somehow I'd managed to stop a terrible thing from happening. *Me*. But something told me it wasn't over yet.

Outside, I was the first to reach the Subaru. A flyer was tucked under the windshield wipers.

"I hate those," Mom said. "We're never going to get a car wash here."

I pulled the paper off the glass. As I read it, I felt the blood receding from my face. I looked up and down the avenue. How had he done it? How had he picked out my car from the sea of other cars on St. Vincent Ave? I thought of the boy bleeding over his pizza box. And now this.

"What is it?" Cheetah wanted to know, hovering around me like a bee.

I pushed him away. "Nothing," I said, crumpling up the paper. "Car wash, like Mom said." Ana gave me a searching look but said nothing. It was only when we were driving away from St. Vincent Ave that I handed the crumpled sheet to her. I didn't need to read it again to remember the words inside: I'll find you in Dobbs Ferry.

4 PETER

MISSING PERSON REPORT

Missing: Randall Wilson **CASE NUMBER #M33456744**

Basic Information	
Race:	Mixed
Sex:	Male
DOB:	May 12, 1999
Height:	5'11"
Weight:	150 pounds
Eyes:	Black
Hair:	Black
Other:	Birthmark on left ear, large hands and feet

Additional Information	
Last seen:	Date: August 20 Location: Yonkers, NY
Last seen wearing:	Gray hooded sweatshirt, jeans, black & white Air Jordan sneakers (fakes)
Miscellaneous:	Randall was last seen in his family's apartment the night he disappeared. He left behind a note, possibly indicating he went away of his own choosing.

If you have any information, please call:	
Agency:	**City of Yonkers Police Department**
Address:	**12 Main Street, Yonkers, NY**
Phone:	**646-555-1212**

5 PETER

THE PIZZA BOX FROM SPICE WAS STILL ON THE kitchen counter where I'd left it at lunch. I couldn't get the blood off, so I scratched away that part of the cardboard. My mouth had stopped bleeding. Luckily, none of my teeth got knocked out, just a cut and some swelling. Even so, I could barely eat. When I did, a picture of those guys came into my head like a bad painting. I'd never seen them before. They didn't hang at the basketball courts or the train yards at night. But they knew who my brother was, they'd called him Mighty. It was him they wanted, but it was me they beat up until that girl came along.

What chilled me, though, was the leader. Forget his stupid rings. It was the tat on his arm. Three lines like the ones painted over Randall's tag. Those lines meant something—a gang, an ID, or else . . . a warning.

On top of that, a few days ago Ma announced we were moving. Just like that, no warning. "Our lease ends this month and my friend is renting her house to us for cheap," she said. And that's when I heard we were moving to Dobbs Ferry.

When she told me, a cold knotty feeling started in my stomach. "How will Randall know where we are?" It was a week since he'd left, and no word from him. I kept thinking he'd climb in through the window, wearing his dark blue hoodie, even though he had left it behind on his bed. I'd been wearing it almost every day, and it still smelled like him, like the shampoo he uses plus something that's plain and simple Randall, like sneakers and dirt and sweat.

"He's a grown-up, Petey," Ma said. "He's got our phone number and e-mail."

But it's not like Randall e-mailed. All I could imagine was him coming back to an empty apartment, or finding someone else here instead of us.

Ma saw my face. "Don't worry. We've moved enough times, he'll know we just moved again. I won't stop looking for him. I promise." Her lower lip trembled. "And maybe one of these days, we won't have to move anymore."

"Have to?" I repeated. But if Ma heard me, she didn't respond. I watched her gather the pizza box to throw away in the kitchen. There was so much more I wanted to ask, like if she didn't want to move, then why did we have to, when we were used to Yonkers, and Randall knew where we were. But I could tell from her face that I wouldn't get anything more out of her. Whatever discussion we were having, it was over.

Soon there were boxes and boxes in the apartment. Ma couldn't get them packed fast enough. One had her wedding dress. Another had her doll set from India, and our photo albums. All my things fit inside two boxes, including the duffel bag, which was still locked, and who knew where that key was. At the end of the week, the apartment didn't look like ours anymore, just empty walls and long scratches down the wooden floor. The only things left were Randall's Michael Jordan and New York City posters. I couldn't take them down just yet.

Tonight we were almost done packing. I could tell Ma was tired. She usually kept her hair up for work, but now it hung down in dark waves past her shoulders.

"You sure your lip is okay?" she asked, frowning. "I don't see how you could fall going up the stairs." We were sitting on the floor eating leftover tandoori pizza for dinner. Only I wasn't eating much. The swelling had come down but not a lot.

"I said I had the pizza box in my hand, so I couldn't see where I was going."

"Well, I'm just praying for my kids. First, Randall, now your face."

"I tell you I'm fine."

She leaned over. "Is that Randall's?" she asked and felt the sleeve of the hoodie I was wearing, as if the fabric might feel like him.

I didn't answer. I could talk about Randall, but I couldn't talk about his stuff.

She changed the subject. "Petey, you'll love the new house."

"Who is this friend of yours, anyway? I've never heard of her." I stared at the flecks of orange paint on my sleeves. They were from when Randall went out to tag, and they never came out in the wash.

"Margaret. She's great—she was always throwing dinner parties, getting people together. She went to Mercy College with Pop and me. We got married and moved out of town, but she settled there. Then she moved away with her partner, but she still owns her house in Dobbs Ferry. That's what she's renting to us. Real pretty, near the water, and you can see the Palisades. And she was friends with Grandma Rose, too, who lived there on Broadway. But I haven't been back in years. Not since . . ." Her voice tapered off. She couldn't finish, but I knew what she meant to say: not since my pop's death.

I'd seen a few photos of my parents at Mercy. Still, I couldn't picture either of them in college. As for Grandma Rose, I'd seen her only a few times before she died. So this place, Dobbs Ferry, meant nothing to me.

On the fire escape, we could hear some squirrels running around, making a racket. Ma looked out and her eyes filled. I know she was thinking about Randall. Which was good. Otherwise, she would seem like a monster. I mean, I knew she cried to herself at night, and she filed a report with the police. And yeah, she went around the neighborhood to ask if anybody had seen my brother. But now we were suddenly moving, with no Randall.

The racket on the fire escape got louder, so Ma went to shoo the squirrels away as I ate the last of the wretched tandoori pizza. One thing packing had shown me was that there wasn't anything left to find. Nothing under the bed, nothing in the closet, nothing behind the stupid door. No clues to where he'd gone. Soon we'd be gone, too, and I'd be no closer to finding my brother.

Plus there was the duffel bag.

Truth was, I was scared of the thing. That day at the train station, when I showed Ma what Randall had painted on the platform wall, I remember the look on her face, like she thought someone was after us. My ma's look was a clue. If you could call it that.

My pop was a construction worker in New York City. He poured cement, laid bricks, and erected giant beams of steel. According to Ma, one day he was on the fortieth floor of a new construction, and he fell to his death when a metal beam hit him in the ribs and the harness around him snapped as he was knocked down to the street below. I was five years old when it happened. Randall was nine.

Two things that didn't make sense:

First, I remember my ma one day pulling everything out of the closets that belonged to my pop, and stuffing them in garbage bags as my brother wailed, "Don't take them to the Salvation Army." My ma missed the duffel bag because Randall hid it under his bed in time. The lock came later. I don't know who Randall was locking the bag from—my ma, me, or someone else.

Second, if you Google my pop's name, Omar Wilson, you'll find an obituary from the *Westchester Times*. It says he was a construction worker found dead on East Fiftieth Street in Manhattan, next to a new construction. It says he fell but it doesn't say anything about what floor he fell from. It doesn't even say he died on the job.

Which is why it came to me, maybe the bag had to do with the way my pop died. Because if he didn't die on the job, what made him fall? And why did Ma tell me a different story from the one in the newspaper?

Was the bag a clue? I wasn't sure. But it was enough to make me scared to open it. Because Randall thought the bag was important. And now he was gone.

6 MYLA

AFTER WE GOT HOME FROM YONKERS, ANA AND I went up to my room to look at Craggy's note. So far we'd figured he knew about Dobbs Ferry because he talked to his mom. And Ana guessed our bumper sticker gave our car away: MY KID LOVES CHESS IN DOBBS FERRY. Which was ironic because Cheetah hates chess, and quit the chess club a month after he joined.

"But will he find me here?" I wondered as I sat on my mattress, which was now on the floor.

Ana was next to me looking on her phone at pictures of Stazi, one of the horses she rides at the stable. "I don't know. But wait. I have a picture of him here."

I sat forward. "The craggy guy from the fair?"

"Yeah, he's next to you. It's the picture with you trying on my hat before I bought it."

Well, I looked ridiculous in the hat. But I already knew that.

Ana enlarged the photo on the screen with her fingers. "Actually, he's cute for an old guy."

"What are you saying? He's creepy. His face is craggy like a cliff."

Ana moved the image around, zooming it in and out to study his face. "Not craggy. Rugged. Like someone who's outside a lot. Maybe he rides horses."

I snorted. "You're just saying that because you were thinking of Stazi." Ana was always thinking of Stazi.

She moved the picture around. "See, he even wears boots."

"That doesn't mean anything," I said. "And those are cowboy boots."

She shrugged. "Fine. Maybe he's in construction." She swiped to the next picture.

"You got the boy!" I exclaimed. She'd been going for the *Om*, but he'd showed up to one side. *You forgot your naan*. Could I have said anything more idiotic?

"His face is blurry." She zoomed in and out. "Why, did you want a picture of him?"

I shook my head. "No, not really." I hadn't told her what happened in the alley. And it wasn't because of the naan comment. It was something I couldn't quite explain. Watching him get struck was terrifying, but I knew it wasn't just the blood. It was the feeling it could have happened to me, that we were the same. I went to my desk and got out a roll of Scotch tape.

"Wait, are you putting up that note? What if your parents see it?"

"They never come in here. And they'd never notice it on The Wall."

The Wall is covered with different types of paper from top to bottom. Some are from school: homework, flyers, notes. But most are pages from my journal. The Wall is like one big jumble of words and sentences, my own personal graffiti. The Wall is something my mom hates. She tells me about *minimalism*, how it's the latest in urban design. But I went ahead with The Wall anyway.

After I stuck up Craggy's note, I walked back until I was near the curtains. "He's left-handed. See how the handwriting slants to the left."

Ana came next to me. "You're right. A left-handed construction worker." She looked out my window. "Wow, it's almost evening. The sun's so pretty from here, Myla."

From my room you can see the Palisades, and the sun setting behind it. When I was little, I would make myself look out because Mom said the best way to overcome your fears is to face them. I'd stand by the window and imagine there was another girl my age out there in the cliffs, and we could communicate by thinking thoughts at each other. She was like the outdoor version of me who wasn't scared of heights and could climb the Palisades, even if everyone knows it's illegal.

"Hey, there's a window open next door," Ana said.

The sky was turning orange, and the ground heaved, but that was just my stomach as I looked out. I took a step back from the curtains.

"You're not going to fall," she said.

"I know," I said sharply. "You're right. There's a window open."

Margaret and Allie had been our neighbors until last summer, when the bookstore they owned went under and they moved away. Their house had been empty ever since. For a moment, I thought of Craggy. You know those scary movies where the bad guy is secretly riding on top of your car and following you back home without you knowing? I imagined Craggy stowing away on top of our Subaru. But of course, that was ridiculous. And why would he be in Margaret's house? Unless an empty house was the perfect place to hide if you were a necklace stalker.

"I wonder why it's open," Ana said.

I wasn't sure either.

We went downstairs. Mom and Cheetah had gone out, but my dad was in the family room.

"Is Margaret back in Dobbs?" I asked him. He was seated lotus-style on his green yoga mat.

Without opening his eyes he said, "No."

"Are you sure?"

"They're hiking in the Swiss Alps. There's a postcard in the kitchen."

The Swiss Alps? Like all the way over on another continent? I stood a minute longer.

I actually liked watching my dad when he was doing yoga, though I'd never tell him. There was something magical about the way he found a pose. Each movement was like a slow reach into the place where his limbs were supposed to go. My favorite was Surya Namaskar, which is a prayer to the sun, where you keep your body in a line, then lean backward and forward, and stretch like a snake. Maybe he would do that now. But he opened his eyes at me, and I knew what that meant.

In the hall, Ana said, "I have an idea. Why don't we use the key?"

At first I didn't know what she meant. Then it dawned on me. "No," I said.

"Oh, come on. Margaret left it for you. We wouldn't be doing anything wrong."

I shook my head.

"We'll close the window. We're doing a favor—what if it rains?"

"But it's not raining."

Ana gave me a look. Ever since she'd found out about the key, she was always saying, *Let's do our nails there, let's have a sleepover,* and I always said no. I thought of all the times I'd been to that house, but not once after they moved away. I thought of Craggy's note on our car. Was that an idle threat? Or was he the kind of person who would follow a twelve-year-old girl home? He had already followed me to a bathroom.

In the end Ana convinced me. All she had to do was bring up braveness—that word for doing things you don't want to. For her it was always easier: school, friendship, talking to others. For me, it seemed to take longer. It was like I was always in the shadows, looking for the sun.

Outside, fireflies were starting up in the backyard. *I can be brave,* I told myself. But even with my feet on the ground, I felt my stomach lurch as we walked across the yard to Margaret's house.

7 PETER

FACT 1: He took $120, not enough for a hotel or rent, so he has to be staying with someone, probably someone he knows.

FACT 2: He doesn't e-mail, so the only way to reach him is through a friend.

FACT 3: He hid the duffel bag, but he left it for me. He trusts me.

FACT 4: He knows how to jump train tracks and land from a distance. His shoes are more scuffed up than mine. He's been practicing—but for what?

FACT 5: His new tag is the same as the first two letters of our pop's name.

FACT 6: If I can find more of his *Om* tags, I can find him.

8 MYLA

BEFORE LEAVING, MARGARET TOLD ME SHE knew what it was like to be my age, when sometimes you wanted to be left alone to figure out things by yourself. So she gave me this beautiful brass key with a loop at the top. She called it a skeleton key and said it opened all the doors in her house.

I left it in the kitchen drawer. The house was a great place when Margaret and Allie lived there, full of nooks and crannies and odd-size rooms. Without them, it was creepy, with shadowy hallways and tiny windows.

"I don't understand why you want to go there," I said.

"And I don't understand why you don't," Ana said.

"There's nothing to see. They've taken everything away."

"It's not what's there. It's *being* there."

"Or *who's* there," I muttered. I tucked my necklace inside my shirt just in case.

The front door opened with the key, although we had to give it a shove. But when we got in, we stopped. All the lights were on. For the first time Ana looked surprised, and even a little scared.

"All right, so someone is here," she whispered.

I could picture it now: Craggy atop our Subaru, then nimbly

cutting across Margaret's yard after we went inside. "Let's go home," I whispered back.

Then we heard a sound. It rattled all the way from the second floor down the stairs to where we were. "Oh," I said, feeling foolish. "Nora."

"Who?"

"The cleaning lady. She comes around once in a while. That's her vacuuming upstairs."

"Oh." Ana sounded strangely disappointed. "I guess we should go."

"Well, we're here, so we might as well tell her to close the window before she leaves."

We went up the familiar winding staircase. When we got to the second floor, the vacuuming had stopped but now I heard something else—heavy shoes on the wooden floor. Not like Nora in her tennies. More like work boots. *Like what a construction worker would wear.* I clutched Ana's arm.

Before either of us could decide what to do, a bedroom door flung open.

A teenage girl stood staring at us. She was the person in the heavy shoes: combat boots, paired with denim cut offs and a black T-shirt a shade lighter than her straight hair that read GIVE ME FREEDOM OR GIVE ME DEATH. "Whoa." She looked us up and down coolly and jabbed a finger at me. "You must be Myla."

I blinked. "I must be Myla? Then who are you?"

"I'm Kai." She jerked her thumb behind her. "Nora's cleaning for the renters moving in."

"Are you cleaning, too?" I asked.

Kai scoffed. For the first time, I noticed a camera dangling from a strap crisscrossing her back. "No, I'm with the *Westchester Times*." She turned to Nora. "Thanks. I'll see myself out."

"No problem, sweetie," Nora said. "Be careful in the hallway. I just mopped."

I tried to digest this information as Kai strode past me. "Who's moving in?" I asked Nora.

"The Wilsons. A woman and her son who's starting middle school." Nora looked me over. "You used to come over with your brother. Huh, you're growing up fast."

"We came to tell you to close that window," I said. I realized how lame that sounded. But I suppose it was better than saying, *Don't mind us, we thought a crazy guy might be hiding here.*

"Sure, of course," Nora said. "I'll close everything when I leave."

I stood in the doorway where I could see Kai walking down the hall, peering into each bedroom and taking photos. She was wispy and small, but her calf muscles rippled powerfully above her combat boots. How old was she? Sixteen? She kept going, taking more photos.

"Not to be rude," I said, "but does Margaret want you taking photos here?"

"I'm just looking." Kai saw my face. "I know Margaret, if that's what you're worried about. I'm here because of the house."

"What's so special about it?" It was the first time Ana spoke.

Kai turned to her. "You live down the street, don't you? You're the family with the Norwegian flag ornaments on the tree at Christmas time."

Ana was speechless. Then she smiled. "That's right. Wow, you know a lot."

"I've been down this street a hundred times," Kai said. "It's my job to know people. As for what's so special? This was the last place Scottie Biggs was seen before he was arrested and thrown in prison eight years ago for stealing diamonds. But since you're like ten years old, you've probably never heard of him."

"Thanks, but you look like someone in high school without a car," I shot back.

Kai looked at me for a moment. "Google me. Kai Filnik. You'll see I'm graduating from Mercy College next spring. You'll find out my mom is Margaret's real estate agent. And my dad's in law enforcement. Between the two of them, I know everything there is to know in this town, including this house. But I'm a journalist, and we like to get all our facts before we write the story. That's why I'm here. Because Scottie is getting out of prison in a few weeks."

"And who is he, that Scottie guy?" Ana asked.

"Only Dobbs's most notorious resident," Kai said, "*and* the head of the Fencers."

Ana's eyes widened. But I didn't want her to give it away that I'd heard about the Fencers from Craggy. "Prison!" I interjected quickly. "Well, he wouldn't be *here*, would he?"

That seemed to work. Also, Ana had become distracted by Kai's camera. "What kind of lens are you using?" she asked her. "Can you take close-ups of animals?"

"Dude, you can do everything with this," Kai said. She opened a closet door, studying its interior carefully, before taking another photo. What was she doing? Was she hoping to find that Scottie guy hiding here? Whatever it was, she was pissing me off.

"Do you ever use your phone to take photos?" Ana asked, following Kai like a puppy dog.

"Not really." Kai stopped at a door at the other end of the hall, jiggling the knob both ways. I frowned. That was the door to the attic. As far as I knew, it had always been locked. But why was it locked now after Margaret and Allie had moved out?

"Nora, this door doesn't open," Kai called out. "Do you have the key?"

"That must be the attic," Nora called back. "And no key."

Kai came back to where Nora was cleaning. "What do you mean, no key?"

"My key doesn't work," Nora said.

Finally I couldn't keep quiet anymore. "You shouldn't be here. Not without Margaret's permission."

"Myla," said Ana, "I'm sure it's okay."

"Don't worry, I'm leaving," Kai said, but she kept trying the door.

I crossed my arms and glared at her.

Kai shrugged. "All right. After you, ladies."

We walked back down past Nora, until we were in the foyer. Kai reached for the front door and stopped. "Wait, how did you two get in?"

My heart started beating. Not because I was scared, but because I had to lie. Something told me not to tell her about the key in my pocket. "The front door was open," I said.

"Well, the door is *locked* now."

I held my ground. "It was open. Maybe I locked it afterward. I don't remember."

"You're sure, Myla? You don't have the key?"

I could feel Ana's eyes on me, but she didn't say anything.

"How do you know I'm Myla?" I asked, changing the subject.

"I know your parents," Kai said. "I know they live next door with you and your brother, who won a spelling bee last year. I know Ana is your best friend, and she lives down the street. I know she rides horses and takes photos of them, which she prints out at CVS. And I know you're scared of heights, Myla. I know your mom tried to enroll you in rock climbing because she thought it would help, but then she had to cancel for a full refund."

I stared at her, my face flushed red. How did she know all these things about me and the people in my life? Also, why did she seem to know only the good things about everyone else, and the most embarrassing stuff about me?

Kai pulled out two business cards. "Listen, you don't realize it, but every town depends on people like you and me to keep us safe. If either of you sees something suspicious about the people moving in—*anything*—let me know. My number is on the card."

Ana felt the embossed letters on the front of the card with her finger.

"What do you mean, suspicious?" I asked. "What's wrong with the new renters?"

For the first time Kai's face softened. "Not sure. Could they be the same Wilsons?"

"The *same* Wilsons as?"

But Kai didn't answer me.

Outside, Ana and I watched Kai get into a small, gray sedan parked down the street. One thing I knew: I wasn't lifting a finger to help that snoop. She'd been looking for something in Margaret's house. Whatever it was, I would figure it out first. If only to prove that Kai Filnik didn't know everything there was to know about me.

9 PETER

THE NIGHT BEFORE WE MOVED, I SLIPPED OUT while Ma was asleep with her earphones on.

They were all there on the side of the parkway, like I'd heard they'd be.

"Hey, it's Petey." MaxD saw my face and laughed. "And he's been eating somebody's fist."

The rest of them greeted me with varying levels of insults.

"You've seen your brother?" asked Skinny as he sprayed some seriously messed-up letters on the wall. He couldn't tag to save his life, but the crew kept him on because he was the only one who was eighteen and could buy paint.

I said no, I hadn't seen Randall.

The Points then speculated about him being thrown in jail, which made them laugh and laugh. I seriously wondered what my brother saw in them. I remembered when they both wanted to be Point. They started fighting over it, so Randall made one of them Point Up and the other Point Down. Which made them sound even dumber, like they were both giving you the finger.

"He's got him those magic shoes," said Point Up. "Those fakes will spring him out of jail."

"Look, I'm flying!" shrieked Point Down, his arms spread out.

More laughing. I didn't get it. I knew they liked Randall, so why were they ragging on him? I guess it was me they hated, pure and simple.

"So none of you hear from him?" I looked at Nike, who kept quiet. He'd recently dyed his hair a rusty brown. But his eyelashes were still dark and long, making his face babyish. He worked at Music Land on Central Ave—the only one of these punks with a job.

They went on painting. I looked at Up, who was spraying a crooked arrow pointing up to nowhere, and Skinny, writing his letters all blown up so they were unreadable. It proved what I already knew: they were a bunch of toys with their crappy hand-styles, painting where no one could see their work, on the wrong side of the parkway. I was about to walk away, when I stopped.

"D, that's not your tag," I said. I tried to keep calm, but I couldn't believe what I saw.

MaxD finished his three black lines. "Maybe I have a new one. You got a problem, Petey?"

I made myself look at him, even though all I could think of were those same three lines slashing through Randall's tag. "I know those lines have a bad stink."

"Moron, these aren't lines. Don't you know a fence?" MaxD reached into his pocket, and my heart seized. But all he pulled out was a comb, and he combed and combed that hair of his, short and mangy as it was. "You tell your brother, he better not show himself here. I have us a new allegiance, know what I mean? And the Fencers will find him as soon as Mighty tags again."

The Fencers? Skinny and the Points looked uneasily from MaxD to me. Seemed this like was news to them.

"Om," MaxD said, full of scorn. Then he turned away. But I couldn't leave it at that, MaxD having the last word.

"It doesn't matter," I said. "Because we're moving away from your tired behinds."

I caught Nike's baby eyes for a moment before he stepped back in the shadows.

The rest jeered at me, and the Points sprayed paint in my direction. Then they went back to cackling and doing their ugly tags, and when I walked away, not one of them called after me.

Later that night I sat on my bed. Three lines made a fence. I didn't know everything, but now I knew the tat guy who punched me was a Fencer. I didn't know why the Fencers were after Randall. But if the tat guy could find me, then he and his Fencer friends would find Randall soon enough, especially with MaxD helping. I was losing time.

I drummed my fingers against the mattress, the locked duffel bag in front of me. I had two options. One was to cut open the duffel bag. It was made from canvas, but nothing a pair of scissors couldn't make a hole through. The second was to find that key. So far I'd packed everything. I'd searched everywhere. I'd even looked out on the fire escape. If Randall had left that key behind, he'd hidden it someplace good.

I stretched out on my bed until my feet hit the footboard. When I was little, I remember my pop lying beside me, his feet resting against the same footboard. I told Randall, and he was all, "You remember it wrong. That was me." But I knew my brother never slept next to me. I knew because Randall never spent a minute more than he had to in my company. He was always out the door with me running to catch up. No, it was my pop's feet I remembered clear as day, his toes long and thin like fingers, every toenail perfectly shaped and clean. Which was weird—remembering his feet when I didn't remember his face, except for what I've seen in photos.

I tried to recall now what Randall did every time he opened the bag. Where had he gone in the room? To the closet? Under his pillow? Over by the window? One by one, I ticked off these places in my mind. Then I closed my eyes and asked for the universe to help.

When I opened my eyes, they fell on the two posters still on the wall. The last items left to pack. Carefully I took down the Michael Jordan poster, which had been taped down on all sides. Nothing but blank space. Next, the New York City poster. But this time I felt a slight bulge in the corner. I peeled away the poster, and something fell to the ground. It was the world's smallest key, but I knew—this was the key that unlocked the duffel bag.

My heart thudded as I inserted the key, crazy thoughts filling my mind. Last year in school we had to research a poet, so I chose John Keats because he and Shakespeare were the only ones left on the shelf by the time I got to choose, and Shakespeare looked too hard. So I read through the Keats book, and there was a poem about a basil pot, and I couldn't believe what was in that pot. I thought of that poem now, because I sure didn't want to find somebody's head.

So I took a deep breath and turned the bag upside down, shaking everything onto the floor. Not the most delicate way, but I was glad a head didn't roll out. Instead, I found a bunch of things, most of which I'd never seen before. I made a list:

1 large harness
8 different types of stainless steel round hooky things
3 metal clasps
Several yards of rope
1 plastic container marked climbing chalk
1 pair of gloves
1 necklace
1 small black book

I picked up each item, the harness, the hooks, the metal clasps. I didn't know what they were, except maybe things a construction worker used. They made me realize, like I had my whole life, how little I knew about my pop. Then there was a necklace. It was all scratched up, a pink-and-purple flower with a symbol in the middle of it.

I wondered if the necklace was Ma's. She didn't wear jewelry, except for her diamond earrings, which had belonged to her grandmother. Ma was born in India, then came to the United States by herself in high school, and stayed with her aunt in Poughkeepsie until she went to college. Ma's parents were still in India, and so far we had seen them twice, once when I was a baby. They were quiet-footed, reading the newspaper and taking short walks around the apartment building. Granny Mala wore a lot of "tacky" jewelry, according to Ma. Maybe this was one of those tacky necklaces Granny Mala gave Ma, and she put it away, first chance she got.

Or maybe the necklace belonged to my pop's side. We have just a few pictures of his family. Like one of my pop's parents at a Fourth of July parade, taken in Connecticut before my grandfather Leroy flew off to Vietnam to die in the war. It's my favorite picture, and sometimes I pull it out when no one's looking, because I always think there's something there, some clue about who we are and where everyone's gone. In it, Grandpa Leroy is wearing his uniform and looking all serious, but he's holding an ice cream cone, and it makes me wonder if he's waiting for the picture to be taken so he can eat his ice cream. Grandma Rose is next to him, and has bright red hair and freckles, and looks a little like my pop around the eyes, but that's what people tell me—I don't remember it myself.

Randall said it was a big deal for Rose and Leroy to marry, because he was black and she was white. That's why her family disowned her, and we never saw them. When I asked Ma, she said, "Rose's parents didn't disown her. They were poor—they couldn't make it out here often. Rose had to do everything on her own when she moved from Arizona." Either way, there were hardly pictures of anybody on my pop's side until my parents got married. There's a photo album of their wedding, but Ma says it makes her too sad to look through it.

I picked up the black book. I went through it, slowly turning the pages, the size of index cards. There were drawings of a bridge, a few cars and trucks, but mostly letters. It was like a little gallery of graffiti, with pages of alphabets, then my father's name, *OMAR*. It changed with the pages until it became *Om*, the first two letters of his name.

"Om," I said out loud. What it meant, I didn't know. But I knew it started there, from my pop's notebook, to Randall painting that tag, and why he disappeared the next day.

10 MYLA

Why Kai was snooping and what I know about the house next door:

— Scottie Biggs was last seen there. He was arrested for stealing diamonds, but that was eight years ago. He's getting out of jail soon.

— Scottie was the head of the Fencers, the people Craggy says are after my necklace.

— Margaret wore the same necklace when she lived next door, called a finders necklace, which was "popular for some time."

— The necklace has an Om on it just like the train station. Is that important??

— The attic is locked and there's no key. Why no key? Why locked?

— Maybe my skeleton key opens the door to the attic.

11 PETER

DOBBS FERRY IS ONE OF THOSE TOWNS PEOPLE call nice. Dinky shops, rolling hills, houses with porches and pointy roofs, and in the distance, the Hudson River and those cliffs called the Palisades. But where we lived, we were down the street from the auto-body shop. You could spit on the sidewalk and no one cared. And that suited me fine.

We were moved in by Labor Day, but Ma had to work, and she wanted me to come with her to the hospital. "I hate that place," I grumbled. I'd only been there once, but I couldn't stand the smell of antiseptic and the lab with those vials filled with blood.

"Just one day, Petey. Humor me. I don't feel right leaving you by yourself the first day."

"If I can walk home from school and stay by myself tomorrow, I can stay by myself today."

She shook her head. "You start tomorrow. Today you're coming with me."

On Monday morning, there was fog along the river, so I put on Randall's blue hoodie. The front door was sticky, and it took Ma a few times before she got the door to lock. We turned down Walnut Street, and it was so steep, for a second it looked like we were walking right into the Hudson.

We kept going down the hill until we reached the train station below. A few people were there already, the ones who were working on Labor Day. Ma didn't look like any of them. She didn't have a newspaper in her hand, she didn't carry a briefcase, and she didn't buy her coffee from outside. Instead she was drinking it in big gulps from her insulated mug.

I looked around for graffiti. There was none. Which made me fidget all around, and Ma told me to stand still. Then, while she was drinking, we heard somebody calling her name. She stopped, her mug halfway to her mouth. "My God." She stared ahead, her eyes goggling.

A tall, lanky guy came toward us. He'd come off the train from the other side.

"Shanthi," he said, this time more quietly. He reached up to take off his shades, his fingernails trimmed with dirt, and I saw that his eyes were a watery gray, like the Hudson. He was wearing boots, which were deep red and muddy, like he was a cowboy dropped down in Dobbs Ferry. Maybe he rode horses. Or he was from somewhere else.

"It's you," Ma said. I couldn't tell, was she happy to see him or not? I searched my brain. He looked familiar, though he didn't give off a Yonkers vibe.

Ma said we were renting Margaret's old place.

"Margaret!" By the way he said it, he knew who she was. Maybe everyone in Dobbs did.

"It's nice to be back," Ma went on. "I was thinking how long it had been since college. What about you, Richard? I heard you had a landscaping company in the Catskills."

He nodded. "Yeah, but I'm here all week working on the waterfront and the Aqueduct."

"Aqueduct?" That was me. It sounded like something to do with your toilet or pipes.

Richard turned his watery eyes on me. "You're Peter, aren't you?"

I froze. Now that was just creepy, this cowboy I'd never seen knowing my name.

Ma ruffled my hair. "He's twelve already," she murmured. She didn't mention Randall, though you'd think if this Richard guy knew me, he'd know him, too. Instead they went on talking till my ma's coffee must have gone cold. I heard the word "college," then something about Pop, which made my ears perk up, but that's when we heard our train coming.

"That's your train," Richard said. "But call me some time." On a piece of paper from his pocket, he wrote down a number and gave it to Ma. "Anyway, I know where you live."

"Thanks, Richard," she said. I couldn't tell from her voice whether she meant it or planned on losing his phone number.

"You all take care." His boots made clump-clumping sounds as he walked away.

Inside the train, we sat down and I asked who Richard was.

"Don't you remember? Of course, you wouldn't. It's been so long." Her voice trailed off. "That's Uncle Richard, your father's cousin."

"Cousin," I said, surprised.

"His mom and Pop's dad were brother and sister."

I let my brain muddle through that. "So why do we never see him?" I thought of the photo albums still unpacked at home. Was Uncle Richard in one of those albums? Or was he part of the black hole that had no pictures at all?

Ma gazed out the window. "He's busy, I'm busy, it happens."

"That's all you can say? Do you hate him? Did he do something?"

"Of course not. Just after Pop died, it was hard to keep it all going." She bit her lip. "You wouldn't understand. Some day you might."

"You think he'll visit?"

"I don't know. Maybe."

Strangely, that "maybe" was the first hopeful thing I'd heard from her in a long time.

Still, seeing Uncle Richard must have shaken her up. For the rest of the trip, all she did was stare at that phone of hers. Then I knew she was really off her game, because how else could she miss the world's most kick-ass tag staring at us right outside our window?

12 PETER

WE WERE PULLING UP TO OUR STOP, WHEN I SAW it blazing in orange on the station wall. "Holy bejesus," I breathed, forgetting all about Uncle Richard and his cowboy boots. Randall!

"Watch your tongue," Ma said, her eyes still on her phone.

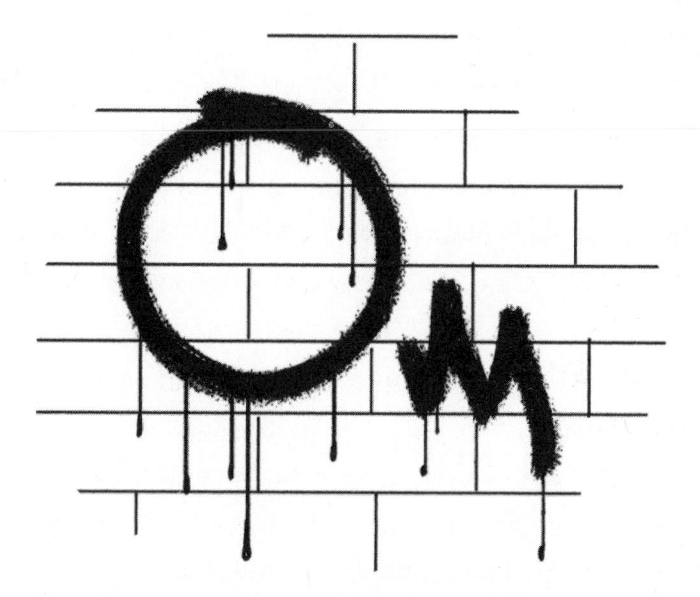

I stared at the orange, drippy letters of the *Om* tag. Who else could have done it? Who else could have made that tag burn like a miracle sun? "Ma, did you—" I sputtered, but she didn't see or hear anything.

As soon as the train stopped, she stood up. "If we hurry, we can make the bus on Lenox."

"But did you see?" I tried again, as we hustled down the steps past waves of people to the street below. Even early morning on a holiday, the station was bustling.

"I'm sorry, Petey, we've got to hurry. Once we're on the bus, we can talk."

I looked around us, at all the people and the traffic filling the streets. Was it really only seven o'clock? "Where are we again?" I asked.

"Harlem," she said over her shoulder. "125th Street."

On the bus, I decided not to tell Ma about the tag. Instead I paid attention to the bus route, where we got on and got off, and how to get back to the train station from the hospital. In the waiting room of my mom's ward, I said I'd go to the cafeteria.

"All right, but I can't come down there to look for you. You'll be back when?"

"An hour. There's newspapers to read." One hour was plenty. At least I hoped.

I'd never been outside the hospital by myself. When I first stepped through the front doors, I felt my breath go faster as cars whooshed past me, honking loudly, and a taxi driver rolled down his window to yell at someone for double-parking. At the corner of 135th, the smell of eggs, coffee, and honey-roasted peanuts coming together from a stand made me want to hurl. For a moment I almost went back to the hospital. But I didn't. Even if I'd never been in the city by myself, I was going to that station. I was going to find out if that tag could help me figure out where Randall was.

Even with Randall's hoodie on, the bus to the station was as cold as a freezer with the air-conditioning. I hadn't noticed it on the way. But now that I was alone, I noticed everything. I was sick with worry, and I was excited, too. *Om*. It was written in my pop's black book, and it had become Randall's tag. Now it was on the wall at 125th. What did it mean? That Randall was alive and okay? Then why didn't he come home? With a pang I realized there was no home for him to come back to. Someone had to tell him where we were, or he'd never know. I'll leave him a note, I decided. I had a Sharpie in my backpack. I'd write something next to the *Om*.

The bus pulled up to 125th, and I got out. I raced down the street to the train station, then up the stairs, past a nun eating a breakfast burrito. I paused. That was something you didn't see every day. Then I rushed on. But when I got to the platform, I almost choked. There standing in front of the *Om* was a cop. I saw the baton hanging from his belt, the sharp look in his eyes, and I knew there was no way of writing on that wall. Above him, the *Om* glowed like an orange halo.

He must have seen me staring because he said, "Kid, you got somewhere to go?"

That was enough for me. I turned around. I walked past the nun again, who was finishing the last of her burrito, and she belched. Great. A belching nun. The universe was giving me a bad sign. I was about to head down the stairs, when I looked back once more and saw someone with rusty brown hair sitting on a concrete bench. I hustled to him. "Nike!"

The rusty brown head turned. "Petey! What are you doing here, man?"

I'd never seen him up close in the day. He wore a T-shirt and running shorts, and sneakers without socks. He seemed more wiry than I remembered, like a wild cat in the jungle.

There was no point beating around the bush. "I'm looking for Randall."

"The *Om* bro."

I gestured to the tag behind us. "I know you saw that. Now, where is he?"

"Stop pointing, man."

"I know you know something." He was the youngest of the crew, and with those long lashes, he didn't scare me. "You have to tell me, or I'll talk to that cop over there right now."

Nike burst out laughing. "You'd pee your pants first." He stood up, rolling on the balls of his feet, the muscles in his legs flexing.

I gave him my best tough look, but I knew he was right. I turned to go when Nike said, "Mighty's gone to study with Tops."

I stopped. "Tops?"

Nike leaned over, stretching his hamstrings, and for a moment I thought he was going to tear down the tracks. I noticed a deep cut on his knee, and it was bleeding.

"There's more to Mighty than that." Nike did a sideways jerk of his head toward the *Om*.

"He's selling dope," I said.

"Sshhh," Nike hissed. "Seriously, are you *trying* to get arrested?"

I doubted anyone could hear us over the noise in the station. "So what is it?"

Then we both heard it. The train horn.

"That's for me, dude. I'm going home to chill out my bones." Nike stretched his legs again, this time gingerly, and I realized he was in pain.

"What happened to you?" I asked, pointing to the cut.

He shrugged it off. "You want to hear what I have to say or not?"

I nodded.

"Parkour."

"What?" Nike and Randall were speaking French? That's what it sounded like.

"I've been training. Mighty has, too. That's because he doesn't want to tag—he wants to fly." Then Nike stretched his arms out and whooped so everyone stared, even the cop. Now who wanted attention? The train was only a hundred yards away.

"Wait, that's it? You're giving me one lousy word?"

"Look it up. You'll see what I mean. It's all part of Mighty's master plan."

I didn't understand. His master plan to do *what*? But the

train was too loud to hear anything else as it came to a stop. Nike got in and saluted me.

"What's that word again?" I called out.

"Freerunning. Try that instead, home boy." The door closed and the train pulled away.

Where was I supposed to look that up? My ma hadn't set up the computer at home. Maybe I could look on the computer in her office at the hospital. The hospital! I flew like the wind. The last thing I needed was Ma worrying about me. As I went past the *Om*, I saw that the cop was gone. I stopped, staring hard at my brother's letters. Think. *Think.* I whipped out my Sharpie and I wrote: Find me in Dobbs Ferry-PW

If anyone noticed what I did, they didn't say. I took a few steps back, wondering if Randall would see the message. Would he know PW was me? Peter Wilson. Little brother. Dobbs Ferry resident. I turned around, my fake Jordans pounding the ground as I ran.

13 MYLA

IT WAS THE FIRST DAY OF SIXTH GRADE. I THOUGHT of all the first days I've dressed for, how I never quite know what to wear, or how to get it right. But this year I had the necklace. So I parted my hair to one side, put on a peacock-blue shirt from Coney Island, and wore my Om pendant. I wasn't sure, but it seemed like for once, everything matched up—hair, shirt, Om—and I might even look decent.

Downstairs, Mom and Dad were talking to Cheetah about the first day of fourth grade.

"You could start using your real name," Mom said to my brother. "Now that you're older."

"No one calls me Chetan," Cheetah said. "Nobody calls Myla by her real name either."

"But just because somebody called you Cheetah doesn't make it your name," Dad said. He and Mom called it "the Great Irony" that Cheetah liked to spell but misspelled his name. It was their favorite story, the one they liked to tell everybody, how my brother wrote his name down in preschool and the teacher thought it said Cheetah. Like who would call their kid that? But that's how the name stuck.

Meanwhile, I was thinking how strange it was that Cheetah and I wouldn't be in the same school anymore, but that Dad and I now would. We'd already gone over the whole thing, like how

I didn't have to call him Mr. Rajan unless I was in his class, and he wouldn't stop in the halls to talk to me. Even so, I was feeling jittery. It was also the first day of middle school, where I had to suddenly juggle teachers, lockers, and upper-class students.

Ana and I wanted to go together, but Dad and I had to drop off Cheetah first. As we left the driveway, I looked over at Margaret's house. I hadn't seen the new renters yet. Nora had said one of them was a boy starting middle school. Maybe he would be in one of my classes.

When we got there, Dad dropped me off at my homeroom. Afterward, I got my locker assignment, and that's when I finally saw Ana. She was wearing her cap from the street fair.

"You look different," she told me. "And you're wearing that necklace."

I smoothed down my peacock-blue shirt. "Is the color too bright?"

Violet Márquez came up to us. "Ana, I *love* your hat. I want one just like it." She stood right in front of me like I wasn't there.

"You'd have to go to Yonkers," I said. "That's where I got this necklace, too."

Ana's eyes shifted from her to me. "Myla's right. That's where we got everything."

I waited for Violet to turn around and notice my necklace. But instead she joined her other friends in the hall and said, "Yeah, like I'd ever even go there, Ans!"

I wondered if I had on an invisibility cloak like Harry Potter.

We'd all gone to the same preschool. We'd done tea parties in the sandbox with twigs and dirt packed into plastic containers, and even when Violet accidentally swallowed some sand and threw up, I didn't judge. I kept playing with her that day and stepped around her barf. But I guess she'd forgotten about that.

Ana looked at me now apologetically. "She's always been annoying. You look great, Myla."

"You look great, too," I said automatically. But I was feeling a lack of greatness in the air.

We walked together to American Studies, and I tried not to think of how tall Ana was, and how short I was, or how we must look next to each other with her straight hair and my frizzy hair, and with her grace, and my what? Instead I tried to concentrate on the blueness of my shirt and the weight of the necklace. I even said Om in my head a few times. I'm not sure it made me any calmer, but it gave me something to do.

When we sat down, our teacher was writing his name on the board in block letters: MR. CLAY. Dad had told me about him. I think the word he used was "caffeinated." After watching him, I thought Mr. Clay was someone who could benefit from saying Om. He was small and jumpy, like he had too many words inside him, and he paced up and down the aisle a hundred times as the class filed in. I got out of breath just watching him.

Finally when everyone was seated, he bounced on the balls of his feet and said, "Welcome to American Studies." He said it like the words were written in flashing lights on a billboard.

"You will all become experts on Dobbs Ferry, then and now. We will study George Washington's revolutionary route from Dobbs to Virginia. We will visit the Historical Society and the famous Croton Aqueduct Trail, and research what life was like for those who worked for the old waterworks system in New York."

The "famous" Croton Aqueduct Trail? Was this the same one down the street from us where Cheetah and I went biking during the summers? The only reason we'd even go was that there was an old house on the trail that was totally creepy and looked haunted, and we'd dare each other to go inside, though neither of us had gone near it except to look inside the broken-down windows. Not exactly my idea of famous.

I was writing in my journal during attendance, when I heard Mr. Clay say, "Myth . . . Myth . . ."

"Myla," I spoke up quickly. "Myla Rajan." No one can say my real name. Only I don't have a cool story about it like Cheetah that my parents tell everyone. The truth is that when I was little, I couldn't say my name either. I could only say Myla. My parents told me Mythili is another name for Seetha, an Indian goddess. I liked that. But I liked Myla better.

Mr. Clay nodded at me, and I couldn't tell if it was a generic nod, or one that said you're-the math-teacher's-kid-and-I've-already-decided-things-about-you. Then he called out a name I hadn't heard before. "Peter Wilson," he said.

"Yeah," said a voice.

I sat up. Turning slowly so it wouldn't look like I was staring, I peeked at the boy across the aisle from me. When I saw his face, I almost jumped out of my seat. It was the boy from Yonkers, the one bleeding on his pizza box. The cut was gone. His face was calmer now. But he was wearing the same hoodie, and his hair was the same mass of dark curls pushed back from his eyes. He met my eyes, and the same jolt of recognition passed through him. He remembered me!

I felt the prick of Ana's pencil through my peacock-blue shirt.

"He's cute," she whispered. "Is he the new neighbor? Nora told us it was the Wilsons."

Oh God. I'd forgotten about that. "I don't know," I whispered back. Was *this* my neighbor? The boy from Yonkers? What could it mean, this boy named Peter moving in next door? Was it another fact to add to my list of strange things about Margaret's house?

I was going to ask Ana if she remembered him from the photo on her phone, but Mr. Clay was looking right at me as he told us about our assignment. So instead, I snuck another look at Peter. This time I saw he had a small notebook sandwiched inside a bigger one. I looked down at my own journal wedged inside my binder. It was something I did all the time last year when I didn't want the teacher seeing me writing in it. And here was someone else who did the same thing.

During the rest of class, I kept stealing looks at him. He was tall and thin, and his wrist bone stuck out from the sleeve of his hoodie. The edges of his sleeves were frayed and speckled with paint, and I wondered why he'd wear something so old on the first day of school. I also noticed the way he spread his thin fingers over his twin notebooks, the nails like white half-moons at the tips, as if he didn't want anyone to see.

Was he cute, like Ana said? He was different from anyone I'd seen in Dobbs Ferry. There was an Indian boy in the grade ahead of me. And someone from Vietnam in our grade, and another from the Philippines, but no one who looked like Peter. His long legs were wedged awkwardly beneath his desk, which made him seem like he didn't fit, that he belonged somewhere else.

When the bell rang, Mr. Clay pulled the blinds. "All of you out while I enjoy my sun therapy," he said. He looked at us over his coffee cup, and it occurred to me he wasn't joking.

We herded ourselves to the door. I wondered if I would have to say something to Peter, but he'd gone ahead, which made me strangely relieved and disappointed at the same time. I searched for Ana but she had moved up ahead, too. Then I saw her bump into Peter in the doorway. A small sheet of paper flew from the stack in his hands and fell facedown on the floor.

"I'm so sorry!" she exclaimed.

He looked surprised. "No big deal. I didn't see you either." He said it nice enough. Not like when he told me to mind my own business.

"You're new? I haven't seen you before. Are you from Brooklyn?"

He smiled a sudden easy smile, and I noticed then how they were perfectly matched, Ana's height and his. "Seriously? I'm from Yonkers."

"No way! I was just there this weekend!" She said it as if she went there all the time. I heard her telling Peter her name as I bent down to pick up the paper off the ground. A strange jealousy gripped me. Had she bumped into him on purpose? Was it because she thought he was cute?

As I handed the sheet to Peter, I saw what was on it: two letters in bright, streaky colors, like an orange sun. *Om*. Like the one in Yonkers. That's when I froze.

But that was nothing compared to the astonishment on his face. "That necklace," he croaked.

My hand went up automatically to my throat. Then I blurted it out before I could stop myself. "Are you a Fencer?"

14 PETER

FOR A MOMENT, I WASN'T SURE I WAS HEARING right. She thought I was a Fencer?

"Of course not!" I wanted to get to the important stuff, like her necklace. Only the crazy girl was having none of it.

"Are you sure? Then why are you following me?"

"Following you?" I asked in disbelief. "I don't know what you're barking about, but you've got some problem thinking it's about you."

"I'm not a dog," she said coldly. "And I'm late for class." Then she walked off.

"And you can stay out of my business, too," I called after her, but even I could hear how lame I sounded. I glanced at the girl named Ana, who was still standing there.

She gave me a tiny smile. "You really pissed Myla off."

"Well, she pissed me off, too."

"I guess so." She tossed her hair as she walked away. "Have a nice day, Peter Wilson."

Have a nice day. I didn't even say anything back to Ana, that pretty girl with the hat. Of all the stupid things. I was still re-membering that conversation from the morning. I was now in sixth period, my last class of the day, and it sucked. Usually I like math, but I was tired and I hated being the new kid. In my old school, you had Latinos and black kids, the mixed ones like me, a few Italians, a few Jewish kids, maybe an Indian or two. Nobody looked like nobody, so nobody cared. Here most of the kids were white. For the first time, I saw my skin was dark, and I looked different.

The math teacher was Indian, though, and he laughed a lot, mostly at his own jokes. At the beginning of class he said, "My name is Mr. Rajan, and this year we're going to make music. Another kind of music, with symbols and equations." And I was like, great. Another freak. My last math teacher was one, too, and it seemed the whole year we did nothing but fractions, and everything was about food and pie and what people ate during the holidays.

I took a seat next to the window, and saw the sky was a creamy blue. I wondered what kind of moon it was tonight. Randall always knew. He would count it out on his fingers. He said quarter moon was okay with clouds, but no moonlight was better for tagging and not being seen.

My thoughts went back to Myla. *She had the necklace.* The same one as inside the duffel bag. And she knew about the Fencers. At least enough so she thought I was one. It made me realize that Ma and I hadn't come to Dobbs by accident. There was something that connected my family to this place. Something mysterious. Maybe it was even the reason why Randall was gone.

I reached into my backpack and pulled out the little black book. This morning, I wasn't sure if I should take it to school.

Then I decided I'd be extra careful. In mysteries, there are always clues everyone overlooks. The book was a clue. I just didn't know yet how it could help me find Randall.

Quietly, so Mr. Rajan wouldn't see, I spread it open on my lap and flipped through pages of letters and tags written over and over. By now, I'd figured out that this here was my pop's black book. All the guys on the crew carried one, even Randall for a while. A black book was where you practiced your tag before throwing it on a wall. You only showed it to people you trusted, because a black book was like your ID—it said what you were. I guess I'd known all along, but the black book confirmed it for me: It wasn't just Randall who was a graffiti writer, but my pop. History repeating itself.

At first my pop wrote in that lean hand style you see on street signs, where you can't read anything because all the letters run into each other:

Then his style evolved, and my pop went from choppy and unsure, to round and strong, with bubble lettering that exploded with faces inside them. In between, he practiced his tag until it went from *OMAR* to *Om*. Randall called that aging. My pop had aged his way to *Om*. Randall had aged from *Speed* to *Mighty*. Then one day he threw Pop's tag on the wall. Not sure if that was aging so much as taking.

There's a place halfway in the black book where the drawings stop, and the rest of the pages are blank. I wasn't sure if this was when my pop stopped tagging or when he stopped living. So just like that, I started drawing on those pages. A little bit in American Studies, some more in English, and now in math. I didn't have a tag of my own, so I practiced writing Om. I didn't do faces like my pop, or make my "O" a sun like Randall. I just did whatever came to me—patterns, whirls, random shapes. And maybe it's weird, but writing those two letters over and over was like a meditation, of being connected to my pop and Randall.

Tucked at the end of the book was an *Om* done on a separate paper. On the back was Skinny's phone number scrawled in Randall's handwriting. When I first saw it I thought, I could call Skinny and he would tell me where Randall was. But he and Randall weren't tight. And I remembered the way Skinny had acted last time I saw the crew. Maybe he was with MaxD.

Maybe he was on his way to becoming a Fencer, too. I looked at the front of the sheet again, at Randall's *Om*. That was the side Myla got freaked out about when it fell on the floor. And I still didn't know why she had on the same necklace.

On the last page of the black book, I'd jotted stuff down. You could call it my Find Randall list:

- Look up freerunning and le park.
- See Uncle Richard again. How?
- An *Om* at every station. Why?

I'd seen the *Om* tags on the way home from the hospital yesterday. I counted ten, one at each station until I got to Dobbs, which was bare. Randall said train stations were the place he could reach the most people. Is that what he was doing? Reaching the most people? I wished he was trying to reach me.

Mr. Rajan walked down the aisle, handing out packets. "We're doing a math assessment. Don't worry if some of it's hard. By the end of the year, you'll know everything. Remember, we're making music." Then his glasses fell off and he had to pick them up, and we all laughed. Right before he got to me, I added one more item to my list:

- Figure out why Mile-a (sp?) has the same necklace.

I went through Mr. Rajan's test, and it was easy. There were fractions, and a little algebra I knew from helping Randall. I remembered those nights when he threatened to cut school, and

I'd change his mind by doing his homework for him. Sometimes it was an essay for English. For math, I had to teach myself whole sections. But I'd pulled a decent job. I'd kept him from failing.

I finished early and went back to the black book. I was getting frustrated. It seemed like I kept looking and looking, and I still didn't find anything. All these tags and squiggles and drawings went nowhere. They didn't add up. They didn't say what. Then I thought of something—maybe I *hadn't* looked at everything after all.

I went back to the early hand styles I couldn't read well. I'd skipped them before, but now I looked at them more carefully. There was one that kept repeating itself. This time I stopped to untangle the letters: T-O-P-S. I looked at the others, and they were all the same: *TOPS*, *TOPS*, *TOPS*. I couldn't believe it. The guy Nike had told me about, the one Randall went to meet.

Then if that didn't do it, I found the last one near the end of the book. When I did, I swallowed hard. I knew I'd come across the biggest clue of all. The tag said *TOPS*, just like the others did. But this one had three black lines running through it.

15 MYLA

EVERY THURSDAY AFTER SCHOOL SINCE LAST year, Dad, Cheetah, and I took a train and bus to West 116th Street in Manhattan so Cheetah could spell words like "sarcophagus." There was a youth spelling club at Columbia University, and it was the nearest one my parents could find. Today Dad had a staff meeting at school. Cheetah and I knew the way, so after much debating, Mom and Dad decided we would be okay this one time by ourselves as long as we stuck to our route. I also had Dad's old cell phone if anything went wrong. So far nothing had, but that didn't stop Mom from texting every ten minutes to check if Cheetah and I were okay.

We were now getting to the place where the train went close to the Hudson River. It was mostly train tracks and water, but there were a few rocky places where you could spot graffiti like *LINK* and *TATTOO*. The cell phone beeped. It was my mom. Reach 125th yet? I texted back: Since 5 min ago? No!

I took out my homework. It was only the third day of school, and they were already piling it on. For American Studies, we had to write an ad for a local landmark. We already had the information in a packet, but Mr. Clay told us we had to convince other people to visit, like a real ad. I chose High Bridge. This was what I wrote:

Visit High Bridge, New York's oldest bridge! Once part of the Aqueduct, this bridge brought fresh water into Manhattan. Now it is a pedestrian bridge between Manhattan and the Bronx. Come see this famous landmark where you can walk, run, and explore, and no one has fallen from the bridge to date!

I supposed Mr. Clay would make me take out that last part, but honestly, if I was visiting a bridge, I'd want to know about fatalities and accidents.

"I met our neighbor," I said to Cheetah. "His name is Peter."

He looked interested. "Yeah, I heard you telling Mom. What's he like?"

"I'm not sure. I haven't spoken to him after the first day." I thought of how I accused Peter of being a Fencer. Not exactly neighborly. After that, we'd pretty much avoided each other.

"Is he Indian? One of their cardboard boxes flew over to our driveway. It said Shanthi Wilson on it."

"That must be his mom. Yeah, he does look a little Indian. Or maybe his mom is."

"I bet we'll be friends with Peter," Cheetah said.

"Why, because his mom's Indian?"

Cheetah shook his head. "Kids are always friends with their neighbors, right?"

"But you don't know a thing about him," I said. I looked at his face in the afternoon light coming through the train window. I remembered when his baby front teeth had fallen out years ago and the new ones came in, and how big they looked for his small mouth, making him seem like a rabbit. But since then, and I wasn't sure when it happened, his face had grown. Now his teeth were the right size, and he didn't look like a rabbit anymore. Sitting next to him in the train, I could see a hint of the person he was going to be.

"It doesn't matter," Cheetah was saying. "I just know."

"Whatever," I said, but I was strangely pleased. So far I hadn't seen any evidence of Peter and me being friends. We hadn't talked to each other and he mostly kept to himself, although I saw him with a few guys at lunch. It had been a long time since I'd made a new friend. And I'd never been friends with a boy.

I started to draw a picture of High Bridge to go with my ad when Cheetah said, "Om."

We had come to a stop, and he pointed to a tag on the outside wall. It was small and done in black paint, but the "O" looked like a sun, just like the one in Yonkers.

"I wonder if it's the same person," I said. "I saw an *Om* tag last weekend."

"It's like all the other ones so far."

The train started to move again. I turned to Cheetah. "What other ones?"

"I've seen one at every station except Dobbs. There was nothing there, I'm pretty sure."

"Why didn't you tell me?" I demanded.

Cheetah looked confused. "Why should I?"

I pestered him: how big, what color? But as soon as I questioned him, he blanked out and couldn't remember a thing. I tried to go back to my High Bridge drawing, but now I was curious. Would there be more?

We reached the next stop. "Another one," I said. This was bigger with an "O" in bright orange. Now that we were looking for them, they were popping up at every stop. Most were small, drawn with thin lines of black and orange paint. Some appeared near the tracks, and some on the walls several feet high, which made me dizzy just looking at them. How could anyone do those, unless they had magical shoes?

When we went to Arizona two years ago, we saw rock etchings left by the Anasazi Indians. Only they were called "petroglyphs," with ancient symbols of people hunting, singing, and playing the flute. I was amazed they'd lasted so long. People say petroglyphs aren't graffiti, but a type of communication. I wondered if the *Om*s were like petroglyphs, like a secret way of communicating.

At last we reached Harlem Station, our stop. Cheetah and I had counted ten *Om*s, including the ones Cheetah saw without me. Then as we came out of the train, I literally stopped in my tracks. "Holy smoke!" I couldn't believe what I saw on the wall.

"It's huge!" Cheetah cried.

Then I noticed something else. At the bottom, someone had added in Sharpie: Find me in Dobbs Ferry-PW. Those words were just like Craggy's note. And yet . . . I caught my breath. The orange paint on Peter's sleeve. PW. Peter Wilson. *Find me in Dobbs Ferry*. It couldn't be a coincidence, could it?

Just then a cop walked by. "No getting lovey-dovey with that. It's being removed."

"Removed?" I asked him before I could stop myself. "Why?"

"Because we're a city that says no to vandalism. No telling when the next one will pop up if we don't take this one down before the next moonless night." He hoisted his buckle.

"Huh?" Cheetah asked.

I watched the policeman walk off. "He means the next time someone paints, Cheet."

"You mean like Dobbs?"

I shrugged. "Maybe." When I first wanted to spray-paint my bed, I went online to look at videos on how to do it. I found tons of stuff on graffiti, too: the best equipment, the best clothes to wear, the best time to paint. One guy said it was when there was no moonlight so you wouldn't be seen. I started telling Cheetah about the videos, but he was in his own thoughts.

"The next moonless night," he murmured to himself.

I looked at the *Om* again. It was like a big, beautiful fireball that lit up the station. But I couldn't help wondering, who was supposed to find Peter? And would Craggy find me?

16 PETER

TOPS. I COULDN'T STOP THINKING ABOUT HIS name crossed out in the black book. So why was Randall training with this guy? Didn't he know about the Fencers? Didn't he see those three lines running through Tops's name? It seemed that Randall had jumped into the lion's den. Unless that's where he was aiming all along.

I was itching to get online. We had a brand-new router at home, but no matter what I did, the connection was dead. Ma said she'd call for someone to take a look. But I couldn't wait anymore so after school on Thursday, I hurried to the library, where I finally scored a working computer.

I remembered what Nike had told me: "freerunning." I looked that up first, and that's how I found "parkour." The other word Nike used. And what was it? A kind of running people did in New York, Cleveland, Amsterdam, Paris, and basically anywhere around the world. But it wasn't just running. In one of the PK videos I watched, this guy jumps the same way Randall did onto the third rail. Then he climbs a concrete wall, leaps over another, and *jumps from one building to another and lands in a roll.* This was what Nike meant: climbing without ropes, balancing on poles, flying like a superman with no one to spot you. Was this how Randall got his *Oms* high up on those walls? But who was Tops? Was he teaching Randall how it was done? The mystery started there.

On the way home, all I could think about was Randall and Nike flying through the air. On the sidewalk, I tried to jump and land on the balls of my feet. I saw a fence, and I jumped against it, and kicked myself away like in one of the videos. Only I didn't go flying in the air. I went flying onto the sidewalk. Face forward, palms scraping the ground. Like a dumb-ass.

"You're doing it wrong," said somebody.

I looked up, still flat on the sidewalk. A girl was standing in the doorway of a store. I got up quickly, brushing myself off. "I tripped, that's all," I said.

"No, you didn't." She was dark-haired, with a look on her face like she knew all the answers. "I know what you were doing." She came over to where I was standing.

"You know what I was doing?" I crossed my arms. How would this girl know what I was doing when I didn't even do it right?

She looked at me for a moment. Then she ran at the same fence I did a minute ago, clomped her shoes against it, and jumped off, landing neatly next to me. Not on her face like I did. "You were trying to do a tic tac," she explained.

"I suppose you're some fancy parkour runner," I said.

"Not really. But I know a little about it, and if you do something wrong, you'll get hurt. That's why I said something. You looked like you were going to skin your face."

Great. So a PK expert was watching me make a fool of myself. I had more privacy in Yonkers. I picked my backpack up off the ground.

"Hey, no hard feelings," she called after me. "You're new, aren't you?"

I turned around. "What, my life's an open book?"

"No, my mom works here." She tilted her head toward the store behind her. That's when I saw it was a real estate agency. "She's the one who gave you the keys. Remember, you came over the weekend with your mom? You didn't see me. I was in the back."

"So you're a real estate agent who does PK," I said.

"No, my mom's the real estate agent. I'm not into that. I'm not even into PK."

"You just know how to do some candy jump off a wall."

She laughed. "You're funny. No, I write. I helped someone write a story on parkour when a new gym opened in Hastings. And I always try to learn on the job. What was your name again?"

I told her, even though I hadn't told her before.

She nodded. "I'm Kai. We should talk again, Peter, since you're learning parkour."

"I'm not learning it at all." I didn't like the way she said it, like she was implying something that wasn't there. I narrowed my eyes. There was something off about her.

"By the way, we just left a complimentary gift for you and your mom at your house." Before I could say thanks or ask her what it was, she went back inside.

I walked home, curious to know what it was. A plant? A cat? A box of chocolates? It was hard to know what people in Dobbs did for hospitality. When we moved to our last apartment, we found broken glass in front of our door. Ma yelled at us not to step on it.

When I reached home, my hands were still stinging. Kai was right. I *had* skinned myself. Not so much that I was bleeding, but enough that my hands hurt. I thought about what she'd done, running at the wall clean like that. She made it look easy, but I was living proof it wasn't. Nike and Randall, they were out of their collective minds.

I climbed up the porch and saw a newspaper delivered. I picked it up, surprised. We never got a paper delivered to our door. Ma said she had no time for the news. Then I saw the note at the top: *Welcome to Dobbs Ferry!* There was a card attached, which read "Kai Filnik, *The Westchester Times*." So this was her surprise. The local newspaper. Well, it was better than broken glass.

I got out my key to open the door. But today the key wouldn't turn. I tried and tried. Still nothing. What was going on? It had worked fine yesterday and the day before. I wiped the key up and down my jeans. Then I spit on it for good measure. Same thing. I swore out loud.

Then I thought maybe the neighbors had a spare. So I went next door and rang the doorbell. No one was home. I guess the universe wasn't coming through for me today.

Back on the front steps of my house, I gave up and sat down to read the newspaper. There was nothing interesting. All local stuff, like the Aqueduct renovations, some prison dude set to be released, and a story about the waterfront. Boring. But I was glad they had the moon forecast. Randall never needed to look at it, but I did so I'd know when he'd be out painting.

Moon Forecast

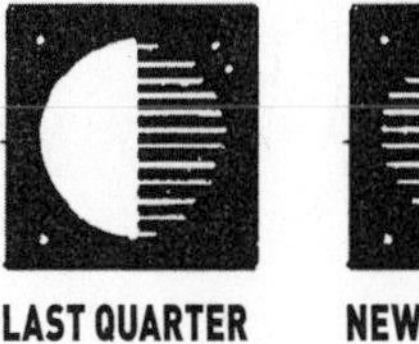

On Saturday, we were coming up to a new moon. Somewhere, Randall was getting ready.

Sometimes I wondered why I bothered. Like, Ma and me, we could coast and let Randall take care of himself. Plus I was getting tired of being the little brother who followed. Wasn't he the one who was supposed to watch *my* back? Wasn't that what big brothers were supposed to do?

Even so, I couldn't help worrying about him. In a way, my family was like a Fencer tag. Three strokes, when there used to be four. If I didn't try hard enough, there would be just two.

I must have fallen asleep, because next thing I knew I heard voices across the yard. It was early evening and the neighbors were home. I scooted off the porch to their house, and rang the doorbell once more. The first person I saw was my math teacher. But more surprising was the person next to him. I groaned and said, "Not you."

17 MYLA

"WHAT DO *YOU* KNOW ABOUT OPENING A STICKY door?" Peter asked skeptically, as I inserted his key into the lock.

I felt a flash of annoyance. "Listen, you can either get my help or forget about it."

There was a moment of silence. "Fine," he said.

"You have to pull the door when you're turning," I explained, then pushed the door open.

Peter stared at the gaping door. "I tried that."

I shrugged. "Margaret should really fix the door."

We looked at each other. "Thanks," he said. "Really."

I'd been thinking about it all afternoon on the way to the city. It was hard to say it, but I did. "Sorry I called you a Fencer. I guess it didn't make sense."

"Yeah, well," he said.

That wasn't exactly the response I expected, but okay. I wasn't good at sorry either. "So why were you so interested in my necklace?" I asked. I waited for him to say he knew the craggy-faced man who was looking for it.

Instead, what he said next surprised me. "That's because I have the same necklace."

It was strange being inside Margaret's house again after only a few days. Already it seemed different. The window shades were drawn and the air smelled like a mixture of incense, candles, and oranges. Peter said I could wait in the dining room, since that seemed to be the only place where there was furniture to sit on. The rest of the house was bare.

"You hungry?" he asked.

I shook my head. I watched as he emptied his backpack onto the dining table. I wondered what he was getting out. The necklace? But it was his lunch bag. From it he pulled out a Ziploc bag of Cheetos. He offered them to me. "Sorry, that's all I have," he said.

"Oh, that's okay," I said, embarrassed. "I mean, thanks." I reached into the bag to have one. The cheesy powder stuck to my fingers like orange paint, which was weirdly appropriate.

He said he would be right back and went upstairs. So I sat down at the table and waited. There were unopened boxes and stacks of clothes everywhere, even on the dining table. I wondered what his family was like. Nora said it was him and his mom. What about the dad? On the table next to me was his backpack, and its contents piled up next to it, and I thought how if I ever did that in my house, I'd get yelled at. But his things seemed to fit right in with the rest of the stuff on the table.

On top of his stack of textbooks and school papers was a thin black book. I recognized it immediately—it was the one he looked at every day when he thought no one was watching. It was old and beaten up, like he'd had it forever. Was it a diary or journal? Did boys even keep them? I had no way of knowing.

Cheetah had a notebook, but it was for collecting new spelling words, which was probably weirder than what anybody else did on the planet.

By now, Peter came back to the dining room with something in his hand. "This is what I was talking about," he said. He laid it on the table in front of me and sat down. His necklace.

"Did you get it in Yonkers?"

He shrugged. "We've always had it."

"Let's look at them together." I took off my necklace and placed it next to his. Now that we were both seated, I was at the same eye level as him. I was glad, because that's the only time I feel like equals with someone. My mom says that's why I'm bossy, to make up for my height. But I don't think I'm bossy. You can't be when you're short. Half the time, nobody hears you, and then you have to repeat yourself.

"Actually, they're *not* exactly the same," I told Peter. I paused, trying really hard to keep my voice friendly just in case he thought I was sounding bossy. "Mine's on black leather. Yours is brown." Mine was in better condition, too, but I didn't say that. I turned his over and there was no "finder" or "keeper." Instead, the word there had been scratched away, and another one was etched over it faintly. "'Shouse.' What's that?"

Peter was surprised. "I didn't see that before." He lifted his pendant and held it to the light.

"It's called a finders necklace," I explained. "Like finders keepers? Each Om necklace has one of those words on the back."

"Om?" Peter interrupted. "*That's* what the symbol is?"

"Yeah. The back tells you whether you're a finder or keeper. I'm a keeper. It's silly, I guess."

I had this sudden memory of Ana in second grade when she lost a Hello Kitty key chain attached to her lunch box. Then Isabel Loch, the one everyone called the Loch Ness Monster, found it and singsonged "Finders keepers, losers weepers" to Ana, and refused to give it back, even when Ana's face was streaked with tears. I was playing on the swings, but when I heard Isabel, I jumped off and gave her a big push. She landed with a thump on her Loch Ness butt and gasped, because even then I was about half her height. Then she gave Ana back her key chain. But I didn't share this with Peter.

He was looking at the back of his necklace. "Then what am I supposed to be? A 'shouse?'"

"No, don't you see? Someone scratched off the word and added that instead."

"Huh," he said. He let the pendant dangle from his fingers as he watched it twirl in the air.

I could still see the orange flecks on his sleeve. I'd been looking at graffiti all my life, but I'd never met somebody who did it. Peter seemed so mild. How could he sneak into the night without getting caught or hurt, or meeting dangerous people?

"Who are the Fencers?" I asked. If they wanted my necklace, maybe they wanted his, too.

He made a face. "Why do you keep harping on them?"

"In case they're looking for me."

"What?" He started laughing.

"What's so funny?"

"Oh come on. Look at you. You're a nice girl in a nice house in a nice town with a math teacher dad. I bet your mom does something nice."

I didn't like the way he used the word 'nice.' "She's an urban designer," I said tonelessly.

"Yeah, well my mom does blood."

"*Does blood*? What is she, a vampire?"

Peter's mouth twitched. "She's a phlebotomist."

Then I don't know why but we started giggling. Peter bent over, and I laughed the way I always do, my head tilted up. We must have looked like opposites in every way, but it didn't matter.

"The Fencers are a gang," Peter finally said. "They're the ones you saw bust me in the mouth."

"The one with the tattoo?"

He pointed to his arm. "Three lines make a fence."

I wasn't sure what he meant. "Weren't you scared? You were bleeding."

He flinched. "Sure. Nobody thinks they're going to get jumped in daylight. But even when it happened, the worst was knowing they were really after my brother."

"Your brother?"

"Yeah." His face darkened. "He's sixteen. He disappeared a few weeks ago. I mean, he left on his own. Nobody made him go."

"Oh," I said. He looked so worried. What would I do if Cheetah went missing? "I'm sorry, Peter. Maybe he'll come back soon." I didn't know what else to say.

"I hope so." His voice was gruff, but I could hear the worry in it.

I tried to change the subject. I didn't want to say something stupid, so I asked the only thing I could think of. "Do you like Dobbs Ferry?"

He looked surprised, then he said, "I don't know. I haven't been here long enough."

"Right, it's your first week," I said.

"It's just . . ." He hesitated. "Does it ever . . . bother you?"

"What?"

"You know. Being the only one."

I was about to ask the only what? Then I got it.

"I've always been the only one," I said. In preschool, I was the only Indian girl in my class. In elementary school, there was a girl named Anjana in my grade, but she moved away. In first grade, my mom read a story on Diwali to my class, and then we made paper lanterns to celebrate the Festival of Lights. But after that, no one noticed I was Indian or asked about it. They forgot about Diwali, and they forgot about me.

Peter nodded. "It was different in my old school." He told me what the other kids were like there, how no one looked the same. It sounded so cool to me.

I felt this strange pulse of happiness, hearing him speak. I'd never known what it was like to talk about being different. It was just something I always carried inside me. Maybe that was why I had noticed Peter. He was someone who was just a little bit like me.

"Well, I'm starting to know people already," he said. "Like your friend."

"My friend?" It took me a moment. "You mean Ana?"

"Yeah. She's in my Spanish class, too. She's really . . . nice." Then was it my imagination, or did he blush?

Of course he did. Because it was Ana, who was tall and pretty. She was the one everyone noticed. And just like that, the happiness I felt went away, like a small animal darting for cover.

I looked away. "Yeah, Ana's nice," I said. And even though it was completely true, it made me sad to say it. Because I knew what we were really saying—that she was the nice one, not me.

"Hey, I'll be right back," Peter said. "I want to put the necklace away before I forget."

While he was gone, I put mine back on, fingering the enamel like I always did now. *Om*. No one had asked about the necklace after all. No one had stopped me in the hall or wondered what the symbol meant. But I was still glad I had it.

I leaned over to look again at the black notebook, still on top of all those school papers. Without thinking, I reached out with my finger and lightly traced the worn cover. It was one of those fake leather covers that feel like the real thing, even though you know it's not.

"What are you doing?" It was Peter standing next to me, watching in dismay.

I stood up, flustered. "I was just feeling the front of your book. I'm sorry."

He reached over and stuffed it into his backpack. "Yeah, well, you can't do that." He looked upset for a moment, and then took a breath. "I mean, sorry. I just get touchy about it, that's all."

"I have one, too," I said.

He looked at me, surprised. "You have a black book?"

"Mine's like a journal. I write down stuff I see. Is that like yours?"

He breathed out impatiently. "I don't think I could really explain what it's for."

"Okay," I said. I'd offended him, but I wasn't sure how. "I guess I should go."

When I said that, he looked relieved.

Outside on his porch, he said, "Thanks for opening the door. I feel like a donkey. Hope I don't have to keep asking you every day to unlock my house."

"I don't mind," I said. The image of a donkey made me smile, but I still felt strange.

"Maybe you've got some special way with keys," he said.

"That's me, the key whisperer," I said.

I was suddenly conscious of the skeleton key in my kitchen drawer. I hadn't told him about it.

"See you tomorrow, Myla," he said. And then he closed the sticky front door.

18 PETER

MA WAS WORRIED. EVERY DAY SHE'D BEEN COMING home from work, with her face tighter than a drawstring bag. She would relax a little when we unpacked in the evenings. But the next day, she'd come back home her tired, stressed-out self. And the more stressed she was, the more coffee she drank. This evening she was making dinner and on her third cup already, with no end in sight.

As I watched her drinking and rolling up burritos, I asked, "Are you getting fired at work?"

She stopped, mid-roll. "Of course not." Her voice was sharp.

"Well, it's *something*." Then I saw her face. "I know, you saw the *Om*s at the stations."

Her hands shook as she placed a burrito in the tray. "That fool will get himself killed," she said. The doorbell rang. It was then I saw how many burritos Ma had rolled. She was expecting company. I hurried out of the kitchen behind her.

Ma had already opened the front door. "Glad you could make it, Richard," she said.

"I'd have come sooner but my car was in the shop and I took the train." He looked at me then, his gray eyes like a cat. "Petey," he said. He even knew my nickname, the one I've always hated.

After Ma put the burritos in the oven to bake, we drank lemonade with crushed ice and little lemon wedges floating at the top of our glasses. Uncle Richard's long legs were folded up under the dining table, but I could see the cowboy boots poking out.

He swirled his glass. "Nice and sweet. I remember your lemonade."

"Omar liked it," Ma said. "I always kept a pitcher in the fridge."

I stared at my glass. I hardly remembered her making lemonade for any of us.

Uncle Richard pulled out a business card and handed it to Ma. "Before I forget, take a look at that," he said proudly. "Designed it myself."

Ma looked at it, turning it over. "Nice. I like the lines crossing at the top."

"Well, I'm no artist like Omar was," Uncle Richard said, but he was clearly pleased. Meanwhile, I wondered just what he meant about my pop being an artist. Did Uncle Richard know about the drawings in the black book? Did he know my pop did graffiti, too?

"It says you're a carpenter and a landscaper," Ma read. "You do both?"

"That's right, Shanthi. I'm a superman," he said, grinning. Then he looked at me and said, "One thing for sure, Petey has got his daddy's height."

"Really?" My voice came out a squeak. I was desperate to know more about my pop, and that artist comment was just a small whiff. "You know Randall, too? Does he look like our pop?" I asked even though I knew the answer.

"I do," Uncle Richard said. "I knew the both of you when you were born. And I've known your ma since college."

Meanwhile, Ma got up to take the burritos out of the oven.

"So does Randall look like our pop?" I asked again. I wanted to see how much he did know.

"The spitting image. You've got his height, and mine. But Randall's got everything else. The same face, the same walk, the same way of moving through his environment."

For some reason, that made me jealous. I wanted to be the spitting image of my pop. After all, I was here, and Randall was gone.

Ma set the burritos on the table, on top of two hot mats. "Careful or it will burn you."

"Thank you, Shanthi," he said. "Nothing like a home-cooked meal."

The burrito was hot and cheesy, and the steam went up my nose, so I waited for it to cool down. But Uncle Richard went tearing right in. He ate and ate and ate.

"Good to be here," he said. "It's been too long, too much water under the bridge."

"Well, you're back now, aren't you?" she said archly.

Uncle Richard chewed and swallowed. "I can't help wonder, did Omar ever find them?"

"Really," Ma said. "Do you ever have a different thought in your body?"

"But don't you wonder the same?"

"Sometimes I think they didn't exist at all," Ma said.

"What never existed?" I asked.

"The diamonds." Uncle Richard looked at Ma. "He knows about them, right?"

I trembled. Diamonds! What were they talking about?

Ma pressed her lips. "No offense, but Rose is dead. It's better to put some things to rest."

"How can you say that? Petey's practically a man. He has a right to know." He turned to me. "Petey, your grandma Rose was the cleverest woman this side of the Hudson River."

"Richard, you don't need to go there," Ma warned. "I hate dredging up all this stuff."

"That's why I'm here," he said. He took a sip of his lemonade. "Call me the dredger."

She sighed. She got up to refill the lemonades, but she watched him like a hawk.

"All right, Petey," Uncle Richard continued. "Picture this: about eight years ago, Scottie Biggs is this guy from the Bronx. He sells cheese. His pop sells cheese. His pop's pop sells cheese. They're a family of cheese-makers. But Scottie's tired of cheese. He's looking for something else."

Scottie Biggs. That sounded familiar. "Isn't he that guy getting out of prison?"

"Bingo," Uncle Richard said. "Same loser. But we're still back eight years ago, when Scottie goes to a jazz festival in Quebec. Two important things happen there. One, Scottie meets a woman selling jewelry. We're talking necklaces with flowers and peace signs. A hippie. Then he finds out she's from Dobbs! Not only that, her real job is diamond-cutting. Do you know who this lady is, Petey?"

I shrugged. "Your sister?"

"My sister! I don't have siblings. Unless you count Omar." Uncle Richard's eyes clouded over momentarily. "But I'm not talking about my cousin, God rest his soul. I meant your grandma."

"Grandma Rose was a diamond-cutter?" I asked skeptically. "Wasn't she kind of old?"

"Age has nothing to do with it, son. She was plenty smart to know what she was doing. Second important thing that happened to Scottie." He held up two fingers. "Scottie was making some connections between a diamond mine in Canada and the Diamond District in Manhattan. He and his buddies were building a network to collect uncuts from Canada, cut them in New York, and sell them on the black market."

"*That's* what my grandma did?" I asked, my eyes wide. "She cut diamonds for Scottie?"

"That was the plan," Uncle Richard said, and took a sip of his lemonade.

I tried to understand. Grandma Rose worked for this Scottie dude. Did that make her rich? Nothing in our life indicated there was anyone from our family who was. And there was something else. "Why get the diamonds from Canada? Can't you buy them here?"

Ma banged her fork down on the table with a sudden vengeance. "*Buy*? Don't you get it, Petey? They were stealing diamonds from one place, and selling them somewhere else for money. That's what Fencers do. That's what they called themselves. And that's where your grandmother came in. She was the one who cut those diamonds for the Fencers. That makes her a thief like them. And when the Fencers came after her, she left behind her mess for your father to take care of."

The Fencers! But these couldn't be the same ones I saw in the alley, could they?

Meanwhile, Uncle Richard was sitting up, pointing at Ma. "I beg to differ! Aunt Rose was no thief. She was protecting her family." He turned to me. "What would you do, Petey? One day Scottie leaves you with a set of stones. He thinks you'll cut them into something fine he'll sell elsewhere. Maybe he'll give you a share of the profit. Maybe he'll make threats to your life."

Ma muttered something from the counter.

"But here's the kicker," Uncle Richard said, ignoring her. "Before Scottie can walk away with the diamonds, the Feds pick him up. The whole fencing network from Canada to New York gets shut down, people on both sides of the border get thrown in jail. Scottie gets eight years! Now here's the important part, Petey. Imagine you're Rose. You've cut the diamonds like Scottie asked. He's arrested, and the authorities can't trace the stones back to you. But the Fencers know you've got them. What do you do?"

"I'd turn the diamonds in," Ma said. "That's the legal thing to do."

Uncle Richard said, "I'm not asking you. I'm asking Petey."

I thought for a moment. "I'd hide them."

Uncle Richard smiled. "You're darn right. And if you were Rose, you'd hide yourself, too."

"She went into hiding?" I asked, excited in spite of myself. It was like a spy movie.

"No, she died, Petey," Ma said.

Uncle Richard shook his head. "The right way to say it is she disappeared, Petey. The authorities found her car gone off the Taconic Parkway, on fire and completely destroyed. Was this the work of the Fencers? Or Rose herself? Nobody knows. They didn't find a body. But at least your family was left alone after that."

"But for how long?" Ma asked pointedly.

"These Fencers," I asked, "are they still around?" It was on the tip of my tongue to ask if Tops was one, but I was afraid. I didn't want Uncle Richard or Ma to guess I had the black book.

Uncle Richard scowled. "Yeah, and they have kids. There's a whole next generation of them. Younger and meaner. They don't know a thing about running the business. They just want to get their hands on the missing loot."

"This is going nowhere," Ma interrupted. "Petey, I can see Uncle Richard is confusing you. He doesn't know a beginning from an end. He just goes spinning in circles."

"Life is just one middle after another, Shanthi. You ought to know that."

They went back and forth, and while they did, a picture emerged. Grandma Rose had cut a set of diamonds she couldn't sell. She couldn't turn them over to the police either, because it was more money than she'd ever seen her whole life. And the police would want to know how she got them in the first place. So she disappeared. And now the Fencers were looking for the loot. But what loot? That's when I realized something big.

"Wait, nobody caught Grandma Rose?" I asked. "What did she do with the diamonds?"

"That," Uncle Richard said, "is the million-dollar question."

I was floored. "No one knows where the diamonds are? And there aren't any clues?"

Richard slurped from his cup. "Oh, there's clues. Rose was a jeweler, wasn't she? The night before she was gone, she left behind a necklace for me, and another for Omar. No explanation, no paper trail, just those two necklaces she said point to where the diamonds are, marked by an *Om*."

"Necklaces?" I stammered. "Like, they have a message on them about where the diamonds are?"

"Like, I don't know what they're telling us," Uncle Richard exclaimed. "I've looked them over and over, and they don't tell a blazing thing."

"Okay, that's enough," Ma said.

"So, wait, you have both of them?" I asked carefully.

"Mine's gone, through no fault of my own," Uncle Richard said, "and your mama says she gave away Omar's to the Salvation Army. What made her do a fool thing like that, I don't know."

Ma bristled but she didn't say anything.

Meanwhile, I tried to make sense out of what Uncle Richard said. "But I don't get it. Why couldn't she just tell you where the diamonds were? Why did she give you those necklaces instead?"

"Because *that's* the way Rose was, Petey," Ma said. "It was all a game for her."

"No," Uncle Richard said. "She was worried about us getting in trouble. This was her way of safeguarding us, of making sure we really wanted those diamonds before we went looking for them."

"Or maybe she didn't *want* anyone to find them," Ma said. "How about that?"

"Well, that's just crazy," Uncle Richard said.

"I rest my case." Ma turned to me. "Now, Petey, I'd like you to go upstairs. Richard and I have some talking to do. In private."

What did they need to talk about in private? It had to be about Randall or me. Or the loot. I felt another tremor inside me. "But the diamonds, Ma," I pleaded.

"Put that out of your mind. Those diamonds have brought nothing but misery to our lives. Who's to say they exist at all, except in our fantasies."

I stared at Ma. It seemed that if there was anything the universe could give us when we had nothing, it was this fortune left by my grandmother. Did Randall know? Was that why he was gone?

Upstairs, I went into a feverish pitch. Diamonds. Where would my grandmother hide them? And did my pop find them before he died? I went to the closet and pulled out the duffel bag. My pop's last things. If he'd found the diamonds, the evidence was here in the bag. Randall must have known that. And yet he'd left the bag behind.

I emptied everything onto my bed. I looked through all of it once, twice. The harness, the ropes, the chalk, the metal clasps. The more I looked, the more frustrated I became. There was *nothing* here, nothing to suggest my pop had found the diamonds. As far as I could see, there were only two items of importance: the black book and the necklace. The black book held the warning about Tops. And what did the necklace say? *Shouse.*

Unexpectedly, I remembered Myla. She thought the Fencers were after her, and I laughed in her face. But maybe she wasn't so far off. She'd been getting a few things right already. It had been a gamble telling her about my necklace, but I was so hungry for more information on Randall and Pop. And now the stakes had gone up tenfold. Could I crack the necklace when my uncle couldn't? Could I trust Myla to help me?

19 MYLA

I WAS WATCHING TV IN THE FAMILY ROOM WHEN Cheetah came in with the newspaper and his tablet. "What do you want to hear first, Myla—the moon thing or the sad thing?"

I looked up from my show. "Neither." Then I saw his face fall. "Okay, the moon thing."

Cheetah held up the weather page from the *Westchester Times*. "Remember the *Oms* in the train stations? And what the policeman said about the next moonless night? That got me thinking. I checked news reports online, and it turns out all the *Oms* painted at the stations have happened on a new moon."

"So?"

"So I looked at the moon forecast in the paper. Saturday is a new moon. Which is when Dobbs will get tagged, because it's the next station on the line that doesn't have an *Om* yet."

In spite of myself, I felt a glimmer of interest. Was Cheetah right? Was Peter going to paint on Saturday night? "Hey, that's pretty smart," I said.

Cheetah flushed with pleasure. "Do you think I should tell Mom? You know how she hates graffiti. Maybe she can do something to stop it and—"

"No," I said, shaking my head. I was still feeling out of sorts about Peter, but I didn't want him to get in trouble. "She wouldn't understand."

"Understand what?"

I sighed. "That graffiti is art, Cheet. We can't stop art from happening."

He nodded. "I guess."

"So what's the sad thing? You said there were two things."

"Oh, yeah." Cheetah handed me the tablet. "It's about how Peter's dad died."

When he said that, my stomach dropped. On his tablet was an obituary, dated seven years ago. I read the article and swallowed. "Are you sure it's his dad?"

"There was only one Shanthi Wilson when I Googled."

I was stunned. Then a vague feeling overcame me, a kind of déjà vu. "I know about this," I said quietly. "It's him, Cheetah."

"Who?"

I shook my head. He wouldn't have remembered the dinner party at Margaret's all those years ago. He was too little. But I did. Hair like black licorice. It was all coming back. I couldn't believe Peter was the same boy. I couldn't believe it was the story of his dad that I'd heard so many years ago.

"Are you okay?" Cheetah asked me anxiously. "I thought you'd want to know."

I looked at him and saw he was freaked out, too. "Don't worry, Cheet. Forget about it. Do your spelling club stuff or something."

"All right," he said, unsure.

After my show was done, I went up to my room. My new

bed hadn't been delivered yet, so I stretched out on my old mattress. I missed my plywood bed. If you sat the right way on it, you could watch the sun setting behind the Palisades. From here, I couldn't see a thing, just the room getting dark as it became evening.

Below I could hear the creak of Cheetah's feet across the family room floor, and Beatles music wafting from my dad's study where he was doing lesson plans. My thoughts crept to Peter. Why did he act the way he did about the black book? Why did he show me his necklace but not tell me about the *Om*s he painted? I thought of his sweatshirt with the specks of orange paint on his sleeves, of what he sprayed in the most improbable places, big splashes of color that were strangely brave and beautiful. I thought of his father falling from that building, and how I'd carried that memory of what happened all these years. Like a permanent tag. Like a stillness inside me.

For years, my dad tried to teach me yoga. We would start with the mountain pose, then tree pose, and finally triangle. But I couldn't keep the lines of my body straight. I was always losing my balance, and to be honest, even standing still was hard—not for my body, but for my mind.

Dad says yoga isn't about holding a pose, but making it last as long as you can. It's a way to bring your body to rest, and your thoughts, too. But I didn't want to rest my mind. I didn't want to rest anything. The most important thing in the world was to move, and to keep moving.

*

In the kitchen, Mom emptied a bag of vegetarian Chinese takeout onto the counter.

"Again?" I asked. I'd come down when I heard her car in the garage and surveyed the items: tofu with peanut sauce, vegetarian wonton soup, and noodles with mixed vegetables.

"Oh, Myla, I barely had any time today," Mom said.

"Well, it's my favorite," Cheetah said. "Let's chow."

"I know, Cheet," Mom said, relieved. "At least one of you is happy."

We assembled around the dining table after Mom and Dad set out the food. I pushed around the congealed tofu on my plate with my fork. How could Cheetah like this stuff? I was tired of takeout. It seemed like that's all we were doing, that Mom was too tired to cook, or Dad would try to make something disgusting with Brussels sprouts, and we would still end up with takeout.

"Hey, I was thinking for the fall colors," Mom said, "we could try Breakneck Ridge again."

"No," I said. I stabbed a broccoli with my fork.

"Why not?" Mom asked. "It will be better this time."

"No," I said again. "I'll stay at home, you guys can go without me."

"She's scared of heights," Cheetah said. "You know."

I gave him a look. "No, I'm not."

"Whatever," he said.

Breakneck Ridge was a hiking trail our parents insisted on dragging us to last summer. We were halfway up when we had to climb across an endless stretch of sheer rock, and I almost hyperventilated. Dad sat in the car with me while Mom and Cheetah finished the trail without us.

Mom turned to me. "We'll only go halfway up."

"I'll still stay home," I said. "And don't sign me up for rock climbing either."

Mom sighed. "How will you get better if you don't keep putting yourself out there? Remember, the best way to conquer fear is to face it."

"I don't need to get better! Next you'll say I have to go bungee jumping."

"Boing boing," Cheetah said, giggling.

"Okay, new subject," Mom said, seeing my face. "How was school today?"

I didn't feel like talking about that either, so we listened to Cheetah's glowing report of how he'd made two new spelling friends in addition to his two best friends who were already spellers. Which, if you think about it, is mind-boggling, unless Dobbs Ferry has the highest proportion of elementary school spelling geeks this side of the Hudson.

"I discovered a problem in class," Dad said. "The math books have the wrong answers."

"What?" Cheetah said. "They solved the problems wrong?"

The answers were correct, Dad said, but listed under the

wrong chapters in the back of the book. "We have to ship everything back. I don't know what Peter will think."

"Why would he care?" Cheetah asked.

"Oh, he's very bright. He knew everything on the test I gave him on the first day."

"Who's Peter?" Mom asked.

"The boy next door," Cheetah said. "He moved in with his mom."

"Oh." She glanced at me. "I ran into her at the station this morning."

"You know them?" Cheetah asked.

Mom cleared her throat. "They were friends of Margaret and Allie."

"Did you know Peter's dad died falling off a building?" Cheetah said suddenly. I guess he couldn't keep it to himself anymore.

"Oh, Cheet." Dad sighed. "It was a long time ago. I think we should all put it behind us."

I stared at my tofu. Why did Cheetah have to tell *everything*? I knew what was coming next.

"Myla, are you okay?" Dad asked.

"Of course I'm okay. I didn't fall off a building."

"Myla, that's not funny," Mom said.

"I'm not trying to be!" Why would anyone think I was joking?

Mom and Dad looked at each other. Mom opened her mouth and then I could see Dad shake his head slightly, as if to say, *Don't go there.*

"Well, maybe Breakneck Ridge would be a good idea," Mom finally said. "A good first step."

Was my mother crazy? "I'm fine right where I am," I said.

But now she was craning her neck to the hall. "Wait, did you hear that?"

"What is it, Rani?" Dad asked.

Mom got up from the table. "It sounded like someone at the door."

No one else had heard anything. But now we were curious, so we followed her to the hall. "The porch squeaked," Mom said. She opened the door and we peered out. But there was no one.

"Maybe it was a cat," Dad said. "Or the wind."

But then Cheetah turned on the hall light. "Look at the door! On the front!"

And that's when we all saw it.

20 MYLA

MOM USED SOAP AND LYSOL, BUT NOTHING GOT it out.

"It's a Sharpie," Cheetah said. "Everyone knows Sharpies don't come out."

Meanwhile, I stood on our porch, staring at the four black vertical lines on the door. I knew what they were. I'd been marked. I looked toward Peter's house. Had he been marked, too?

"Myla, where are you going?" Mom called out as I walked quickly down our front path.

"She's going to the neighbors," Cheetah said. Then I heard him walking loudly behind me.

"Stop following me. You're being too noisy."

He jogged next to me, stepping on twigs. "How do you know they've got those lines, too?"

"I don't. Shush!" We stopped short of Peter's porch, which was unlit, but the streetlight was bright enough to see their front door.

"Nothing," Cheetah said. I walked back and forth slowly to make sure. He was right.

Back on our porch, Mom was waiting. "Come inside. I have no idea who did this, but that doesn't mean you have to go around the neighborhood looking at everyone's door."

"We weren't going everywhere, just next door," Cheetah said. "Right, Myla?"

"Buzz off," I said.

He gave me a hurt look, and went inside.

"Myla, that wasn't fair," Mom said. "Remember, he's your little brother."

"But he's always in my face. Sometimes I have to figure things out on my own."

Mom tried to put an arm around me. "You don't have to do it all on your own," she said softly. "What's bothering you?"

I shrugged her arm off. "Nothing!" I ran back inside.

The whole conversation made me angry. I didn't want my mom's help. But more than that, I was angry because she was right. I was being horrible, but I couldn't stop myself. I was worried, and Cheetah had this uncanny way of knowing how I felt, even when no one else did. Soon he would be announcing to Mom and Dad how Myla was afraid that the lines on the door were meant for her.

Inside, I overheard Dad and Cheetah talking and cleaning up in the kitchen.

"It happened a long time ago," Dad was telling him. "But it left an impression on her."

"But why didn't she tell me?" Cheetah wanted to know. "I would get it."

"We know that. You're a great brother. Just give her some time, Cheet."

I caught Cheetah's eyes, and I knew they were talking about

me. I'd heard it all before: He was a great brother, and I was the worst sister in the world.

Ever since I could remember, I was walking into conversations like that where one of my parents was explaining to Cheetah something awful about me that wasn't his fault. When I wouldn't let him go trick-or-treating with Ana and me, or watch *Pirates of the Caribbean* with us when she came for a sleepover. Or how I didn't share my roasted marshmallow with him after we made it in the backyard grill, even when I threw half of it away in the garbage.

It's a phase, they would say. *She doesn't like to share Ana*, they would say. And I would pretend they were right so I didn't have to think about it. But the truth was, I felt bad every time, and I wondered what was wrong with me. Why was it so easy for Cheetah to be friends with my friends, or find kids who were exactly like him, when I had to work so hard to get what I had? And by the way, that marshmallow took me *ages* to crisp exactly right. It wasn't my fault it gave me a stomachache afterward.

I couldn't listen to Cheetah and Dad anymore. So I went to look at the front door again. *Three lines made a fence*. Now I understood what Peter meant. But there were four lines on my door. Did that make a difference? Craggy had said the Fencers would come after me. But how did they know where I lived? Unless someone else knew, someone who was marking my door for them. I shivered.

I had to talk to somebody. It was too late to call Ana, and I wasn't sure I could talk to Peter. Not after the way he acted with the black book. But there *was* someone else. As much as I loathed the idea, I needed her help. So I went to my room and took down the business card stuck to The Wall.

She came immediately. I waited at the window so she wouldn't have to ring the doorbell.

"That's four lines," Kai said as soon as I opened the door. No hi, just right out with it.

"I know. I told you that on the phone already."

"Then it's not a Fencer tag. I've seen them before. It's always three lines."

I waited. "So what does that mean?"

She was about to answer when Dad came down the hall. "Oh, hello, Kai!" he said, surprised.

Kai's face slipped for a fraction of a second. "Hi, Mr. Rajan."

"What are you doing here?" he asked.

"Kai's helping me with American Studies," I said quickly. "We have to write about a historical landmark. She works at the newspaper, so she had some information for me."

"Really?" Dad asked. "Working there at your age?"

Kai's eyes darted at me. "Oh, you know me."

"Kai was in my math class a few years ago," Dad explained to me. Then he said to her, "Now look at you! In high school! Time flies!"

I threw a look at Kai, who shrugged.

"Well, I'll leave you two to it. You want to work in the study?"

"No, how about your room, Myla?" Kai asked, already walking to the stairs.

As we went up, I said accusingly, "You lied about college. You're really in high school."

"Fine. So what?"

We got to my room and I stopped. "I'm not even sure I should trust you. Maybe you don't know anything about the Fencers. Maybe you don't even work for the newspaper." I saw Cheetah standing outside his door, watching us. Kai saw him, too.

"Can we talk inside?" she asked me. We went in my room and Kai shut the door. "Okay, I lied about my age. I'm sixteen. But everything else is true. I do work for the newspaper. I'm an intern, but I do everything the other writers do. I've been following this case with Scottie Biggs and the Fencers ever since I was young. I really do know everything about it. And maybe this will be the first article I write and publish completely on my own."

"So?" Her publishing an article had nothing to do with the four lines on my front door.

"So . . . ," Kai said evenly. "That's not a Fencer tag on your door."

"You already said that."

"It's someone who drew it wrong. Somebody trying to make the tag, maybe to scare you. Is there someone like that you know?"

I didn't say anything.

I saw Kai staring intently at The Wall. I was suddenly conscious of everything up there—all the pieces of graffiti I had copied, the notes about her snooping and what I knew about the house next door, and the moon forecast I'd cut out from our newspaper. But it was the note from Craggy she zeroed in on. "Who's trying to find you, Myla?" she asked.

I still didn't say anything.

"How are the new neighbors?"

"They're nice," I said.

"You met Peter yet?"

"Yeah, he's nice, too." I was discovering how useful the word "nice" was.

Kai sighed. "I'm here because you called. And if we work together, you can be safe." She sat at my desk. "I'll start with what I know. Because I know what the Fencers are looking for."

"That's the craziest story I've heard," I said when she was done. "Diamonds hidden here."

"But Scottie lived in Dobbs," Kai answered. "And next door was the last place he was seen before his arrest. So why shouldn't the Fencers look for them here?"

"Yeah, but to say Scottie gave the diamonds to Rose."

"Consider the facts. Rose lived in Dobbs. She was a diamond cutter. And she was Margaret's friend."

"What does that have to do with anything?"

"Scottie was last seen in Margaret's house!" Kai exclaimed. "One of them had the diamonds, Scottie or Rose, and they hid them *somewhere*. Diamonds don't vanish into thin air."

I thought over what she said. Actually, it was kind of exciting—something that valuable, hidden all these years in the town where I lived. But it still didn't explain why the Fencers wanted my necklace. Isn't that what Craggy had said? Could the diamonds and the necklace be connected in some way?

I debated, then I told Kai. "There might be another reason the Fencers are looking for me," I said. I held up my necklace. "It started with this." Then I told her about Craggy following me in Yonkers.

"Interesting," Kai said. "Rose made those finders necklaces, you know."

"Really?' I asked, surprised. "Peter has one, too."

Kai nodded. "Makes sense. She's his grandmother."

"But what do you think it *means*, Peter and I having the same necklace?"

Kai wasn't sure. "It doesn't all add up . . . yet."

"So what do I do?"

"We need to work together. We need to figure out why your necklace is important to the Fencers. But in the meantime, don't tell Peter anything. Don't tell him you know about the missing diamonds. For all you know, he's the one who marked your door."

"Peter wouldn't do that," I said quickly.

"Yes, but I don't think we can trust him yet. We need to

make sure he's not working for the Fencers. Don't look so shocked! Keep an eye on him, see what he knows, learn his routine. Who does he talk to? Maybe he carries a phone or a notebook to school."

"I haven't seen a phone, but he does have a small black book," I said slowly.

Kai sat up suddenly. "Well, there you go," she said.

"What, spy on Peter? That doesn't sound like much of a plan."

"No, isn't it obvious?" Kai leaned forward. "You have to take his black book."

"What!" I exclaimed. "I can't do that!"

"Myla, think. What if there's something in there—a phone number? Names?" She paused. "And graffiti writers carry black books, too. Maybe Peter's the one painting all those *Oms* recently."

I was amazed by how Kai made that leap. But I didn't like this change in direction. "I'm not taking Peter's black book," I said.

"Well, maybe you *won't*," she said as she stood up from my desk, "or maybe you *can't* because you don't have the guts. In which case, I'll do it for you instead."

My eyes narrowed. "Wait, why would you? And you'd never get to it. He has it with him all the time, including school."

"Don't worry. I'll find a way."

What way was she talking about? I started jumping on her to explain, but she wouldn't answer any more questions.

"I have to go. Just keep your mouth shut and I'll take care of the rest."

I ran to my door as she was walking out. "But what's in it for you?" I asked.

Kai just smiled. "I would hate it if something happened to you because of the Fencers. Especially if we had a chance to stop it."

Then she left. I saw Cheetah watching worriedly from behind his bedroom door.

21 MYLA

THAT NIGHT I TOSSED AND TURNED. FINALLY I sat up, wide awake, staring into the darkness. Kai wanted me to steal Peter's black book, but it didn't make sense. I was sure Peter wasn't a Fencer. I thought of us sitting at his table yesterday afternoon, how we were serious one moment, laughing the next. I thought of the bag of Cheetos he offered. And I remembered how the cover of his black book felt, bruised and battered, and like the most important thing he owned. How could I take something like that away from him?

I couldn't shake the feeling that it was Kai who wanted the black book. And she was using me to get to it. I turned on the light, and went over to The Wall. I found the list I'd made last week, of all the things I knew about Margaret's house. It was where Scottie Biggs was last seen. And it was where I found Kai searching room after room, taking photos. What had she been searching for?

"The diamonds," I whispered. Did she think they were hidden in the house? Or was she looking for clues? Either way, it was the diamonds she wanted. And maybe she wanted to write her story, too, but imagine what she'd write if she actually found them.

But why did she need the black book? What was the rest of the story she told me—how there were rumors that the diamonds were hidden and marked by an *Om*. Is that what these tags were? I'd thought they were some kind of communication. But what if the *Om*s were something else? Like a trail leading to the jewels? Kai seemed to think that Peter's family was the link to the diamonds. Maybe she also thought the answer was in that black book.

I paced back and forth across my floor, thinking and thinking until I grew tired. One thing I knew for sure. Kai wasn't getting that black book through me. I was done asking for her help. Instead, I would talk to Peter tomorrow. I would ask him about the diamonds and the four lines on my door. I trusted him a lot more than I trusted Kai. Maybe Peter and I could figure some of this stuff out together.

I fingered my necklace. Om. It was a word that was supposed to bring you peace. Yet this piece of jewelry had complicated my life in so many ways. I took it off and put it in my desk drawer. Maybe it was better that way . . . at least for tomorrow. Then I turned off the light and went back to bed.

In the morning, when I came downstairs, Mom had colored over the black Sharpie lines on the door with a red Sharpie so you couldn't see them from far away. But that didn't help me. I hadn't slept well, and in the bathroom mirror, I saw circles under my eyes.

Cheetah noticed. "Kai really freaked you out last night," he said to me on the curb as we watched Dad back the car out of the driveway.

"No, she didn't," I said not very convincingly.

We got into the backseat and Dad pulled out onto Cherry Street.

"Forget about her," Cheetah whispered. "Anybody that scares you is bad."

Dad fiddled with the radio and tuned to NPR.

"Life doesn't always work that way," I whispered back to my brother.

"I-n-s-t-i-n-c-t," he said.

"What, now you're spelling words at me?"

He shook his head. "It's not just a spelling word."

Like that helped.

22 PETER

IT WAS FRIDAY MORNING, AND I WAS LATE TO class. I had trouble sleeping, thinking about last night's conversation with Uncle Richard, the diamonds, and Grandma Rose, and how a new life was waiting for us if we could solve the puzzle she'd left behind. Meanwhile, Mr. Clay was asking everyone to take out their ads. I barely got mine out when he called on me to share. Really? Was it because I was tardy? I knew some teachers who worked that way. I looked at Myla but she was writing something in her notebook.

"I did mine on a person, not a place," I said. "The Keeper of the Aqueduct. Here it is:

"Come one, come all! Come see how history gets made, as water from Croton Dam gets pumped forty-one miles to the city, quenching the scorching thirst of New York's finest residents. As a Keeper, I make sure there are no cracks or leaks in the pipes, nothing to stop the water from getting where it's going. I'm careful and I work hard. At the end of the day I kick back at my house with some malt beer. Maybe you'll join me and see why my job is the most important one in all of New York!"

Mr. Clay smiled. "I see you're also advertising malt beer, one of New York's famous beverages. And *scorching*? Is that a reference to the Great New York Fire?"

"Wasn't that one of the reasons for the Aqueduct?" I asked. "There wasn't enough water to put out fires in the city?"

He nodded. "Save that thought," he told me.

After everyone was done and we turned in our ads, Mr. Clay told us how normally we would watch a movie next, but that this year we were doing something different.

"We're fortunate to have one of our alumnae here today to tell us more about the Aqueduct." At the door, he motioned to someone. Then who should come in but Kai Filnik.

A parkour real estate agent talking about the Aqueduct? This I had to see. I checked if Myla found this as hilarious as me. Instead, I was surprised to see another type of expression on her face. She was positively horrified. Like it was Christmas in hell. Like any minute she was going to keel over and die. Really? All because of Kai Filnik?

"I'm so excited to share my honors project with you guys," Kai said. "Mr. Clay used to be my teacher, too, and he was totally cool."

Okay. Snooze time. But then she started her slideshow, and even though her voice was like nails going down the blackboard, what she showed us was kind of interesting. First, she put up slides of the Aqueduct getting made, and the stonemasons who came from Italy and Ireland to build the Croton Dam. Then she showed us how it all got put together, with miles and miles of brick tunnels laid down that carried the water from Croton River to Manhattan.

"Gravity moved ninety million gallons of water a day," Mr. Clay interjected. "And no one even saw it or heard it. It was like a precious resource for everyone, hidden underground, like . . ." He paused. "Like the earth had a secret."

Kai smiled. "That's right, Mr. Clay. And there were other people in on that 'secret.' They were called 'keepers' like I heard Peter telling you while I was sitting outside. They were stationed along the Aqueduct, and maintained the pipes and tunnels."

I glanced at Myla again, who finally looked at me. She smiled, but it was a weird smile. Then her eyes flickered back to the screen. It was the most confusing thing. Was she mad at me? Or what? I looked back at the screen, too, and whoa. I was startled to see something I actually recognized.

"This is High Bridge," Kai explained, "which just reopened over the summer. The bridge carried Aqueduct water over the Harlem River to Manhattan."

Randall had been asking to see this bridge all summer, but Ma didn't have time. I'd never noticed how beautiful the bridge was.

"High Bridge is the oldest standing bridge in New York City," Mr. Clay said.

"Older than the George Washington Bridge?" someone asked.

"Yes," Mr. Clay said. "And it's a beauty."

I looked at the way the arches under High Bridge went up

and down like a McDonald's sign. Then something about that made me stop.

The lights came on as Mr. Clay thanked Kai for sharing her presentation with us.

"If you don't mind, I'll stay and listen," she said. "Your class is the best."

I don't think I'd seen a bigger smile on Mr. Clay's face. He started talking to us about our assignment for Monday. Meanwhile, I spread open the black book inside my American Studies textbook. There was something I had to check, something from Kai's slide that triggered an image in my head. It didn't take me long to find my pop's drawing. And I saw I was right. It wasn't just some bridge he'd drawn. It was High Bridge, with the same arches, and the letters "HB" underneath. Not only that, there was a line with a dot in the middle that ran from it to another drawing, like a wall with steps attached to it, and the letters "CD" . . . Croton Dam! But what was my pop sketching these for?

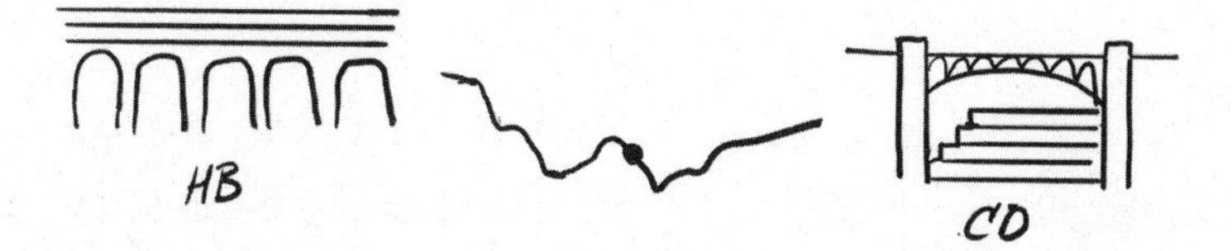

Then class was over, so I closed the American Studies textbook on my table with the black book still inside. That's when Kai stopped by.

"How's it going, Peter?" she asked. "You all moved in?"

I looked up at her. "Yeah, we're moved in. I thought you were going to do some PK for us."

She laughed. "No, that's for another day. I was talking to Mr. Clay. I asked if he had you, and how we wanted to make sure you and your mom were all set up in Dobbs."

"How thoughtful," I said. "Like your newspaper subscription."

By now, Myla came over, too, with her textbook in tow. She moved in front of Kai, almost pushing her out of the way. "I'm going to get a hernia carrying this," she said setting her book down heavily on the table next to mine. We'd got our textbooks yesterday, and Mr. Clay had warned us that they weighed seven pounds.

"Yeah, we'll probably be bench-pressing it in PE," I said. We both glanced at Kai, wondering if she was just going to stand there. It was awkward, us wanting to talk and the parkour girl not getting the hint.

"You're not wearing your necklace?" I said to Myla.

"Not today," Myla said. She looked like she wanted to say more, but she didn't.

Then, would you believe it, Ana came over next. She and Kai exchanged hellos, so I guess they knew each other, and now I was surrounded by three girls at my table. I'd say it was a compliment, except it wasn't. There was something fishy going on.

Plus with Ana there, I felt my palms start to sweat. She had on a dark blue shirt that looked like velvet, something I've only read about, but you know it when you see it.

"Myla said you're neighbors," Ana said to me.

"Yeah, small world," I said. "Next you'll say your ma is the French teacher."

Ana laughed, and her laugh was just like the sparkly earrings she wore.

Kai laughed, too. "He's funny, isn't he?"

"Except Ana is Norwegian," Myla said flatly. What was up with her? Was she trying to make me look stupid?

"That's right, I'm Norwegian," Ana said. "It gets me in all kinds of trouble."

"I don't see you as trouble," I said. And then I felt myself blush. I better shut up, that's what. But the way Ana smiled back, it made something inside me lift high.

Meanwhile, Myla was fading like a day-old flower. She was wilting and wilting. And I don't know, it was making me feel bad, too, so I was lifting and sinking at the same time.

Kai seemed to notice also. "Myla, are you okay? You don't look so good."

Ana turned to her. "Are you okay?"

"I'm fine," Myla said. Then all of a sudden she was like, *Gotta go!* She grabbed her book off the table and hurried out. We all looked at one another.

"I should check on her," Ana said, and followed her out.

By then, Mr. Clay said we had to leave because the next class was coming in. So I headed out, too. At my locker, I tossed the King Kong textbook inside where it could stay all day, and shut the door with a bang. And that's when I remembered the black book.

23 MYLA

ANA CAME UP TO MY LOCKER. "ARE YOU OKAY? You ran out like you were about to puke."

I set the American Studies book carefully on the middle shelf inside my locker.

"What? I'm fine." I paused. "I just don't like Kai."

"She is kind of nosy," Ana agreed. "But your neighbor is soooo nice. Yesterday he sat next to me in Spanish class, and we tried to write notes to each other in Spanish."

I swallowed. "Oh, yeah?" I tried to sound interested as I looked into the recess of my locker. It seemed like the rest of me was somewhere in there, too. Because I felt empty, except for the sad feeling rising in my throat.

"If you don't feel better, let me know," Ana said. "I can go to the nurse's office with you."

I gave a half smile. "I'm okay, Ana. Really."

She hugged me, and my tears almost spilled over because she was my best friend, even when I was grumpy or annoying, and because she was being nice to me now, like she always was. I told myself it was silly to cry, because there was nothing to be sad about.

Then right after Ana left for her class and I was wondering what on earth to do, Kai came up to me. "Well done, Myla."

I watched her warily. "What do you mean?"

She nodded at my open locker. "I saw what you did. It was very clever."

I sniffed. "I have no idea what you mean," I said, even though my heart was beating fast.

"In class now, you took Peter's book." She pointed to it. "That's his book."

"Really? They all look the same."

"You can't fool me. I know what's inside that textbook. It's his black book. You put your textbook next to his. Then you took his when you left."

"If I did, it was a mistake." I closed my locker shut. "I'll return it as soon as I see him."

Kai tilted her head. "Don't you think you should share the black book with me? I can help you. I can figure out if Peter's working with the Fencers or not."

I pointed a finger at her. "You're lying. You want the black book for yourself. But you're not getting it. You'll have to write your story without me."

Kai paused for a moment. "Fine, have it your way. We could have worked together. You could have been part of my story." She tossed her hair. "Now you're on your own."

"Even better!" I called out to her as she walked away.

The bell rang. I was late to English. But I waited until Kai was gone before I opened my locker again. I stared at Peter's American Studies book sitting on the middle shelf. The thing is, I didn't intend to take the black book. Not after all the thinking I did last night. Then seeing Kai in class today totally unhinged me. I never thought she would find a way to get to Peter, but she did. And maybe she really would have taken his black book, unless I did something to stop her.

But deep down, I knew Kai wasn't the real reason I did it. It wasn't because I wanted to stop her, or because I was scared of the Fencers, or that Peter was working with them. It was seeing him and Ana together—Ana, who was my oldest friend, and Peter, who was my newest. While they were laughing and joking, I could see that goofy look in their eyes. It was the kind of look that meant I'd vanished in the process. And I was so tired of that, of wanting to be taller and louder and prettier. If only there was something I had—something that would make me stand out and feel better about myself. Then I couldn't help seeing how Peter's textbook was right next to mine. It was just a matter of speed, and the little black book was now in my locker.

I fished it out and I felt monstrous, holding the worn cover between my fingers. I could give it back right now, as soon as I saw Peter. I could do the right thing and then everything would be fine. And maybe Peter and I would go on being friends, and we'd figure out what the four lines on my door meant. And he and Ana would pass notes in Spanish class, and then American Studies, and then they'd walk home together because she lived down the street from him, too. And that would be the end of me knowing Peter better than anyone else in Dobbs Ferry.

Or . . . I could go inside his head a teeny, tiny bit. I could find out what was so important that he had to hide what he wrote inside his textbook. It would be just a small peek. Then I'd give the black book back to Peter.

The rest of my day went like this. English: flip through black book. Technology: flip through black book. Science: flip. Math: flip. By Spanish, I'd flipped through everything multiple times. I'd tried so hard to look just a little bit, but in the end, I saw it all.

And what did the black book tell me? Nothing about the diamonds. Nothing about the Fencers. But it did tell me about Om. And that Peter loved graffiti. Like me. And that he was obsessed with words. Like me. There were lots of *OMAR* and *Om* tags. Maybe it was Peter's tag. Or maybe he was writing them to remember his dad. When I thought of that, it made me sad.

There were also things in the book that were nothing like me. Lyrics from songs I'd never heard, drawings of cars and trains, and faces inside letters with their eyes closed. Then, halfway through the book, were the strangest drawings of all. It took me a moment to figure out that "HB" stood for High Bridge and "CD" stood for Croton Dam. I wasn't sure what the line and dot were. I traced my finger along the curving line, puzzled.

But I think I finally realized what I'd been searching for. It wasn't clues about the diamonds. It was whether Peter and I were meant to be friends. It seemed if I found enough things in here we had in common—like caring about graffiti—it wouldn't matter how I talked or looked. Peter would still think I was special. Instead I found words and drawings I didn't understand. I found the last traces of a father who was never coming back. Then I knew you couldn't find friendship by looking through someone else's private book. So I shut the black book and put it away.

I could hardly concentrate on anything after that. It seemed like I was in a fog, and the teacher was talking somewhere behind it, far away. Finally I wrote this in my journal:

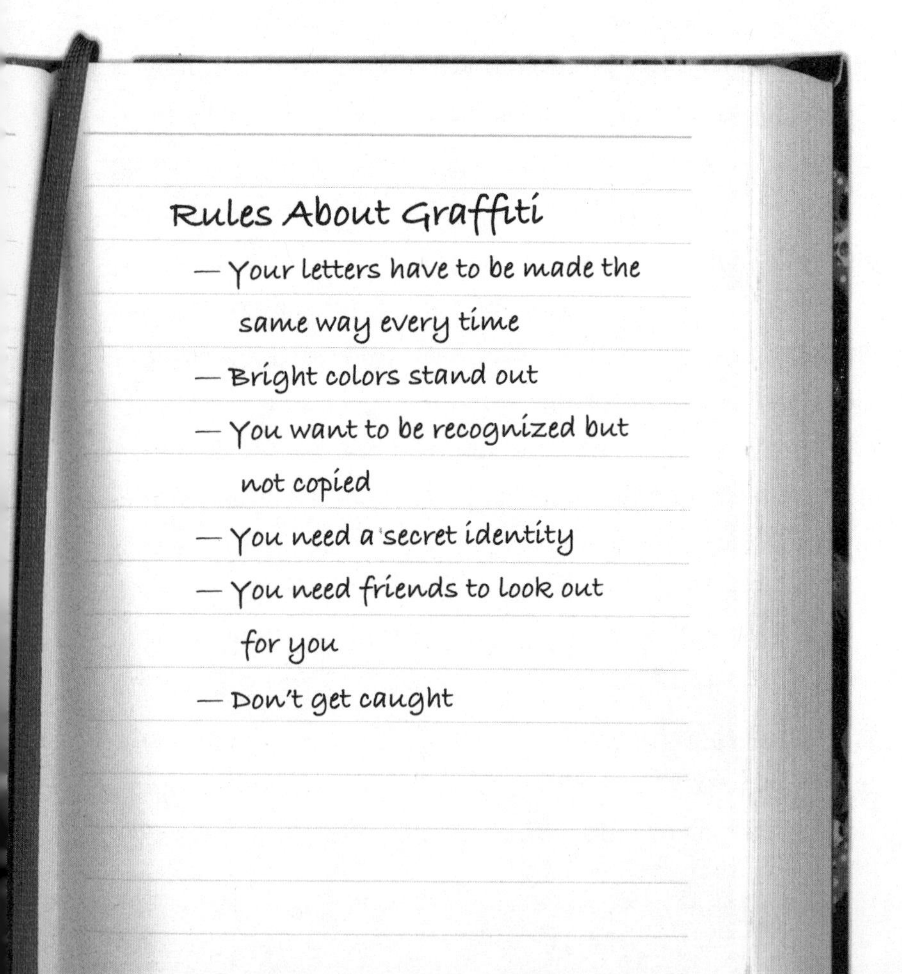

I don't know why I wrote them, except there was a part of me that wished I could do what Peter did. Most of all, I wanted to feel like I learned something to make up for the terrible fact that I'd looked through his black book. The shame of it followed me as I hurried to my dad's class after Spanish. That was where I knew Peter would be.

Dad saw me and came to the door. "Myla, aren't you supposed to be in woodshop?"

I cleared my throat. "Is Peter here?" I looked around as my shame grew and grew.

Dad glanced behind himself. "As a matter of fact, he isn't. I was about to take attendance."

"But he was in my class this morning," I said. I came in and walked down the aisle while some of the students looked at me. I was conscious of how weird I looked, trolling their classroom. But Dad was right. Peter was nowhere to be found. The shame had now turned into a dark cloud hanging over me as I walked out of the room. And then I was left carrying the weight of Peter's American Studies book, with no Peter.

24 PETER

ANYONE WHO CAN GET SEPARATED FROM A black book between American Studies and French has talent. For being a loser. Soon as I noticed, I hightailed it back to American Studies. Mr. Clay came to the door. "Hi, Peter, did you need something?"

"I think I left my book here," I said, my voice wavering.

"There weren't any books left behind."

"I mean, I have my book, I just had something in it that's missing. Some . . . notes."

"You were all talking, and your books were on the table. Maybe they got switched?"

"Switched?"

"You never know." He smiled faintly at me and went back to his class.

A switch. Why didn't I think of that? I hurried to my locker and pulled out the American Studies book. I turned to the beginning page and there it was in the top corner, written in pencil: *Myla Rajan*. This was her book. Which meant she had mine.

Maybe it was a simple mistake. Maybe Myla would be waiting for me in the hall or back at my house. *Oops*, she would say, smiling as we exchanged books. But the reality was I was cold with fear. Fear of her looking at it, seeing all those *Om*s, and doing what? Putting together stuff about Pop and Randall, and the hidden diamonds.

There was another problem. Finding her. I scouted in the halls between classes, but no luck. Then I decided to go home and wait for her in the one place I knew she would be, eventually. I wouldn't budge till I saw her reach her front door.

As I walked home, the air was crisp, like the kind of autumn day when you should be eating apples and drinking cider, though my family never did any of that. My Jordans were starting to pinch around the heels, and a hole was working its way through my right shoe, near my big toe. But they still had spring. They still had action. I thought about that night in Yonkers when Randall jumped on the rail. Truth was, I thought about that night all the time. I thought about my brother's crew, and what they were doing, if they were scheming like that MaxD, or in Randall's corner like Nike.

By now, I'd got to Walnut. Just halfway down and a left on Cherry, and I'd be home. As I walked, I saw an old house up ahead. I didn't know what it was, only that people were doing construction there. Then I scrambled back, crouching behind a car. Uncle Richard was talking to somebody in front. Not just talking but working.

Shoot, he would be working on Walnut Street, as the universe would have it. There was no way I could pass by without him seeing me. Then he'd know I'd cut class and tell my ma. I stayed a hair longer behind the car, wondering what to do. Maybe it was closer to the end of school than I thought.

What if I had a free period and I was walking home? I would act like I was supposed to be here, that's all. I continued. As I did, Uncle Richard and the second man crossed the street to the other side. For a moment I hoped I might miss him after all. But as I walked on, he turned at the last second and our eyes met. He gave me the barest smile, but he didn't call me over.

I let out my breath. When I got home, I eased onto the porch, not bothering with the door just yet in case it stuck like yesterday. That made me think of Myla, and I felt the bile rise inside me all over again. I had to get the black book back. Randall would kill me if anything happened to it. Even though I had to find him first before he could do that. If only I knew who Tops was.

Down the street, I saw a car. That is, I heard it first, then saw it, a beige-colored sedan with a sound like a plane taking off. I watched as it made its way and then turned unbelievably into our driveway. The door on the driver's side opened, and out stepped Uncle Richard.

"Hey, Petey." He stood behind the door, resting his elbows on top. "Home from school?"

"Yes, sir." I don't know where that "sir" came from. I guess I was tense.

He looked at the house next door. "You met your neighbor yet? With the green Subaru?"

I shrugged. "Yeah, an Indian family. There's a girl my age."

Uncle Richard nodded. "Indian like your mom?"

"I don't know. Just Indian, I guess."

He looked back at the house. "You know which room is hers?"

I blinked. Why would I know that? I shook my head.

Uncle Richard nodded. "Get to know your neighbors, Petey."

I frowned. I didn't know what he was getting at, and I was still wondering why he was here.

"I suppose you've been thinking about what I told you last night. Well, listen, I came to tell you we'll find your brother and he'll be okay. Now, if there's anything I can do, let me know. I'm here to help, son. I'm family."

He stood there with a smile on his face, like he understood everything about my life, even though he was a complete stranger. I was about to pick up my backpack as a signal for him to leave. He was making me nervous on my driveway, like being at my house, but not. Then a thought came to me, and I breathed in and out, terrified by my idea. "Actually, there's something you could do," I said slowly.

He leaned forward. "Is there? Tell me. I'm on it."

I looked one last time down the street for Myla. She wouldn't be home for an hour, and if I sat here waiting, I'd go crazy. I said to Uncle Richard, "It's Randall's friend. I think he could tell me where Randall is. Only I have to see him to ask."

"You need someone to take you?"

I nodded.

He motioned to the car with his head. "Get in."

25 PETER

THE SOUND WAS WORSE INSIDE. WHEN I WALKED home, no one noticed me. But when driving with Uncle Richard, everywhere we went we got looks from people, like we were a plane taking off from JFK. "What's wrong with your car?" I asked at the traffic light.

Uncle Richard chuckled. "Bad muffler. I took it in last week, and no worries, she's fine."

The car kept gunning as we waited for the light to change green.

"Now, you going to tell me who we're seeing?" he asked. "What's he know you don't?"

There was a lot I could ask my uncle. But I didn't want him to know anything about me in the process. "He's one of the last people who saw Randall," I said carefully.

Uncle Richard nodded. "You mean he's one of them."

I swallowed. Had I said too much? "You know what Randall . . . does?"

"That he paints? Sure. What do you think, I'm some ninny? I know what he does. Because long ago, your daddy and I did it, too." The light changed and we were off. *Vroom! Vroom!* I gritted my teeth against the sound. On either side, houses went by, then a fire station and a big grassy field. We were only a few minutes away from Central Ave. "You find out from your friend what you can. Just don't get involved."

"I don't do that stuff," I said stiffly.

"I see that, Petey. You're a good kid." He reached over and patted my arm awkwardly.

"Uncle Richard, are you married? Do you have kids?"

He laughed. "Sorry, son. No time for a family life."

"And do you know somebody named Tops?" I didn't want to ask before, but I couldn't pass up the opportunity now. My uncle might be the only one who'd tell me anything. What I didn't expect was his reaction. I wanted to take cover, his face got so mean.

But it wasn't me the meanness was aimed at. "Tops," he said like the word was a piece of meat gone bad. "That's one person you can't trust. Steer clear of that dog breath. That's something Omar should have done."

I waited, fearful of his next question: How did I know Tops? But my uncle was too seething mad to notice the nuances. "What's so bad about him?" I finally asked.

Uncle Richard pulled over to the side of the road and slammed the brakes. I was stunned because there was really no place to do that on Central Ave. I waited for somebody to come crashing into us.

"Promise me, Petey," Uncle Richard said, putting his face close to mine. "Don't go talking to that Tops. He's running from a jail sentence. Hear me? He's nobody you can trust, not you, your brother, or your mama." He paused. "Is that what this is all about? Randall's got mixed up with the likes of him?"

I shook my head. "No—c-c-course not," I stammered. I wasn't sure why I said that, when I was thinking the same thought. But something told me that my uncle would turn around and drive me back to Dobbs if I made mention of Tops again. And I really needed to see Nike.

It took Uncle Richard a moment. "All right then," he said. He pulled back into traffic, and I started breathing slowly again. Then we drove and drove with that muffler, and the world staring at us until we got to the Music Land in Yonkers. That's where Nike worked after school. And by this point, I was just happy to get out of the car.

"Remember now, you're just here to ask questions," Uncle Richard told me as we entered the store. "Soon as you're done, we leave. Don't know what your ma would say about me with you."

I nodded. I didn't know what she'd say either.

My uncle walked toward the classic rock section. "You come for me when you're done. I'll be here with the shades on." With that, he pulled out a honking pair of sunglasses and slid them on. He looked like some whacked-out seventies guy. But I said yes, and I searched for Nike.

It didn't take long. Near the subwoofers and amps, I spotted the familiar rusty hair.

"Petey!" He jumped a mile high at the sight of me. "I swear, you're following me. Like, you'll be standing some day on my grave."

Even now, after him running out on me like he did, it was good to see him. Nike was all about Randall and me and where I was from. "I'm not following you," I said. "I'm here to talk."

"Yeah, well, maybe I don't have time to talk to you."

"Just a few minutes. Don't you have a break or something?"

"A break for what?" Nike sneered. "This isn't preschool."

He turned to go. I reached over to pull his sleeve. "I don't know the next time I can come like this. Today I got a ride. Please, Nike."

He looked at me curiously. "You're not here with your mom?"

"No man, she works."

"Oh, right. The blood lady." He snickered. "Who's your ride, then?"

"See him with the shades? That's my uncle."

"Huh," he said, looking over at Uncle Richard. After a moment he said, "All right, follow me. There is one place we can talk." A second later, we were out behind the store, near the trash bin. Nike turned to me. "You've got exactly two minutes."

"Where's Randall?"

He looked annoyed. "You're asking me that again? I told you, he's gone to learn with Tops."

"Who is he? Is he a Fencer?"

Nike looked at me like I was smoking out of my ears.

"Then who is he? Why can't you take me to him?"

Nike shook his head. "That's not how it works. The point is, it's not who he is, it's what he can do. Training. Did you look up what I told you?"

I shrugged. "Yeah, parkour. So it's cool, and—"

"*Cool*? You think this job is where it's at? I'm practicing PK hard until I'm so good, I'll fly out of here and land in Santa Monica. They've got a stunt gym out there and everything."

"And that's what Randall is doing? Trying to get to Santa Monica?"

"Course not, you idiot. That's *my* dream."

"But where's Randall, then? You still haven't told me where to find him."

"Look, I can't. Why don't you follow the *Om*s?"

"Follow the *Om*s?"

"Sure. A moonless night is coming. That night, he'll be at the first clean station on the train line, because that's where he'll be doing the next *Om*. That's his latest thing."

"Dobbs." Why didn't I think of that? And the new moon was . . . "Tomorrow."

Nike nodded. "You be waiting there for him."

Okay. So I had a plan. But there was one thing Nike hadn't told me. "How does that . . . ?"

"It doesn't. I'm just telling you how to find Mighty. Now why's he training with Tops? That's easy. To make himself a better finder. He wants to find those diamonds and make your family rich."

I stared at him. He'd said the D word. Which meant he and Randall knew the story about my pop and grandma. My head was spinning. But why would parkour make Randall a better finder?

"One last thing. And this one's important, Petey. That uncle of yours. Don't trust him."

"Wh-wh-what?"

"I don't know what rock he crawled out from, but people don't just show up, hear?"

I stared at Nike's baby eyes. I remembered the times I'd seen him with the crew, his quiet way of whispering his tag in the dark—a wing for victory.

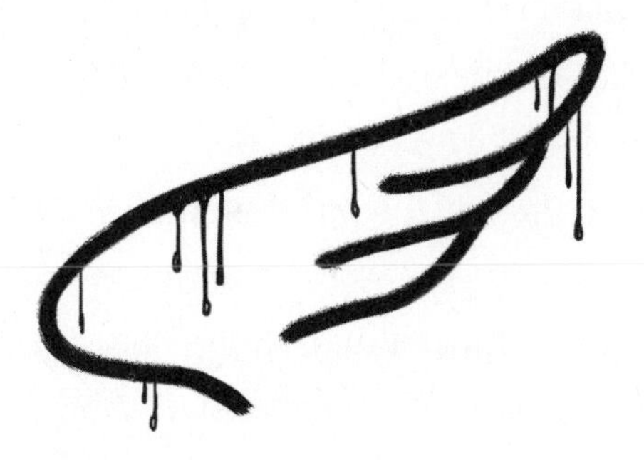

He had a little brother, and parents who spoke Spanish. I didn't know a single other thing about him except he was Randall's only real friend.

"Listen, this is my last day at the store," he said. "So don't come back here, okay?"

He turned to go when I stopped him.

"Who is he, Nike?" I whispered. "My uncle, that is?"

He shrugged. "I don't know. Just don't him tell him nothing about Mighty. *Nothing*." Then he disappeared inside the store.

26 MYLA

I WAS WALKING TO MY LOCKER AFTER THE LAST bell when Mr. Clay saw me from his door.

"Did Peter find you?" he asked.

I stopped. "Was he looking for me?"

Mr. Clay was drinking coffee as he spoke. "Well, he was looking for his American Studies book. We thought it got switched with someone else's, like yours."

So Peter had figured it out already. I guess I wasn't that shocked.

"Okay, I'll talk to him," I said, smiling weakly. "He lives next door to me."

"In Margaret's old place?"

This surprised me. "You know her, Mr. Clay?"

He nodded. "Sure. She used to come sometimes with her friend to the Historical Society when I was volunteering there."

"You mean Allie?" I said.

He shook his head. "No, that friend of hers, Rose. The diamond cutter."

So Mr. Clay knew Peter's grandmother, too? I wondered who else or *what* else he knew. He was the local history teacher, wasn't he? "I guess you've heard about Scottie Biggs," I said.

He lowered his coffee cup. "Oh, him. I don't know if we can believe everything we read. It's just too bad that Rose got her name involved, especially with what happened to her afterward."

Kai had told me about Rose's car accident. "Yeah," I said.

I looked down where students were streaming out the front doors. In a few minutes, the halls would be empty.

"And Rose knew a lot," Mr. Clay went on. "So did Margaret, but Rose came more often."

"What was she doing at the Historical Society?" I tried to picture someone who looked like Peter and made diamonds, talking to Mr. Clay about landmarks. It was a little hard to imagine.

"I don't think she was *doing* anything. She just liked history. She was someone who got it."

The halls were empty now except for the sound of one pair of footsteps. I saw my dad approaching us. "Got what?" I asked.

"That we're living in history," Mr. Clay said. "We're surrounded by it. At least, that's what I try to teach you kids. Buildings are our map back."

Buildings are our map back. I looked at him when he said that. I actually liked it. I'd have to write it down before I forgot.

"There you are," Dad said. He and Mr. Clay nodded to each other. "I hope she's keeping out of trouble," Dad said lightly.

"Oh, I have my eye on her," Mr. Clay said. "Myla's a sharp one."

I was surprised he said this. Mostly I was surprised he even knew my name.

"See you later, Mr. Clay," I said. In the parking lot, I dug out my journal from my backpack, and started writing down what Mr. Clay said.

Dad watched me. "Can't that wait? You can do it in the car. I've got a dental appointment in a little while."

"I'm almost done," I said.

"Peter does the same thing, you know," Dad observed. "I see him writing in his little book all the time. Just like you."

"Oh, yeah?" I asked. I could feel the guilt starting to bubble inside me again. I had to return Peter's stuff as soon as we got home. But first I stopped to read over what I'd written. *Buildings are our map back.* And just like that, seeing those words on the page, I thought of something else. Why didn't I see it before? "A map," I said softly.

"What did you say?" Dad asked.

I shook my head. "Never mind."

In the car, I drew it the same way I'd seen it in Peter's black book, right under Mr. Clay's words: High Bridge and Croton Dam, with a line and dot in between. It was a map of the Aqueduct Trail. And the dot? Maybe that was where we were. Maybe it was Dobbs Ferry.

I watched the buildings go past us as we drove down Broadway. I was still feeling bad about reading Peter's black book. But there was also this small glimmer of satisfaction in me that I'd solved one of Peter's puzzles. It wouldn't help me know him better, and it probably wouldn't make a difference to anyone else. But I'd still done it. I'd made sense out of something strange and mysterious. I turned to Dad. I wanted to tell him to step on it, but I didn't. "Hurry," I said instead. Then I added, "Please."

27 PETER

NOTHING COULD GET ME HOME FAST ENOUGH, least of all Uncle Richard's craptastic car.

"Petey, not following here. He can't tell you where Randall is?"

The car idled like a crazy thing at the traffic light.

"That's what he said." I kept a poker face.

"You mean, he doesn't know, or he doesn't want to tell you?"

"He doesn't know." I searched for something to tell Uncle Richard so he'd stop with the questions. "He said to watch the moon."

That seemed to work. Uncle Richard nodded. "We had this thing, your pop and me, about moonless nights. There's a way of knowing when they come up. Counting on your fingers."

"Really?" I asked, interested in spite of myself.

"Your pop liked to plan. Soon as we saw the full moon, we counted. Fourteen days later is a new moon."

"I didn't know my pop was the planning kind."

"He was. Even with the *Om*. But that was really a way of him having a conversation with your grandma."

"Wait, what? *Talking* to Grandma Rose?"

We crossed the parkway, and a sign greeted us at the light: WELCOME TO DOBBS FERRY.

"Yessir," Uncle Richard drawled. "Let's just say the dead can talk. And sometimes the living can't. Omar was trying to figure out which was which."

Huh? I had no idea what Uncle Richard was shooting out of his mouth. Right now, I just wanted to get home.

I waited for the rat-tat-tat of Uncle Richard's car. He was in my driveway, engine turned off, doing what, I didn't know. I didn't want him seeing me at the window like I was waiting for him to leave. So I sat in the kitchen, listening instead. Was he under the hood with a monkey wrench? Taking a siesta in the backseat? Finally I heard the gunning of his motor echo down the street. With that noise, the folks in Texas were covering their ears.

I walked across the yard with Myla's textbook tucked under one arm, and I was seized with a nervousness I didn't expect. I knocked on the door, then remembered the doorbell. *Idiot. No need to pound the house down.* The door opened, and there she was. Behind her was her brother.

"Oh, Peter," Myla gulped, seeing the book. "I stopped by before, but you weren't home."

"I came for my American Studies book." I held it out. "This one isn't mine." I paused, but I had to be sure. "Mine's got something else inside it. The black book."

Myla nodded. "I know," she said. She looked up at her brother, who seemed to be hanging on every word. "Cheetah, can you leave us alone for a sec?"

Did she call him *Cheetah*? I watched as he hurried upstairs. After he was gone, she turned back to me. "You mean the black book I saw in your house?" she repeated nervously.

I gave her an exasperated look. "I only have one," I said.

"Right, of course. Wait here," she mumbled. She ran up the stairs.

Meanwhile, I stepped inside her house. She hadn't exactly invited me in, but she'd also left the door open. The wall along the staircase was the strangest green. Like being in the woods. But it was trimmed with a shiny white, and there was a tall vase of leaves, which made me think everything was done on purpose, by somebody who knew how to decorate.

Upstairs I could hear voices going back and forth. Then: "Cheetah, quit bugging me!" I thought of calling out, but I made myself wait. Then I took one more step in. From here I could see the TV turned on to a cooking show with no one watching it, and behind the TV set, the deep purplish haze of the living room walls. Purple? Everything was done in velvet, the sofas the color of red wine, and there were wooden elephant statues on either side of the fireplace. Opposite the window was a print of the Taj Mahal. Nobody in my family had come close to seeing it, though Ma had a paperweight version on her nightstand. I remember playing with it when I was little, then dropping it on my toe. I had a bruise for a week. Meanwhile, the talking overhead had stopped.

"Myla?" My voice traveled up. Nothing. "You there?" Still nothing. "I'm coming up, okay?" When I got to the top of the stairs, I spotted Cheetah looking out from his bedroom. The moment he saw me, he shut the door. On the other side of the hall, Myla stood in front of her room. She wasn't holding the black book.

"Peter, I'm really sorry." There was a catch in her voice. "I don't have what you want."

"What?"

Her face was blotchy and red. "I mean . . . you see . . ." She didn't know how to finish.

I pushed past her, then stopped. There were words of every size and color popping out at me. It was like drowning in paper. "What kind of crazy place is this?" I muttered.

"It's my room." Myla's voice went up a pitch.

"Just give me the black book," I said impatiently.

"Peter, you don't understand."

By then I saw the American Studies book lying on a mattress on the floor. Without waiting for her, I kneeled down and leafed through the pages. Then I held the whole book by its spine and shook it. But nothing fell out. There was no black book. Just a big, ugly textbook that weighed a freaking ton.

"Can I just say something now?" Myla asked.

I jumped to my feet. "All my life I've never seen such a dumb thing!" I could see her shriveling in front of me like a dried fruit, but so what.

"I'm so sorry." She did sound genuinely sad, her eyes round like two moons. "It's completely my fault. But I think I know what happened here."

I leaned in so I was shouting in her face. "Like you dropped it somewhere? Like the Fencers have been in your room?"

She held her hands up. "You don't have to yell. Remember my necklace?"

"Who cares about your stupid necklace?" My pulse quickened. There was a silence. "Fine. What about it?"

"I told you I bought it in Yonkers. But I didn't tell you this man followed me while I was there because he wanted it back." Myla rushed through, her voice squeaking like a mouse on speed. Around us, the cut-up words hovered, and I thought of one that described them perfectly: *claustrophobic*. "Only I wouldn't give it to him," she squeaked on. "And he left me a note on my car saying he'd find me."

"And you were stupid enough to tell him where you live?"

Now Myla was glaring. "I'm not *that* stupid."

I glared right back. "I better go before you waste my time about some crazy fool after you."

"Waste your time?" Myla looked at me with disbelief. "That 'crazy fool' is the one who took your black book." She leaned over and yanked open an empty drawer from her desk. "And he took my necklace, too."

28 MYLA

PETER DIDN'T WAIT FOR AN EXPLANATION. IF HE had, he'd see I was upset, too. "Maybe we can find the man," I called out, running behind him. "We could talk to that lady who sold me the necklace. What if there's another fair in Yonkers, and we can—"

He glared at me over his shoulder. "We are NOT going back to Yonkers. At least not together. You've done enough already."

"Please listen to me," I pleaded as he barreled down the stairs. "Look, I thought it was the Fencers, too. You didn't see my door. It was marked. But then his note is gone from The Wall. Don't you see—it's his way of saying it was him. It has something to do with the necklace and the *Om*s in the train stations."

Peter halted so suddenly, I almost crashed right into him.

"What?" he asked.

"The *Om*s in the train stations. You painted them, right, like the ones in the black book? Unless . . ." I stopped, and it dawned on me. "Unless that's not your book." I saw his face and I knew I was right. "It's someone else's."

Peter turned white. "You had no right looking through that book. Thanks to you, my brother will never speak to me again. If I ever find him." He stormed out, slamming the door behind him.

I was thunderstruck. *His brother*?

I clapped my forehead with my palm. It suddenly became clear. The book was his brother's. Which meant, those were *his Om* tags, not Peter's. Now his brother was missing, and Peter wanted to find him. Maybe the black book was his only clue. Until I came along.

A wave of grossness washed over me. It was bad enough the necklace was gone. But so was the black book, maybe Peter's only link to his brother. Why didn't I give back the necklace that day when I had the chance? Now it was so much worse with Peter involved, and it was all my fault.

"Myla?" Cheetah called out softly. "Is he gone? Can I talk to you?"

"Not now," I said.

"But Myla," he said miserably.

I sniffed loudly. "Not now, Cheet. Okay? I've got to think through stuff by myself."

I went back to my room. This was where it had begun. If Peter had just let me explain, I would have told him what I had pieced together. Like the gap on The Wall where the note had been. And my open window, which I never locked. From there, I figured it all out.

Craggy had used the metal trellis to climb onto the garage. Then, he used the painter's ledge we'd left on the side of the house when we had it painted last year. It was small, less than a foot wide, but the ledge ran from the garage all the way to the end of the house, right under my window. And then it was only a matter of pushing the window up and climbing in. Just thinking about the whole thing made me faint, like the world was tilting, and I was slipping down one side.

More than the necklace, it was that awful look in Peter's eyes that haunted me. I'd told him we could look for Craggy, but in my heart, I knew it was impossible. Craggy had found me, but the truth was, I couldn't find him back.

"And now Peter might never find his brother," I said aloud.

I went to look out the window again. My stomach lurched but it felt good, like I was correcting something that had gone wrong in me. Here I'd been thinking about me, me, me. Even when I was looking through the black book, I was looking for things I liked, that Peter had in common with me. But it went further back. I'd been thinking about myself even when I bought the necklace in the first place, how it would make me look, how it would make other people in school notice me. I'd given no thought to Craggy and his feelings. I knew he'd wanted that necklace but I still went ahead and bought it. And when I had a chance to give it back to him, what did I do? I ran out the door. Of course, Craggy wasn't an angel. But all these problems hadn't started with him. They had started with me. And now it was up to me to fix them. I studied the painter's ledge and the trellis nailed to the side below. And slowly, an idea began to form. Tomorrow was Saturday, right? There *was* one way I could help Peter after all. If I was brave enough.

The next day dragged by as I readied myself for basically the most terrifying adventure of my life. Then night fell, and it was ten o'clock, as I paced back and forth in front of my window.

Cheetah was in bed. My parents were in the family room. The house was mostly quiet except for the faint murmuring of my parents' voices downstairs. It was their habit to read in the evenings, sometimes to each other, after we went to bed. It was the only thing they ever did together. And like my dad's yoga, it was a time Cheetah and I weren't supposed to interrupt.

No problem. It meant no one would be interrupting me either.

I raised the window all the way. It slid easily. It was brand-new, something my parents had replaced two summers ago. But then I looked outside, and for a moment I thought I was going to throw up. *I can't do this*, I thought. I was the person who couldn't even sleep on a bed. And I was climbing out of my bedroom window? I covered my eyes with my hands, ready to give up and crawl back to my mattress. But when I covered my eyes, I saw Peter's face. The expression when he found out his brother's book was gone. *It's your fault*, I told myself. *You have to fix it.*

So I opened my eyes and carefully slung my leg over the sill. I thought of my necklace. I wished I still had it. Sometimes just wearing it, feeling its cool enamel resting on my skin, calmed me down. But I didn't have it anymore. So I thought of my dad instead, and what he'd told me about Om. Then I breathed in and out, and let my mind go still. And more still.

I moved the other leg out, and hung from the window sill by my hands, sliding slowly down until my feet reached the painter's ledge. All good. Surprisingly good. I steadied my breath, thinking about the next task. Walking along the ledge. I could do that. No looking down. Breathe in and out.

Outside, it was dark. No moon, no streetlights. A slight wind picked up, then subsided. I inched my way along the ledge. Closer and closer to the garage. The next moment, I was there.

This was the part I wasn't sure about. Whether I could hoist myself onto the roof. It took a few tries. For one panicky moment, I felt my foot lose traction. Then I was able to get my knee on the edge, and I was up. I paused, astonished by the sudden view. From here I could see down our street, to the far end where Ana's house stood. Was she sleeping? Could she see me if she looked out her window?

Then I looked at my own window, and imagined me looking at myself out on the roof. The curtain shifted, and it seemed there *was* a face looking back. Wait . . . I stared hard, but whatever I saw was gone. I debated. I couldn't go back and check if it was my brother. I'd made it this far, but I wasn't sure I could do it again. Besides, I knew Cheetah. He would have called out if he saw me climbing on the garage. I decided to put it out of my mind, like with everything else.

Above me, the sky was amazingly clear. I pictured staying here, sleeping with my head pointed to the stars. I could be out all night, and no one would know. Of course, this reverie lasted about twenty seconds. I scaled back to the edge of the garage. The sudden drop made me dizzy.

But I hung myself over like I'd done with my window, ignoring all the alarm signals going off inside my body. After a moment, I closed my eyes. It didn't matter—I wasn't looking with my eyes. I was feeling for the trellis with my foot. I thought of my dad again. He told me that yoga is about finding the pose with your mind. I never understood it before. But I understood it now as I felt with my eyes closed for the beginning of the trellis. A moment later, my foot came to rest on the crisscross shape, and I was balanced. Then I was climbing down.

29 PETER

THE PROBLEM WITH THE DOBBS STATION IS there really isn't any place to hide. There's nowhere to conceal yourself on the way there either. It's just one big winding street down to the water, very few trees, and a parking lot on one side of the tracks. So you feel like a walking target the entire time, except there's nobody outside, and it's quiet as a coffin.

I got to the platform around ten thirty, according to my watch. There wasn't anything on the walls, so I figured Randall hadn't come by yet. But would he later? And how long could I wait? I should have brought a blanket. All I had was Randall's hoodie, and it was cold out. I saw the signs, one pointing to New York, the other to Poughkeepsie, and sat on the New York side behind a trash can. From here I had a good view of the platform, and anyone getting off the train in either direction.

I couldn't help but feel a swell of excitement. It was a sweet plan. And sure, Nike suggested it, but I was the one here, testing out the theory. Of course, I thought of all the angles. Like who would be stupid enough to tag train stations every new moon. Wasn't that asking to get caught? But maybe the cops didn't care about systematic graffiti writers. Not enough to connect the dots.

Also when he saw me, would Randall say, *I knew you'd be here tonight, Petey Boy.* Or: *I did everything I needed to do, I'm coming home with you.* Who was I kidding? I leaned my head back against the brick wall. Getting Randall home was the biggest challenge. Especially if he was after the diamonds.

I looked at my watch. Was it really only eleven?

By eleven thirty, some interesting things began to happen. First, several cars came in the parking lot. Some of them were picking up passengers on the 11:10 from New York, and some on the 11:18 from Poughkeepsie. But there was one car that came into the parking lot around 11:00, and didn't go back out after the trains arrived. It made me nervous. *Probably waiting for the next train*, I thought. But I couldn't shake the feeling that somebody else was waiting like me.

Then the 11:40 train came, and I realized something so idiotic, I don't know where my head had been. Here I was sitting on the New York side, which was for trains going *toward* the city. But the person getting off the 11:40 train to Poughkeepsie was on the other side, because he was *coming* from New York. I was on the wrong side of the tracks.

My eyes bugged out at the person on the other side now. After all these weeks, it was like an electric shock. There he was and everything I knew: his walk, his way of hanging his arms by his sides, that familiar bulge in the front pocket of his hoodie which could only be a spray can. My voice stuck in my throat. I thought of calling out, but I didn't want to startle him. In a minute I would get up and cross to the other side. For now I just soaked in the pure joy of watching him in action.

He walked along the station wall, running his gloved hand across the surface. The gloves were new, something I hadn't seen him wear before, but I knew what he was doing. He was scoping. He always did that before he started a tag. Plus he was looking for a dark spot, a place where the platform lights didn't reach him. That wouldn't be until the far end, almost off the platform. By then, he was out of my vision. I couldn't see him, but I heard it: the sound of spraying. That sound brought back all those warm nights in Yonkers: of sweat and insects, and that sharp smell of paint you get in your nose so you're almost high, and Nike bringing up the rear and making sure I didn't fall behind while we tracked along the Saw Mill Parkway. My brain couldn't help but leap forward. Would Randall walk up the winding street back to Cherry with me? Would he sleep in the bed made up for him in my room, the one that hadn't been touched? What would our ma say in the morning? That we were a family again. I jumped to my feet, but in an instant I froze.

There were more sounds now. Voices. And then I couldn't believe it. A girl's voice rang out in alarm. "Run!" she shouted. "They'll catch you!"

I flattened myself against the wall, not knowing who it was or who could see me.

Lights fell across him. Flashlights? Randall looked up, startled. And then a click. I couldn't believe it. Someone taking a photograph. Then a man's voice called out, echoing from a megaphone.

"Stop what you're doing! This is a police order!"

That was all Randall needed. Before anyone could say another word, he bounded off the platform, throwing the spray can behind him. And sweetness—Randall was fast. Here I thought there was nowhere to hide, but my brother managed to hide himself in the bushes next to the train tracks. He had a way. I'd seen it before. He could walk in the woods between trees without snapping or bending a twig. That was who he was. Someone you couldn't follow if he didn't want it. Meanwhile, I didn't make a sound. I couldn't run like Randall, and I couldn't hide myself half as good. So I stayed put next to the trash can. The last thing I needed was to get arrested. *Run, Randall.*

Then something crazy happened. The car I'd seen before—the small sedan—pulled up near the edge of the platform and the driver yelled out of his window: "*MIGHTY*!" An instant later, Randall scrambled into the back of the car, and it screeched away. I stared, dumbstruck. He had escaped! The policeman ran to his car in the parking lot, but I knew what was what. That cop could kiss his chance of catching Randall good-bye.

Down at the platform, the girl's voice sounded again. And she sounded plenty mad.

"You set him up!" she cried out. "You were waiting here with your camera and the police!"

Another girl spoke to her—I couldn't see any faces. "Why did you yell 'run?'"

"I had to," the first girl said. "Somebody had to warn him about you."

I shifted my seat so I could see them better. And then I

nearly had a heart attack. It was Myla and Kai, the parkour girl who wrote for the newspaper! I remembered then Myla talking about the train stations. She knew about the *Om*s. She had seen the black book. It was worrying me, what else she knew. Maybe she had told everything to Kai. But then I realized, Myla was the one who shouted "run." She was the one who had saved Randall.

Kai was checking her camera. "Listen, you have to hide. If my dad sees you, he'll take you back home in his squad car, and you don't want that."

"Where?" Myla's voice had gone down to a loud whisper.

"I know. Get into my car. It's unlocked. *And don't say a word.*" I watched as Myla darted inside a car parked in the first row of the parking lot.

Just then, the police car circled back. He rolled down his window to talk to Kai. "No luck," he said. He paused. "Where did that girl go? The one who was here."

"Oh, she ran off. I tried to stop her, but she's gone."

They spoke some more, then he told Kai to get back in her car and go home. A few minutes later they both drove off. As soon as I saw their cars pull away, I jumped out from behind the trash can and made a beeline for home. When I reached Cherry, my heart was thudding in my chest. Randall. So close. And he didn't even know I was there. I was happy he didn't get caught, and I'd seen him with my own eyes. But where was he now? When would I see him again?

As I came close to my house, I saw Kai and Myla parked in

front of Myla's house. I didn't want them seeing me. So I waited behind a tree. The car door opened and Myla got out. Kai drove off, passing under the streetlight and disappearing around the corner. Meanwhile, Myla was feeling for something in her back pocket. When she pulled it out, I knew what it was. She was going back inside her house, and she'd brought a key. Not like me who left the basement door unlocked.

Myla was smart. She was the kind who thought to bring a key. And she had figured out so much on her own. Most of all, she was the one who saved my brother from the cop. Sometimes you think you can do it all on your own. Sometimes you think the universe will come through for you. But now I was tired, and here was this girl that came all the way down to the station to save somebody else's brother. I watched her walk toward her house, and then I stumbled forward. I called out to her, "Myla, wait!"

30 MYLA

SUNDAY MORNING, I WAS HAVING CHEERIOS while Mom and Dad read the *New York Times* and Cheetah slept in. I cleared my throat. “I was thinking of what you said about first steps.”

Mom looked at me absently over the newspaper. “That’s nice, Myla,” she murmured.

“I was thinking instead of Breakneck Ridge, which we’ve already seen, that we should see High Bridge. So can you take me there today?”

“What?” Mom put down the travel section to look at me in astonishment.

“We’re studying it in Mr. Clay’s class,” I said quickly. “It’s not too far from here. And it would be really good for me, too.” I tried to sound convincing.

“I know all about that bridge,” Mom said, nodding. “And it would be a great first step for you. But I’ve got tons of laundry to do, plus grocery shopping. I’m sorry, I just can’t do it today.”

“I have to go!” I exclaimed. “My assignment is due tomorrow.”

Mom and Dad looked at each other. Then Dad finally offered to take me since it was for school.

“Peter wants to come, too,” I added. “He’s in the same class.”

So it was decided: Dad, Peter, and I would leave right after lunch. Cheetah had a playdate, which was even better because

I didn't want him there with his commentary on "Myla's fear of heights."

It was all part of the plan that Peter and I came up with last night on the front lawn. Which was hard to believe, since just the day before, he was so mad he was ready to bonk my head with his American Studies book. We talked about Randall escaping and who drove the getaway car, and if Kai was a double-crosser, or just bizarrely committed to news reporting. Then I listened to Peter's side and I said, "Don't you see, if you want Randall home, you have to find the diamonds. If you find them, he'll come home."

"Me?" Peter was taken aback. "How would I even do that?"

"You've got your dad's bag, you know what's in the black book, and you have the necklaces. At least one of them, and you've seen the other. You just have to figure out what they all mean." I paused. "And I'll help."

"You'll help me solve the clues?"

"I'll help you find the diamonds." I stopped. Was I really going to get involved with stolen diamonds and criminals and a family I barely knew? And what chance did we have of solving a mystery almost as old as us, without knowing where to start except for those necklaces? But somehow in the middle of the night, in the company of this boy, it felt right. For the first time since I'd lost the black book, I was feeling better about myself. Even though I couldn't get Randall back at the train station, I'd stopped him from getting arrested. Not only that, I'd climbed down two stories, and nothing happened to me. If I could do that, I could do anything.

"I think we have to start with the map of the Aqueduct in your dad's black book," I said.

"I don't know how you got that from a squiggle and a dot," Peter said. But he agreed that the drawing seemed important. That's when we came up with the idea of visiting High Bridge. Not only was it part of the map, but Randall had wanted to go there in the summer. We didn't know what we were looking for exactly, but we decided we'd know it if we saw it.

After lunch, Peter came over and we headed out. In the car, Dad listened to Ravi Shankar while Peter and I stared thoughtfully out of the car window. Okay, correction: Peter stared thoughtfully while I was trying not to have a meltdown. I told myself, what was one little pedestrian bridge spanning the Harlem River?

"Did you know High Bridge is one hundred and forty feet tall?" I asked. "That's almost the width of a football field."

Peter looked at me. "Well, at least it's not the length of one."

"But there was one fatality last year."

He raised his eyebrow. "Oh, yeah?"

"An engineer fell off the bridge while inspecting it. Can you believe that? I'll have to get my ad back from Mr. Clay and fix it. I only found out this morning when I was Googling."

"Maybe you should have done the horse water trough in Dobbs instead," Peter said. "Nobody's fallen off that."

We found parking on Amsterdam Avenue. At the entrance to Highbridge Park, Dad turned to me and smiled. "Ready?" It occurred to me how nice he was being. I knew he had grading to do this afternoon, but he'd brought us anyway. Now he and Peter were on either side of me like two guardsmen as we entered the park, and I felt a strange feeling I didn't experience at Breakneck Ridge or anywhere in my life. It was excitement. What would Peter and I find when we got to the bridge?

There were lots of people, some taking pictures, some looking at the view. As we got closer, the Harlem River came into sight. It was dark and murky, the color of mud inside a bottle, but the water was amazingly still. There were buildings and empty lots bordering the river on one side, while cars zoomed on both sides, the roadway closest to us called Harlem River Drive. I breathed in and out. Then we started across the bridge.

There's something funny about walking the width of a football field above the ground. After a while you forget. There are so many people around, it's impossible not to watch them. And the brick walkway was a beautiful color, while the black wrought-iron fences on either side gleamed.

Mom would have been impressed with everything. She would have told me all the stuff I'd already read, like how High Bridge looked like a walkway, but under the brick was an enormous pipe that once carried water over the river from the Bronx to Harlem. She would have told me how it all stopped one day when New Yorkers needed more water from somewhere else, and the Aqueduct was finally shut down. Since then, the bridge went into disrepair and closed for forty years until now when the city finally restored it.

But it was good to imagine everything on my own. What did it feel like to have millions of gallons of water rushing by, right under your feet? Was it like a vibration? Like the earth moving? Or time itself moving?

Halfway across the bridge, Peter stopped to look at the Manhattan skyline. Between him and the edge of the bridge was the wrought-iron fence. Beyond that, stood another one, a safety fence higher and more impenetrable. I joined him as close as I dared. When I got near the edge, my head started to swim. But I was getting better at this. There was a trick I discovered: Just concentrate on one thing, and it keeps you grounded. I concentrated on Peter's curly hair.

"The view's beautiful all right," he said. "But I don't see anything."

"Maybe we need to keep walking to figure out why this place was important to your dad."

He shook his head. "A wild goose chase."

The three of us continued, my dad lagging behind to read the circular plates on the ground that revealed facts about the Aqueduct. At every plate, Dad would stop to take a picture of it with his phone to show Mom and Cheetah afterward.

As we got closer to the Bronx side, we came to the section of the bridge that was supported by the stone masonry arches. They were the same ones I noticed every time my family and I drove past them on the highway. It seemed impossible I was here on the bridge when months ago I wouldn't have left the car. I scanned the horizon, then my eyes traveled down the last length of the bridge before it joined the Bronx. Inside the curve of the final arch, in faded black and white still impossibly there, was a face painted inside an "O," and next to it, a leaning "m."

"Peter," I gasped.

He saw it the same time I did. We all did. For a moment, no one said anything. When you see a word appear in the most improbable place, you can only think of how it got there. Then you think of the person who put it there. And in the end, maybe, you might think of the word itself.

Peter kneeled down and stretched his hand through the spires of the fence, as if he might touch it, this single word left there like the voice of the dead. But the *Om* was beyond his reach. We could all see that. Watching him made my heart twinge.

Dad touched Peter's back. "Careful, son," he said, in spite of the twin fences holding us in.

"I'm okay," Peter said.

When he stood up, Dad looked at him gently. "You know what that word means?"

I saw Peter pause. I wondered what he would say. How would he explain the way he'd behaved? "It means we're here," he said. "Us, and the person who made it."

Dad looked surprised and nodded. He smiled at Peter. "It must be very old, too. Look how faded the letters are. I'm surprised the city let it remain."

"It lasted," Peter said in a small voice.

"Yes, it's a miracle," Dad agreed. Just then, his phone rang. He walked ahead, and I could hear him telling Mom about the *Om*.

"It was him," Peter whispered as we walked behind my dad. "It was Pop who put it there."

"But how?" I wondered. "The bridge wasn't even open all these years. And the fences."

"You should see his duffel bag, Myla. It's filled with climbing equipment. I thought it was because he was a construction worker. Now I get it. He was a climber, too. If anyone could climb this bridge, it was my pop." I heard a fierceness in his voice I'd never heard before.

I considered. "But Peter, why did your dad leave it there where no one can reach it? Is it just one of his tags? Or is it telling us something important?"

Peter frowned. He didn't have an answer.

*

In the car we were all silent, immersed in our own thoughts. My dad was probably thinking about yoga, I was reflecting on how I'd walked across an entire bridge without puking, and Peter? What was he thinking? I saw him clenching and unclenching his fists.

I got out my journal and wrote, *Om on High Bridge. What does it mean??*

31 RANDALL

THE APARTMENT WAS DARK WHEN I WOKE UP ON the couch, sweating. I'd been this way, jumpy and waking up for no reason, ever since I almost got caught in Dobbs the other night. It was three weeks since I'd left Yonkers, and I was staying in a tiny apartment on West 173rd. The kitchen was just two burners and a fridge, plus a microwave that blinked. It could be worse. At least Tops gave me somewhere to stay. There was only one good thing about the place: From the window I could see High Bridge. But it wasn't the funky arches that made me look. This bridge had a secret.

I imagined Pop strapped to a rope, with those hooks and pulleys from the duffel bag to keep him in place. I didn't know how to use that stuff, because you don't use equipment in parkour. But I knew Pop did when he climbed. That's how he must have painted that *Om* on High Bridge, easing down the side of the bridge with his ropes like a superman.

He would always mix his own spray paint. I saw it myself, him on the balcony, swirling together a cocktail of oil paints and chemicals. He said it was how to make it permanent. I supposed that was why nobody was able to wash his tag off. Not even with all the money they spent fixing the bridge. That's what made his tag so sweet, the way it's lasted. Pop landmarked on High Bridge.

I was at the window when the front door opened and the light was switched on.

"Good, you're awake," Tops said. "Let's go while it's early."

"Early?" I squinted at the time blinking on the microwave: 3:15.

Tops grabbed a few water bottles from the fridge. "In ten minutes, we go running."

Three thirty on a Monday morning, there's not many people in Highbridge Park. Even the dealers are off sleeping. Technically the park's closed, but that doesn't stop two lunatics from running in the dark.

"Keep your feet light," Tops said. "Don't pound your feet." Then he overtook me, and it seemed like all I could see were the bottoms of his shoes. I looked down at mine, at the fake Jordans Ma wheedled off somebody in Yonkers. I can't even explain the shame of knowing my ma was scraping by just so she could buy us these crappy sneakers, the ones the Points called out on day one. Nobody respects you for wearing fakes.

I stared at Tops's back—that black, ratty shirt he was wearing, the half-sweats. Looking at Tops, you wouldn't guess he could train anybody. He had a gut, he was as least as old as my ma, and when his hair wasn't in a ponytail, it was stringy and thin. But you should see him work the walls: He flew like a bird and landed like a cat.

Tops first approached me at a PK meet-up in Central Park. It was early August, and Nike and I were practicing wall runs and climb-ups when who should start running next to me but this dude with the ponytail and flab. I knew who he was. Nike said Tops was the best PK runner in the city. I wasn't so sure because parkour is this graceful sport and Tops was ugly as hell. But I knew Tops because he and Pop were friends way back. They ran in the city, and Pop told me Tops was the one who trained him to vault and precision jump. But that's not the only thing I knew. In Pop's black book, near the end of his writings, I'd seen Tops's name with three lines through it. On the street, three lines meant you were a Fencer. I didn't know if that's what Tops was, or just plain bad news. So I tried to ignore him. I didn't have time for losers.

But that didn't stop Tops. "Great climb-up, Mighty," he called out to me.

"Yeah," I said, not like a question but a statement, because I still didn't want to talk to him. So he shut up, and I thought that was that. But while we were taking a break on the rocks, Tops sat next to me, and that's when I found out.

"Mighty," he said. "There's something you need to know, something about your dad."

What he told me, I didn't see coming in a million years. It started with parkour and him and Pop, and ended with the strangest story of all: diamonds hidden and marked by an *Om*. By my *grandmother*. Not only that, Tops said the final thing that was the noose around my neck—he'd help me find the diamonds, because I was Omar's son.

Nike, who was sitting on the other side of me, his eyes as

big as dinner plates, was right away, "Dope!" But I didn't crack a smile. If somebody tells you he knows your pop's secret and he's going to help you, likely he's after the same thing. "So you want me to find my grandma's *Om*?" I asked. Maybe that was it. I was a pawn in his game of Find the Diamonds.

"Forget her," Tops said. "I think your dad found the diamonds and hid them somewhere else. Then he marked it with his own *Om*."

Now I was blown away. "You're tripping. We wouldn't be sucking it if my pop had his hand on real money like that."

"Maybe he died before he could figure out what to do. It's not easy selling stolen diamonds."

Well, he had a point.

"Look, we talked about it all the time," Tops said. "What your dad would do if he found the diamonds. He said he'd never endanger all of you. He would keep them away somewhere safe."

He and Pop talked *all the time*? Sure, they were friends, but nobody my pop was really down with. Who was this guy? "If Pop found the diamonds," I said, "how come he didn't tell you?"

Tops puckered his face. "I can't say. But the way he was training with me made me think he wasn't just running—he was *looking*. Looking and writing stuff down in that black book of his."

At the mention of the black book, my pulse quickened, and it even seemed like the air around me stirred as Tops watched carefully to see my reaction. But I said and did nothing, as motionless as the rock I was sitting on.

Finally, Tops went on. "My theory is he was looking for a place most people can't reach, a place where he could hide something without it being found. Tagging was his way of marking the spot for himself. A spot that's out there, Mighty, waiting for us to find it. Now, if you believe me, I'll train you. Just like I trained your father."

"Train me?" I wasn't following. "I'm already training with Nike here, and we're fine."

"No, this stuff's amateur. We'll train harder, go further. After that, we'll check out your dad's PK runs—where he went all the time when he was alive. We'll see if he left anything behind. A clue, a tag, or who knows, the real thing. But you'll have to learn a lot more PK. So are you in?"

I looked at his stringy hair, his gut hanging over his waistline, and the sweat sliding down his face. "Do I have to call you Tops?" I asked.

He and Nike laughed, and that's when I decided. Not because I wanted to be Mr. Parkour. It was because there's this thing about training. It loosens you. And I don't mean your joints. You train with somebody, you find yourself telling things. That's how Nike knew so much about me. So I figured, a few weeks with Tops, and he'd be spilling it all. Then I wouldn't need his help. I would find my pop's secret hiding place on my own. I'd collect the diamonds and make our family rich.

But there was something more than that. And this was the

part I didn't tell anyone, not even Nike. It was the way Pop died, falling from a building when he was at work. Like some fool who didn't know how to strap on a harness right. Like someone who didn't know the first thing about climbing, or how to landmark an *Om* on High Bridge and live to tell about it. It never made sense to me, my pop dying a sorry way like that. I knew there was something else, starting with that phone call Ma got the night after Pop died, the one that had scared us all. Were the diamonds behind that phone call? Were they behind the way Pop died? Here was my chance to find out. Not just about the diamonds, but how my pop had been taken away from me.

Long as I didn't keel over now.

Just when I didn't think I had another breath left, I saw the playground up ahead. Tops made his hands into a foothold in front of the fence enclosure. I knew the drill. We'd been doing it every night. With a grunt I hoisted myself up off his hands, but as usual I couldn't reach the top.

"You keep trying too hard," Tops said. "Aim for the right place with your foot."

Again and again I tried, until my palms got sore. Finally I heaved myself over.

I watched as Tops took out a ball of chalk from his pocket and rubbed his hands with it. Then he ran at the fence. I knew the science, how your foot has to find the right place to reach the top. So far, I'd never done it by myself. But Tops's foot hit the magic mark, and he lifted himself in one move. Then he flipped himself over the fence like a trapeze artist and dropped down near me.

For the next hour we worked hard. We did everything: jumps, vaults, rolls. The playground was perfect with metal bars, slides, and play equipment, and different levels to practice jumping. Tops said you had to start small, and there was no place smaller than a playground.

"You've got to roll more at an angle, where the meat is on your body," he explained. "Remember, when you land from somewhere, the roll is what absorbs the shock, not your bones."

We took a break as Tops drank from his water bottle and I took out a Sharpie. "Leave no trace," he said, watching me. "That's the parkour way."

I narrowed my eyes. "You never tagged?" I was thinking of his tag in Pop's black book.

Tops shook his head. "Omar sketched out my tag. But it wasn't me." He shifted his weight. "Also, have you forgotten the other night? At the train station?"

I shrugged. "I didn't get caught, did I?"

"Because of me!" Tops exclaimed. "I was the one who drove you out of Dobbs."

I thought of him there. Normal people would be grateful, but I wasn't. It meant I owed him, and I hated that. "How did you know? I never told anybody."

Tops laughed an ugly laugh. "Mighty, you're as predictable as the moon."

Predictable? I didn't like that. I wasn't a dog doing tricks. I uncapped my pen. I worked the outline slowly . . . it was important to get the "O" right, with enough roundness to make it a circle, not an egg. In my mind, I always pictured a sun. The "m" was different. It was low, like a lion in the grass. But without the grass.

Tops was still watching me. "A few weeks ago, when I saw one of your *Om*s at a subway stop, I knew it was you. I thought, that has to be Omar's kid."

I felt my chest tighten. I thought of when I first started painting Pop's tag. How those two letters made my father come alive for me. But since I'd met Tops and heard the story of the diamonds, something had changed. Now I also thought of the person who called my ma. I thought of that caller telling her Pop was dead because he had something he shouldn't. Was it the diamonds, I didn't know. But whoever that caller was, he could eat dirt. And every time I painted an *Om*, every time I left one in plain sight, it was me telling the world that.

Tops finished his water. "Do you even know what Om means?"

"It means," I said, "what it means." In the morning, a piece of Pop would be here along with this stone. And it would be the bad-ass stone of the playground.

Tops shrugged. "Well, this was your dad's favorite training spot. Maybe he wrote about it in his black book?" He said it so casually, I knew right away something was up.

"I don't know," I said. "I never saw it."

"But your dad always carried one. And then he stopped. That's why I was wondering."

I kept quiet. I could hear the change in Tops's voice, the way he was reaching. But I was like a steel trap, and I knew the black book was safe with Petey. I didn't have to tell a thing.

He cleared his throat. "Did you guys ever run here? Since Omar liked it so much."

"We ran." I finished up the shadowing of the letters. "Just not here."

Pop and I didn't exactly run together. He'd slip out at night and run along the parkway, and I'd follow without him knowing. He'd climb up walls, and scale the top in a way that left me breathless and scared and busting with pride. The only time I didn't follow him was when he went on the train. I'd go as far as the station and see him sitting inside a lit compartment. Then it was like he and the other passengers were shuttled away like ghosts to someplace else in the universe. Those nights were sad, and I'd have to go back home. Then one night I met Nike, and that's how it started, my dance with paint, my street bombing with the crew.

Tops stretched his leg muscles. "This is where your dad told me your grandma's secret."

I capped my pen. "I suppose we'll meditate on that for another month." So far, my time with Tops had been a big fat zero. We hadn't even started looking for the diamonds. When I asked, he was all "In due time, in due time."

He smiled faintly now. "You're ready to kill me, I can see

that. Your landings are shaky, and your foot placement needs work. But your roll is decent and you've got good balance."

"So?" Was this his way of telling me I sucked?

"So, you're ready. At least ready enough. We start your dad's PK run tomorrow night."

In spite of myself, I got excited. But I would be a cool cat, watching and waiting for Tops to make the first mistake. The sun was starting to rise as we headed back, when Tops got a call.

"No, we're busy," he said on his phone. Then, "Fine, give us an hour."

I stared. "Who are we meeting?" I was feeling my eyes close. I was ready to crash.

Tops tossed his empty bottle in a recycling bin. "Some guys who'll help us find the diamonds. They call themselves the Fencers."

32 RANDALL

"THE FENCERS!" I REPEATED. WHAT COULD those punks tell me about the diamonds? I didn't know much about them, but in Yonkers, my crew and I would see those three lines and stay away. We weren't interested in a turf war. We wanted to be left alone to do our paint. But now things were suddenly different. I was getting a bad feeling in my gut.

Tops saw my face. "Relax. They'll tell you everything you need to know. It's not easy finding diamonds in the great state of New York. You'll need their help—how to avoid the police, how to know what's real and what's fake, and how to sell them when the time comes."

It sounded like a bogus list. "Tops, are you a Fencer, too?"

He tried to laugh it off. "They're the ones who know about the diamonds. Not me."

That didn't exactly ease my mind. But in the end, I went along with him. Maybe it was important to find out who these guys were. If they knew about the diamonds, then they were after them, too. And if they were, maybe they were planning to ambush me soon as they saw my face. On the other hand, they might know something about Pop and the way he died. It was worth going, even if I was walking myself into danger.

Besides, Tops would be there to help me. I still didn't know why he thought I was his key to the missing diamonds. But I saw the way his eyes lit up every time the black book was mentioned. Maybe that's what he wanted, and until he got his hands on it, he'd make sure I stayed in one piece. The black book was my one protection. At least for now.

We were meeting them at a coffee shop on St. Vincent Ave in the Bronx. Inside, the shop was empty except for a dark-haired girl near the window reading a book, which was kind of weird, but maybe she was on her way to school, and at the other end sat three people drinking coffee. One of them was old, like he was a crime boss wearing glasses, and the other two were young and trashy-looking. These were the Fencers? They looked like somebody's grandpa and loser cousins hanging out for . . . that's right, coffee. Okay, maybe this meeting wouldn't be so bad after all.

At the counter, the lady asked, "What will it be?"

"One cappuccino for me," Tops answered. "What about you, Mighty?"

"I don't drink that stuff," I said.

While his coffee was being made, he said quietly, "The old one's met your grandmother."

"No way," I said, surprised. I checked him out over Tops's shoulder.

"He'll have info for you. But I'll tell you now. They won't make it easy for you."

"Why, they don't like talking to urban youth?"

"No, because you're Rose's grandson. The trick is to tell them just enough to—"

The counter lady set the drink down with a bang. "Three bucks," she said.

"—make them happy," Tops finished with me. "Got that?"

I nodded, even though I wasn't sure just how I was going to do that.

"Morning, Michael," said the crime boss guy when we sat down.

Tops glanced at me as if to say, *Yeah, that's me*. "So he's here like you wanted," he said.

The other two stared at me. Now I was near them, I saw they were my age, but bigger and heavier, like they could kick my ass any time. They had identical tattoos on their fat biceps: three black lines made a fence. And just like that, I started to get nervous again. *We're in a coffee shop*, I told myself. What could happen here? But that didn't make my uneasiness go away.

Crime Boss looked like an owl behind his glasses. "You've got a name, son?" he asked.

"Mighty. What about you?" I might as well know who I was talking to.

"You can call me Bernie," he said. Meanwhile, the other two sat on either side of me with their fence tattoos, so it was like I was fenced in.

"He's famous," said one of them. He was butt-ugly and wore a ring on each finger. At first I thought he meant Bernie was famous, but then I realized he meant me. Why would *I* be? I watched as the guy reached for a folded newspaper on the table but stopped when Bernie shook his head.

"So you're Rose's grandson," Bernie said.

"Yeah," I said. I'd almost forgotten what she looked like. But I remembered her hands were rough, her fingers thick with calluses. "She died when I was little."

"Died!" said the guy with the rings. "More like she cashed it in."

"Jimmy," said Bernie. "Show respect."

"And the word is she left it behind," Tops said, "or else we wouldn't be here, right?"

"Well, the 'word' is that Scottie's getting out of Sing Sing next week," said Jimmy. "And we're wasting time. No disrespect, but you should let us take care of this our way, Uncle Bern."

"You kids. Always want to solve everything with your fists." Bernie turned to me. "Look, it's like this. We've got no bone to pick with anyone—not you, not the police, not my brother, Scottie. We're just a family, and we want to go on doing our business."

"And what's that?" I asked.

Bernie looked at me for a second. "Why, we're cheese guys. We sell cheese. What else?"

Tops gritted his teeth as the Fencers let out a guffaw.

Bernie's face became stern. "In all seriousness, who do you think has been running this operation for the past eight years? It's certainly not Scottie, sitting over in Sing Sing behind bars. It's someone else, someone with grit and smarts. And you're looking at him right here."

Grit and smarts? It sounded like something you ate for breakfast.

"You're great, Uncle Bern," said one of the Fencers. "Scottie's got nothing on you."

"Yeah, nothing on you," the other one agreed.

Bernie nodded, looking satisfied. "Now, Michael's brought you here," he continued with me, "because there's an . . . outstanding balance left by your grandmother, and then your father. We're ready to look the other way if you can . . . clear the balance."

Clear the balance? I looked at everybody, and then Bernie's words started to sink in. They knew my grandmother and she was dead. They knew my pop and he was dead, too. Now here I was. I felt my mouth go dry. Did I really think I could walk in here and get out of this?

Jimmy leaned in. "Remember, you've got your family to think about."

"What do you mean?" I asked warily.

"Me and Tyson know they moved from Yonkers," he said, the fence rippling on his arm like a snake. "But not before we caught up with your little brother. Him and my rings."

I sprang up. "What did you do to him?" I shouted.

Tops reached out to touch my arm. "Sit down, Mighty," he murmured.

I did what he told me, my heart in my throat.

"Someone tell him the floor number," said Tyson.

"Yeah, forty floors is a long way to fall," Jimmy sniggered.

I was stunned. The memory of that call came back like a punch in the gut: Petey and me at the dining table, crying and crying, then Ma picking up the phone. The person on the other end had said the same thing: *Forty floors is a long way to fall.* And that was why Pop was dead. Because he had something he wasn't supposed to have. The next day Ma moved us out of our apartment. From then on, we kept moving. First Tuckahoe, then Mt. Vernon, and finally Yonkers. Since then, nobody's ever known the floor number, not even the newspaper. Nobody but Ma, Petey, and me. And whoever was on the other end of that call. But now I knew. It was a Fencer who made that call. It was a Fencer who told us about the fortieth floor.

I looked around the coffee shop. Did nobody notice? Did nobody care that a couple of thugs were coming down on a young bro? But there was only that girl with her book.

Meanwhile, Bernie turned to me. "Mighty, all we want to know is where the graffiti is."

For the first time the girl looked up. She wore shorts and tall boots, a weird thing to notice while I was getting hammered. Was she listening? But what could she do for me?

When I didn't respond, Tyson leaned in. "You know, the *Om* that marks the spot. Did your daddy tell you where to find it, Mighty?"

"You think I'd be here if he did?" I snapped, finding my voice finally.

"All right," Tops said. "Just tell Mighty what he needs to know so he can clear the balance."

I didn't know a thing about clearing a balance. But something else was clear. It was time to get the hell out of here. Bernie must have read my face because he laid a hand on top of mine. It was warm and dry, and I might have pulled away, but it had a weight to it, like he might be my grandfather telling me about a fishing trip.

"I remember when I met Rose," he said. "She worked at Rosen & Smith, right in the Diamond District. She was good. She was probably the only female diamond cutter on that street. Now, maybe she didn't know what she was getting into. Maybe she didn't know it was only a matter of time before Scottie would be caught." He lifted his hand, and I felt a cold spot where it had been. "Son, you saw what happened to your grandmother. You saw what happened to your pop. Now, if you know where that *Om* is, you've got to tell us. Scottie's getting out next week, and I've worked too hard to let it all slip away. So find me what I want and we'll clear the records, and *your* life goes on. If not, Scottie will find you. Or I will." Then his face hardened like cement. "Especially if you're painting train stations. That will lead us to you like a trail of bread crumbs."

A ringing started in my ears. How did Bernie know it was me? Still there was this weird satisfaction I felt tingling under my skin. "Well maybe I was looking for you," I shot back. "Maybe I was the one who was onto you all this time."

Tops pulled me back. "Listen, we got it, Bern. What Mighty means is we'll scout for that *Om*. I'll help him."

Bernie was glaring. "I don't care what he meant." He turned to me. "You've got a week."

"And I'd watch my back if I were you," I said angrily.

Jimmy made a move toward me, but Tops got in between us. "Let it go, will you?" he whispered to me. I crossed my arms, but that was so nobody could tell I was shaking.

And just like that, the meeting was done, as if nobody had said nothing at all.

"Michael, the boy can go," Bernie went on, "but I need a word with you."

Tops made the angriest face I've seen. For one scary second, he looked like somebody else. But he pulled it all in and said, "Fine. I'll see you back at the gym, Mighty." Then he turned his back to me, which basically meant leave now.

Outside, the air filled with car horns and exhaust as I raged at the world around me. I'd put on an act of bravado in there, but now that I was alone, I was feeling a fear rise up in me. I wondered if I should get on a train and never see Tops or those losers again. I could disappear. I could hide out somewhere in Westchester where no one would know my face.

Then a breeze blew an old newspaper onto my feet. That's when I remembered Jimmy reaching for the paper and Bernie stopping him. I picked it up and opened to the front page. My stomach clenched in my throat. "Oh, man," I said out loud.

33

The Westchester Tim

Dobbs Ferry Gets Meditative

By Kai Filnik

DOBBS FERRY—A graffitist was seen late Saturday night at the train station, spray-painting an *Om* before being chased away by a DF police officer, Stuart Filnik. The graffiti follows a series of *Om* tags appearing at Hudson River train stations every new moon since August.

Coincidentally, Scottie Biggs is scheduled for release from Sing Sing, a maximum-levelpenitentiary, next week. Biggs, the head of the Fencers, a diamond-smuggling network, was sentenced to eight years in prison for embezzling more than five million dollars' worth of diamonds from Canada. A stash of unrecovered diamonds, estimated at a value of two million dollars, still remains at large. Rumors have persisted for years that the diamonds are hidden at a location marked by an Om similar to the one at the train station. Om is a symbol and word used in Eastern meditation.

When asked if the diamonds might be hidden in Dobbs Ferry, where Biggs resided for more than twenty years, Officer Filnik said he doesn't "entertain rumors." What we do know for sure: Dobbs Ferry isn't an Om for graffiti.

34 MYLA

MY PARENTS WERE TALKING ABOUT THE *OM* TAG on High Bridge on Monday morning while I was in the hall packing up for school.

"I thought graffiti can be removed," Dad said.

"Not always," Mom said. "Sometimes the paint seeps too deep into the masonry. Traces will still be there, like a ghost. That's probably what you saw. What a shame. All that money spent on the bridge and the graffiti stayed!"

I couldn't hear Dad's response because Cheetah came up to me and held the front page of the *Westchester Times* in front of my nose.

"Cheetah!" I batted the newspaper away from my face.

"Thought you'd like to see this before Mom and Dad do."

I looked at the cover photo and almost dropped my backpack. There it was, Saturday night with the *Om* at the train station, and Randall's startled expression under the bright lights of Kai's camera. Thank God the *Westchester Times* wasn't delivered on the weekends. Otherwise, my parents would have seen this by now. "Give me that," I said.

Kai had promised she wouldn't mention my name, but I had to see it for myself. I scanned the *Om* article and was relieved to find no mention of a short Indian girl who'd foiled the cop.

I tried to be casual. "So what? Why shouldn't Mom and Dad see it?"

Cheetah's eyes shifted. "No reason."

Then it came to me. "Wait, you saw me. It was you at my window."

"I wasn't trying to spy, honest. I came to your room because I had something to tell you, and you weren't there. Then I saw the window open. I couldn't believe it. You! Climbing!"

I grabbed Cheetah by his arms and stared hard at him. "You can't tell Mom and Dad."

"I was so scared," he whispered.

"I'm fine. Nothing happened. Promise me you're not telling Mom and Dad."

"I promise," he said. "But I knew where you were going, because we'd talked about it."

I'd forgotten he was the one who showed me the moon forecast in the first place. I let go of his arms. "Well, it's not important. I'm surprised you remembered."

"I remember everything you tell me," he said.

Later in the car, as we were driving to school, I thought of what Cheetah said. It couldn't be true, could it? He couldn't remember *everything*. But he did seem to know things I never said out loud to anyone. I remembered his worried look in the hall when Kai came. He was always watching. Normally I found it annoying, but today I felt unsettled as Dad and I dropped him off at his school. How much did I remember of what he said to me?

In American Studies, everyone was talking at the same time. Peter pulled me to one side and got out the same paper

I'd stashed in my backpack. He said that as soon as he saw the front page, he hid it from his mom. "But that's not the worst part. Even if she doesn't see it, everybody else has."

"Yeah," I whispered, "now they know Randall's face."

"No, they know about the diamonds!" Peter hissed.

Wait, what? I turned around, and that's when I noticed what other kids were saying.

"Do you think it's in the train station?" asked a boy named David.

"That's just a copycat one that boy did," said Sam, who sat next to him. "The real one has to be somewhere else important, like the library."

"My mom thinks the church on Broadway," said Lauren, a girl in the back.

"I'm not even saying where I think it is," said Violet.

By then Mr. Clay asked the class to be quiet as he took attendance, but that didn't seem to work. Then after a while, even Mr. Clay got into the discussion about where the diamonds could be, because he said missing treasure was "the stuff great history is made of."

"Where do *you* think they are, Mr. Clay?" asked David.

Mr. Clay's voice dropped to a murmur. "I don't know. If Mr. Biggs hid them, you have to consider his time and place roughly ten years ago. Where was he going? What was he seeing?"

"The Cedar Street Café," said Ana. "That's been around for ten years." She checked my face to see what I thought. She had seen Peter and me talking earlier, and I knew she was curious.

"The bank," said Violet. "Nobody's thought of hiding them at the bank."

"You can't do that," Sam said scornfully. "Not if you're a criminal. They take your account away, don't they, Mr. Clay?"

"You're all forgetting about the *Om*," said Lauren. "You have to find the *Om* if you want to find the diamonds."

"What's an Om?" David asked.

Then the class went into a discussion about yoga. A girl named Allison said Om was what you said before praying, because that's what her ballet teacher said. Violet, who was in the same ballet class, said Om was a way to "get in the zone." David thought it was a kind of exercise. I kept raising my hand. I wanted to explain how they were all wrong, that Om was what you said to clear your mind. It was what you said to make your body still. At least, that's what I'd figured out by watching my dad. But everyone was getting so carried away with their theories that they didn't hear me or one another.

Then I saw the dismayed look on Peter's face, and I knew what was going on in his mind: What if someone found the diamonds before us? Would Randall ever come home?

35 PETER

MYLA WAS WAITING FOR ME AFTER SCHOOL SO we could walk home together and talk about the diamonds. In all my classes, kids were whispering about it—what if they were hidden by the train tracks, or under a brick at the library, or behind a painting hanging in the Historical Society? Myla said she kept hearing the same thing, too. "But don't worry," she reassured me. "We're still far ahead of everyone else." I wasn't so sure.

At the light, we passed by a school bus. I recognized Dan and Theo from math class, sitting at one of the windows. They waved and I waved back. Was I starting to, like . . . know people here?

Myla noticed. "You know them?" she asked.

"Yeah, don't you?"

She shrugged and kept walking. I couldn't tell, was she pissed? She was this mixture of open and closed, loud and soft, brave and timid. I had no idea how her mind worked at all.

We turned the corner and she asked, "So, have you ever . . . painted anything?"

"Why, do I look like a tagger?"

She looked at me, considering. "No. You look too scared."

This annoyed me. "You can't tell just by looking at somebody."

"I know. That's why I asked." She ran her hand along the side of a building as the road sloped.

This was where you could see the Hudson and the cliffs on the other side. I thought of George Washington standing here with his troops more than two hundred years ago. Mr. Clay says we're crossing the footprints of Washington all the time in Dobbs. There was something magical about that, my Jordans crossing over where Washington's revolutionary boots had gone.

"I like graffiti," Myla said. "Sometimes I write down what I see."

"Yeah, like what do you see?"

She named the ones everybody's heard of, like *CAP2* and *NINETY*. When she said *Mighty*, I was startled. How could Randall, all the way in Yonkers, reach this girl in Dobbs Ferry?

"No kidding," I said slowly. "You like *Mighty*? Because he's my brother."

"Get out of here!" Myla didn't believe me at first. "He's so cool! So is your dad's *Om*. I guess graffiti runs in the family?"

I snorted. "It skipped my ma and me. The only thing she draws is blood!"

Myla laughed.

Meanwhile, I was thinking of our trip to High Bridge. Even though Myla and I hadn't found anything left behind by Grandma Rose, I'd found something else just as important: Pop's *Om*. That still sent chills through me. Except for the duffel bag, I hardly had anything left in our house that he'd touched. But the *Om* on High Bridge was a piece of my father that had survived the rain and snow and who knows what else? Last night, I'd got out the duffel bag and tried on my pop's harness.

I put on the gloves and ran the rope through the pulley, and it sounds crazy, but I stood at my open bedroom window and imagined Pop climbing the side of that bridge. Last thing I'd do was something crazy like he did, but the power of it, feeling the harness strapped around me went right to my head, leaving me giddy.

Just then a shop door opened as we passed by and Kai appeared.

Myla stiffened. "Careful or she might take a photo of you," she said.

"Maybe she can do a class on how to rat someone out with a camera," I suggested.

Kai sighed. "Don't be sore, guys. Myla, I said I wouldn't mention you, and I didn't."

"Yeah, but you endangered someone else's life," Myla said. "How do you feel about that?"

"Oh, that guy. He's in bigger trouble." She saw my face. "Wait, do you know who he is?"

"Don't say anything, Peter," Myla warned. "Or she'll print it next in the paper."

I sighed. At this point, Kai had done her worst. "He's my brother. He's been missing."

"I had no idea." Kai looked genuinely concerned. "I saw him this morning."

Now it was our turn to be surprised. "Where?" I demanded.

"On St. Vincent Ave in the Bronx. Meeting the Fencers. I went there early to drop off a stack of newspapers where I know they have coffee every morning. I wanted to see their faces when they read the front page. Then who comes in but your brother. He was with someone—Michael."

"Who's that?" Myla asked.

I didn't know and neither did Kai.

"But the Fencers think your brother knows where the diamonds are," she said.

"He doesn't!" I exclaimed. "If he did, he'd be home."

"Well, they're giving him a week to find the diamonds for them."

"Or what?" Myla asked.

From inside the store, someone called for Kai. "I have to go. But Peter, if your brother knows where the diamonds are, you have to tell him to turn them in. It's his only way to be safe."

"How can I do that if I don't know where he is?" I shot back at her.

Kai shrugged. "Then find him."

After she went back inside, Myla and I walked on, shell-shocked.

Then Myla said, "Let's forget the diamonds—let's find Randall. Maybe that friend of his, Nike, knows where he is."

I shook my head. "I tried that and it didn't work. And now I can't reach him anymore. No, we stick to our plan. We look for the diamonds."

"But isn't Kai right? Whoever finds them should turn them in."

"You know what? I'm tired of all these shoulds. Randall is in even more trouble than I thought. If we find the stones, that's the only bargaining chip we have with the Fencers, the only protection. Unless, of course, this dumb town beats us to it."

Myla looked at me quickly. "Listen, Peter, I know you're worried about everybody looking and what chance you have. But everyone thinks Scottie Biggs hid the diamonds. They're trying to read his mind, think the way he does. They don't know about your grandmother."

"So?"

"So, you know her better than anyone else. That has to make a difference. Just think, did she tell you *anything* that would help us find her *Om*?"

It was so long ago, Grandma Rose was more like an outline than a real person filled in. "The only thing I remember is a purple sweater she wore. Ma said it was her walking sweater, that Grandma Rose walked a lot. I wanted a walking sweater, too, when I was little, just like her."

"Okay, a purple *walking* sweater. That's important. Where would a walker hide diamonds in a small river town?"

"In her apartment?"

Myla shook her head. "Your dad would have checked all the usual places—her apartment, the bank, whatever. Think—where else?"

"I don't know! Don't you see? I'm new here. Everyone else has a head start over me."

"I'm not new."

I didn't say anything. But I couldn't help thinking, what could two kids really do?

At last we turned onto Walnut, where Uncle Richard worked. But thankfully I didn't see him, just construction equipment and two-by-fours lying on the ground next to the old house.

"They're renovating," Myla said as we passed by.

"I know. My uncle Richard works here."

"My brother and I used think this place was haunted." Myla looked thoughtful. "Would your uncle ever let us take a look inside just for fun?"

Something about Uncle Richard crossing paths with Myla made me nervous. Actually, Uncle Richard crossing paths with *anybody* made me nervous. "He probably doesn't have a key," I said.

"Of course he would. And I bet the key would be funky, too. One of those with the loops and . . ." Her hand went over her heart like she was going to pass out. "Oh, Peter. I just thought of something. Why didn't I think of Margaret before?"

"Margaret?" Why did that woman's name keep coming up? It was as if she was still here in the house, like some spirit we couldn't see, but we knew was there.

Meanwhile, Myla's eyes were wide open. "Peter, I know exactly where we should look for the diamonds!"

36 RANDALL

TOPS'S GYM WAS LOCATED ON THE UPPER EAST Side, between a baby store and a hair salon. Inside it was pretty chill with lots of space and sunlight. Even so, the whole day I was flipping out. Maybe I shouldn't have taunted Bernie. Maybe I shouldn't have told him to watch his back. I'd pissed him off, and the other Fencers, too. But I couldn't help it. I hated their smug looks. I hated being given orders. Most of all, I hated how no one cared that they had destroyed my family. It seemed the only choice for me was to get even. But what could a sixteen-year-old guy do in the dark world of diamond thuggery? Worst of all, I was sick thinking of Petey, or what would happen to him and Ma if I didn't deliver the diamonds. If I found them at all.

Monte, one of the gym assistants, found me downstairs. "Mighty, we need you, ASAP."

So I hauled myself upstairs. It was the pact I'd signed with the devil: Tops and I looked for the diamonds, and I worked in his gym for free. The second floor was decked out with purple and red mats, graffiti walls, fake brick, ladders, railings, metal bars, and stoops at different levels. Like what you'd find outside but a hundred times nicer with no rust, gaps, or broken glass.

"What's wrong?" Monte observed. "You've been dragging your feet all day." So I tried to hustle as we moved mats. On the other side of the room, Monte's brother, Dominic, was teaching.

"You've seen climbers use this," Dominic said, holding up his hands all covered in chalk. "It's great for keeping the sweat off, and for giving you a grip. But some parkour purists don't like chalk. Any guess why?"

One guy said, "You slip on metal."

"Not really," Dominic said. "Gymnasts use it all the time, right?"

Another guy about a foot shorter than everybody said, "Leaves a mess?"

"Right. Remember the PK motto: Leave no trace." Dominic clapped, making a cloud of dust. "But chalk washes off. So it's okay. Personally, I love the stuff. So does the owner of the gym."

I thought of the chalk in my pop's duffel bag. Sometimes he left it lying around the apartment. The first time I thought it was for writing on the sidewalk. When I told him, he laughed and laughed. Only later I realized he used it for parkour.

"Quit daydreaming, Mighty," Monte said. "Grab the other end of the mat."

I sighed and did what he said. Though with all the worrying I was doing, you couldn't call it daydreaming. It was more like living a nightmare.

Tops called me to his office after he got back from the Bronx in the afternoon.

"How to avoid the police," I mimicked him. "How to tell reals from fakes."

"Oh, that." Tops took out an egg salad from a brown paper bag, and a Snapple. "You don't mind, do you? I missed lunch. Listen, I had to say something to get you to come. Bernie really wanted to see you. Now he has, maybe he'll get off my back. We'll go on as we planned."

This surprised me. "Wait, are you saying this morning was just a show?"

"You got it."

I looked at him. "What does he have on you? Else you wouldn't be jumping to his beat."

Tops took a bite of egg salad and washed it down with Snapple. "You always have a way of saying things, Mighty. I'm not jumping to anyone's beat. But I've got a gym to run. And it's a nice one, right?"

"Sure, it's dope."

"Well, it doesn't come free. I did some stupid stuff as a kid—stealing gas, lifting auto parts. I got in trouble, but I cleaned up. Still, you think a bank is going to give a loan to someone like me?"

"I guess not."

"So I had to turn elsewhere."

"The Fencers."

He shrugged. "I couldn't have started this place without Bernie backing me financially."

I watched him eating his egg salad. "No offense, but what's in it for him?"

He wrinkled his eyebrows. "I guess it helps I'm related."

I sat back. "So I was right. You *are* a Fencer."

Tops shook his head. "Bernie's my uncle. But he's into . . . cheese. I do parkour. Two totally different things."

"Yeah, but isn't he also Scottie's brother? I bet he's just waiting for Scottie to get out of jail so they can be Kings of the Diamonds together."

Tops snorted. "Are you kidding? Bernie wants the diamonds before Scottie gets out. He wants to stay on top, and he's only got a week."

"But they're brothers." I thought of Petey. I hope we'd never scheme against each other.

"Well, they're not nice brothers," Tops said. "Sometimes the world works that way. And Bernie's running out of time. Once he saw you were tagging *Om*s in the train stations, he had to find out if you knew where the diamonds were. It was like seeing Omar all over again."

"And I guess that's where you come in," I said quietly. "Bernie's right-hand man. I was wondering why you showed up at a PK meet-up for 'amateurs.'"

Tops put his bottle of Snapple down. "Forget about Bernie. Forget about the Fencers. I meant it when I said I'd help you. Because of *your* dad. It's the right thing to do."

"But your uncles—if they're paying for your gym, they could take it away?"

"They could."

"So Scottie and Bernie get the diamonds and you keep the gym."

He sighed. "That won't happen, Mighty. Stick with me, and we're gold."

I frowned. The whole time we were talking, we were avoiding

the elephant in the room. Which was that my grandmother and pop were dead, and Bernie was threatening my life, too, and my family's, if I didn't comply. What was Tops going to say about that?

But it wasn't something I could put into words. It made me sound desperate, and I wasn't going to stoop to begging Tops to save us. But also because there are some things that are just so awful, you don't want to put them out there. So I just sat and stewed and stewed and hated Tops.

I guess he sensed my thoughts. "Mighty, you've got to trust me. I'll watch your back. Your family's, too. I know what it's like to have Bernie breathing down your neck." An expression flickered across his face. It was like that angry look he made at the coffee shop when Bernie told him to stay back. But it went away as fast as it came. "Just tell me what you know. Anything you think that would help us find your dad's hiding spot: notes he left behind, something he said." He paused in a super-obvious way. "Or the black book, if you know where it is."

There it was again, the infernal black book. If there was one tune Tops hummed, it was that one. What was so special about that book, I didn't know. But I knew the moment I owned up to it, any protection I'd have from Tops was gone.

When I didn't say anything, he nodded like he was answering some question inside his head. "So do you believe me? That I'm here to help, not to hand you over?"

I looked out the window, at the tree blowing in the breeze. I began to wonder if Pop had ever told Tops his secret. Why would he trust this bozo? It was Tops befriending my father all along, trying to weasel out information from him. Now he was doing the same with me.

But I could play that game, too. If Pop really hid those diamonds on one of his PK runs, I'd go on every run with Tops, I'd learn every PK move from him, and find the diamonds first. And who was to say I wouldn't keep painting more *Om*s along the way?

I stood up. "Yeah, we're cool," I told him.

"Good. We start at six sharp," he said. When I left, Tops was still eating his egg salad.

Outside his office I wondered how I would kill time until then, when I saw who was in the lobby. I grinned and gave him a fist bump, our knuckles meeting in the air. "Nike," I said.

In the men's room, I showed Nike the newspaper I'd stored in one of the lockers.

"Mighty Man, you're famous," he said. "Course, I know it already because I was there."

"What?" I was surprised. "What do you mean?"

"*I was there*. Exactly that. Who do you think sent your brother to that train station?"

"Petey was there?" It was only two days, but I didn't remember much. "And a girl."

"You better believe there was a girl. She's the one who saved your behind."

"She told me to run," I said slowly. Who was this girl that

tipped me off about the cop? And the flash of those lights—camera lights I knew now. "Was there a news reporter, too?"

"There was a whole army. I've never seen so many people."

I sat down on the bench. "Tell me what happened."

Nike described Petey coming to the store, and talking to him about where I'd paint next. Then Nike decided to go to the station to keep an eye on him. He was stunned by everyone he saw.

"But why didn't you warn me about the cop?" I asked. "Why'd you let a girl do that?"

"Are you crazy out of your mind? Besides it happened so fast. Then Tops came and got you. That was him, right? So I followed Petey home. Turns out he and the girl are friends. Turns out they're neighbors. Hear what I'm saying? *I know where Petey lives*. I know where your family is."

I got it. "Is that why you're here? You're coming to take me home?"

He held his hands up. "Look, it's a free country. Petey asked where you were, but I didn't say. That's your decision. I couldn't come see you yesterday, it being Sunday, when my ma and me go to church. Don't laugh. I don't disrespect her."

I didn't say a word. I knew there was another side to Nike.

"So," he went on, "you coming home? Maybe forget about the Ds."

"Forget about them?" My voice went up.

"Yeah, it's been a month, bro."

I sighed. "There's more. But not here." We headed outside,

not stopping until we got to Fifth Avenue. I told him the stuff that went down this morning.

"If you come home, maybe the Fencers won't know where you are," Nike said.

I waved that off. "They'd find us."

We reached the Metropolitan Museum and sat down on the front steps.

Nike looked thoughtful. "What you need is another plan." He pointed to a banner:

16TH-CENTURY EUROPE AND THE FINE ART OF JEWELRY MAKING

"You want to go to an art show at the Met?"

"Course not, fool. I'm saying, what if your pop never found the diamonds? Then they're still where your grandma hid them. It's time to figure out what *she* was doing."

Was Nike right? Here I was, going with what Tops said all along—that Pop had found the stones and hidden them somewhere else. But what if Tops was wrong? What if it was Grandma Rose we should be tracking? I felt a glimmer of hope. If she was the answer, then I wouldn't need Tops after all. And I couldn't wait to get rid of him.

"Fine," I said to Nike. "In that case, I know where to go."

37 MYLA

WHEN I GOT HOME I RUSHED TO THE KITCHEN. I grabbed the skeleton key from the drawer and stuffed it in my pocket just as Dad and Cheetah came in. "You took a long time," Dad said. "Wondered where you were."

"Peter and I were talking," I said. I was impatient to get to his house, where he was waiting. "I have to go. Peter and I are doing homework together."

"Okay, won't stop you," Dad said. "But before you go, take a look at your room."

I stopped. "Why? What did you do?"

"He didn't do anything," Cheetah said. But he smiled like something was up.

"Mom was the one who stayed home until lunch," Dad said. "To let the delivery guy in."

"Delivery guy?" Then I suddenly knew. "But it's too soon. I have to rearrange my room."

"You can do that now, Myla. You'll like the new bed. Don't worry."

"Who said I'm worrying?" I asked. "A bed isn't a big deal."

"Then why did you make one out of stuff from the garage?" asked Cheetah.

"Shut up. It's your fault my bed broke."

"Myla," Dad said.

I let my backpack land on the ground with a thud. "Look, I'm *not* afraid, I just don't like having a fancy bed, all right?"

Dad and Cheetah looked at me like I was bonkers. So I hurried up to my room.

As I pushed the door open, a sweet smell came from inside, like a mixture of pine and fresh laundry. There was the new bed, pushed up against the far wall, covered by a cream-colored bedspread with matching pillowcases, which I'd seen in a magazine. I heard Dad come in behind me.

"Do you like it?" he asked. "Mom wanted to surprise you with the bedspread."

"It's . . . nice." I didn't know what else to say. The bed was gleaming and gigantic and airy all at the same time. It was bigger than I'd expected.

Dad gave my shoulders a squeeze. "Well, I'll let you get going to Peter's. And Myla, it's a beautiful bed. Enjoy." He went back downstairs.

I sat down on it after he left, feeling the mattress spring under me. I remembered the last time there was a real bed in here. The frame was mahogany, with a Strawberry Shortcake bedspread. Every night Mom would tuck me in, put on different night lights, and sing songs. It didn't matter. I would still end up in my parents' room. Sometimes I woke up, yelling. Mom wore glasses all the time because she was too tired to wear her contact lenses. Then one night, silence. The next morning, they found me asleep on the green rug. That's when they put the mattress on the floor and moved the mahogany frame to Cheetah's room. Everybody slept fine after that.

As I walked to the stairs, I saw Cheetah on the floor in his room, surrounded by paper. Seeing him there all by himself made me pause. "What are you doing, Cheet?"

"Spelling club stuff."

I looked at the sheets filled with rows of words. "How do you remember all of that?"

"I remember patterns. Like how words look."

"I could never do that."

"You do it all the time. It's like seeing *Mighty* and *Om* and *KINK* when we go out."

"Those are tags, Cheet."

"But don't you remember them by the way they look? Spelling's the same way."

I wasn't sure. Like, wasn't spelling all about Greek and Latin roots? But for the first time I realized Cheetah thought about words as much as I did. I don't know why I never saw that before.

"Are you going to sleep in your new bed?" he asked.

I glanced at the clock on his desk. I was supposed to be at Peter's. I knew he was dying for me to get there. Even so, I let myself slide down onto the floor next to Cheetah. "I don't know."

"But you're not so scared of heights anymore."

Was Cheetah right? But how did he know these things about me? I scooted up my legs and tucked my arms around them. "Maybe. But I'm still a weirdo."

"I don't think you're weird."

"Yeah, well." I thought for a moment. "Cheet, this morning, what did you mean when you said you remember everything I say? I mean, you can't remember *everything*."

"Mom and Dad are busy," he said. "They don't have time to hear everything we tell them."

"And you do?"

"It's not like that. It's more like . . . you don't say a lot, but you still want people to notice you. So you leave clues. Like your wall."

I sucked in my breath. I wasn't sure I entirely liked that my little brother, who could barely watch a Harry Potter movie without getting scared, could say things with such certainty about me. So I said, "That's not true." I paused. "Well, it's not completely true. And anyway, what about you? Don't you want people to notice you, too?"

He shook his head. "Not really."

I watched him as he sifted through his spelling word sheets. Some of the words flashed at me: "segue, seminary, sequester." All these words he has mastered in his quiet way. And he didn't want to be noticed for it. "'The Great Irony.' Like Dad and Mom say."

"Not really." He looked up at me. "You want to hear a secret? I lied about spelling my name wrong."

"What?"

"I knew how to spell my name already in preschool. But my favorite book was on cheetahs. Mom was reading it to me then. Seriously, I'm going to write my name wrong when I'm four?"

Um—didn't most four-year-olds not know how to spell their names? But he wasn't like most four-year-olds. Now that I thought about it, I wondered why Mom and Dad didn't catch on sooner. "You wrote Cheetah instead of Chetan on purpose?" I asked in surprise. "Why?"

"Because I *wanted* to be called Cheetah!"

He'd lied? And let Mom and Dad tell their story over and over again? I grinned. It was seriously the most awesome thing I'd ever heard.

"You're looking for the diamonds now, aren't you? With Peter."

"Wh-wh-what?" I wondered if I'd ever be able to lie to him now that I knew he was the world's greatest liar. I shook my head. "I'm not even going to answer that."

Cheetah was looking at me in a strange way. "What's so great about Peter?"

"What do you mean? Peter's great because . . . he's my friend." Then this thought came to me. Could Cheetah be jealous? But why? It wasn't like Peter was going to be my brother. "A lot of bad stuff happened in his family, Cheet. He needs people to be nice to him. He's a good guy."

Cheetah watched my face carefully. Then he nodded, almost to himself.

When I got up, he was bent over his sheets, his thick,

wavy hair an unkempt mess like Dad's, his legs splayed like a marathon runner stretching for the big race. It's weird, but he seemed like a different person. Or maybe I was the one seeing him differently.

38 PETER

MYLA CALLED IT A SKELETON KEY. IT WAS HEAVY and long, with a cloverleaf pattern at the top.

As we went upstairs, I remembered last week when Ma asked me to help her with the attic door. But I didn't want to get up from my bed, I wanted to sit there and sink into a pile of sadness. Randall and I shared a room as long as I could remember, and here I was with two beds and no Randall. So I said no. A few minutes later I heard her dragging our suitcases down to the basement. And we both forgot about the attic. Until now.

"What do you think is up there?" Myla wondered.

"Well, it isn't Scottie Biggs. We know where he still is!"

Myla inserted the skeleton key in the lock and the door opened easily. Inside, the wooden stairs were covered in dust. As we went up, I don't know what I thought I'd see—cobwebs, creaky floors, a dark room that looked like a coffin. Certainly I didn't expect bright sunlight. The attic was bathed in gold, the afternoon sun blazing through windows unblocked by trees and houses.

"Look, the Palisades," Myla said, going near the window. "You can see them better from here than my room." Then she took a step back. "Yikes, we're far up."

"That's right, you're scared of heights."

"No, I'm not." She looked at the boxes stacked on the floor around us. "Let's get to work."

First we had to agree on what we were doing. We couldn't go through all of Margaret's and Allie's belongings. Not unless we thought it would lead to the *Om*. Which made our search daunting, except for one thing. Every box was labeled.

"Margaret is very organized," Myla said. "Everything in her pantry had labels." We glanced through the boxes: *Margaret's Freshman Comp Notes That Helped Her Get an A*, *Allie's Clothes to Be Donated If New Diet Works*. The rest were labeled in the same bizarre way. My ma barely got our stuff in boxes before we moved out, forget about labeling. But Margaret seemed to understand the exact details of her life with Allie. Still, where did we start?

Then at the far end of the attic, away from the windows, we came across a cardboard box and a suitcase that had no labels. Myla brushed the dust from the box.

"This has to be something important, Peter," she said excitedly, "because it's *not* labeled." She got on her knees and inspected the box from various angles.

"Hurry up," I said impatiently.

"I want to take the tape off slow," she explained, "in case we have to put it back. I don't want Margaret and Allie to think we're snooping."

"Course not. Never mind our footprints all over the place in this dust."

Myla looked around. "Oh well, we can't help that. If I do it slowly the tape won't rip."

Then I discovered by "slow" she meant something akin to the melting of the polar ice caps. So I turned my attention to the suitcase. I laid it down on its side and unsnapped the clasps. I raised the suitcase lid. "Myla," I whispered.

There in front of me were clothes—flowered shirts, a peach-colored silky blouse with a ruffle, a blue pin-striped skirt. Each item seemed to make me want to burst a little more. Then I got to the bottom and pulled it out. "Myla," I said more loudly.

By now she had removed the tape and opened the box. "Peter, the *Om*s!" she exclaimed.

I turned around quickly. "You found the *Om*?"

She reached inside the box. "Not just one. Many!" In her hand were several necklaces like ours. "Look, here's one that says 'finder.'" She paused. "What about you?"

I held it up. It was heavy, with thick cables, and it still smelled of detergent. That's what stopped me more than anything. It was the smell I remembered, of my grandma in our apartment, holding me on her lap, her laugh like a clap of thunder. Could a smell do that, take you back in time? "It's my grandma's purple sweater," I said. "This suitcase is full of her clothes."

The next few minutes we went through the suitcase and box more carefully. The box was filled with Om necklaces. The suitcase was mostly clothes, except for a heavy, rolled-up piece of cloth. When we unrolled it, we found different-size steel bits and discs, and something that looked like a small cylinder with a magnifying lens at one end.

"These must be diamond-cutting tools," Myla said. She took out something from one of the inner pockets. "Look, a bunch of New York postcards. They have 'Om' written on them, and nothing else. And they're all addressed to Margaret."

I took them from her. There were six. And Myla was right. They had no return address, no message, nothing but the Om and Margaret's address—which was this house. "You don't think they're from . . ."

"They have to be," she said. "Who else would send an Om postcard?"

Then I noticed something really strange. "Look at the dates, Myla." I laid the postcards down for her to see. "The oldest one is eight years ago. But the newest one is from two years ago."

Myla furrowed her brow. "That's weird. Is that possible?"

Just then, we heard a noise downstairs. Was my mom back from work early?

We put away everything quickly and went down. We'd just shut the attic door, when we saw Cheetah coming up to the second floor. In his hand, he held the black book.

39 RANDALL

NIKE PUNCHED ROSEN & SMITH INTO HIS PHONE. "Lucky you remembered their name."

I shrugged. "When Bernie told me at the coffee shop, I was thinking Rosen sounds like my grandma's name, Rose. And Smith is well . . . Smith."

"West Forty-Seventh. We can walk forty blocks, right?"

This was Nike talking. For him, forty blocks was nothing. But I didn't have a choice, so I said fine, and we started down Fifth Avenue.

"So I want to know," Nike said, "why you switched tags. *Om* is your pop's tag, not yours."

I stopped to trace a tag with my finger on the side of a bench. *LONESTAR11*. I liked the way the "L" was done, loopy like a shoelace. "I'm still Mighty," I said. "But I paint *Om* to keep my pop's memory alive. And also, to remind the Fencers they can eat dirt."

Nike nodded. "Because you think they dissed him."

We started walking again. "It's more than that. Now I think they killed him." Saying that out loud for the first time sent a shiver through me. It made the world scarier. And more unforgivable.

Sometimes I imagine what it would be like if Pop were still alive. Like maybe we'd be walking together in the city checking out tags. Or he'd think I was old enough to join him on his runs. He'd see I could PK sure enough as anybody else. Maybe he'd be proud of me. Maybe he'd say, quit hanging with that loser, Tops.

It was strange having this convo with Nike about Om, because I'd had a similar one with Pop years ago. We were lying on the couch. It was soon after Grandma Rose was dead. Pop wasn't himself. He sat staring into space when he thought no one was around, or wrote in his black book, which he stored in his blue duffel bag under the bed in his and Ma's bedroom.

So when he told me to take a look at what he was writing, I jumped at the chance. I didn't know much about tagging, though I'd seen him spray-paint a city wall when he didn't know I was watching. "Why *Om* and not *Omar*, Pop?" I asked. "What's Om?"

"It's a way of thinking of my ma," he said. "It's a way of talking to her."

I thought of his words now. It was true I was tagging *Om* to get back at the Fencers in my own way. But I also hoped that my pop would know I was talking to him, too.

Nike was quiet. "We'll get to the bottom of it, Mighty," he finally said. "You and me."

We walked and walked, block after block, the sun beating down on us. Then finally we were there. There were two posts on either side of Forty-Seventh Street, with metal diamond shapes on the top. At the corner was a store with a window display of rings of every size, and necklaces strapped on blue velvet boards. Past that, the street was lined with stores with names like "Diamond Exchange" and "Gold & Platinum Inc."

Nike whistled low. "The Diamond District. Where dreams are bought and sold."

Maybe. But now I was feeling queasy. "I can't do this," I said.

"What do you mean? We're here."

"Look at this place. Don't you see?"

Nike scanned the street. "See what, the boogeyman? I don't see nothing."

"You see anyone like us? We'll be thrown out soon as we set our bony feet on the sidewalk."

Nike let out a groan. "Seriously, Mighty, it's a new century."

"You weren't chased by a cop two days ago."

"You were doing something illegal, dude. This isn't illegal. We have the right to walk inside a store, just like anybody else. I'm tired of the same sad convo I hear from all of you—the Points and MaxD. How nobody's giving you respect. Well, nobody's giving you respect, unless you own it."

I wanted to tell him he was wrong. I had my whole life to prove it, the respect I didn't get from my school, from my mother, from anyone. There's only that fraction of time and space when you get a piece on the wall, when you exist. And everyone who walks by knows you do. Until somebody else writes over your piece, or an a-hole washes it away. Then your moment is over. But that's the only respect there really is.

Nike started down the street. "Don't you want to find out

what your grandma did here?" And though I didn't agree with what he'd said, I found myself following him anyway.

We saw the sign at the same time: ROSEN & SMITH, EST. 1948, PROFESSIONAL DIAMOND CUTTERS. Inside, it was dark, with a video camera pointed at the entrance, and an old guy sitting behind a glass, his body stuffed inside a uniform. He slid the glass open. "Can I help you?"

"We wanted to talk to Rosen or Smith," Nike said.

"You have an appointment?"

Course we didn't have no appointment.

Nike said, "We're trying to find out about his grandmother who worked here."

The security guard looked at us mildly, leaning his fat head on his fat hand.

Then Nike said, "Her name was Rose Wilson."

And okay, you should have seen Mr. Security's face after *that*.

"I haven't heard that name in years." He sat up. "Which one of you is her grandchild again?"

"Him." Nike pushed me forward.

The guard looked at me carefully, and I said the obvious. "She married a black man."

His face broke into a huge smile. "Oh, I know she did. You've grown up. Rose showed pictures of you when you were little." He held two fingers up to his forehead, one on each side. "Don't tell me. It's coming to me." He squinted, thinking hard. "You're Petey!"

Nike burst out laughing.

"Shoot, you remembered my name." I didn't know what else to say.

"I'm like an elephant," said the guard.

Nike, the grinning fool, asked, "Can we go in? Petey has questions about his grandma."

The guard scratched his face. "I can't let you in. That's their policy. But maybe I can ring someone down." He closed the glass and we could see him on the phone. A minute later he slid back the glass. "One of them will be down to see you."

Nike clapped my back. "Isn't that great, Petey Boy?"

A moment later a woman with silvery hair stepped out. "Yes, can I help you?"

So we went through the whole spiel, and she let us in through the door. We sat down in some kind of lobby with chairs and a few magazines on a table.

"I can't tell you much, Peter," she said. "Rose worked here . . . almost ten years ago? She was a jeweler, but she made mostly artisan jewelry—silver, leather, enamel, that kind of thing. Once she came on board, she learned our craft quickly. No easy thing. Diamond cutting is an extremely difficult and precise job."

"Did you fire her?" I asked. "Because of Scottie Biggs?"

She looked at me carefully. The ends of her fingers were rough and callused. Grandma Rose's hands had looked the same way. "Is that what this is about? Look, dear, I didn't know Scottie. You saw we have security. No one gets in without an appointment. Did he give Rose diamonds to cut? Nothing indicated so, and we never had trouble with Rose before. We do background checks. We don't let just anyone into our shop. My husband and I are honest people."

Nike leaned in. "Are you Smith or Rosen?"

For the first time she smiled. "I'm Smith, he's Rosen."

"You think my grandma took the diamonds? You think she was a thief?"

Smith looked uncomfortable. "Rose was eccentric, you could say. But she seemed like an honest craftswoman. If she had cut illegal stones here, we would have known. It's a small shop."

There was something I didn't understand. "What do you mean cutting?"

Smith blinked. "Don't you know what we do here?"

"You're diamond cutters," I said. "But I don't know what that *means.*"

Smith looked thoughtful. "Have you seen a real diamond? Like your mom's wedding ring?"

"She doesn't wear one," I said, "but she's got diamond earrings from her family in India."

"From India?" she asked. I could see her trying to wrap her head around that. I didn't look Indian. "I bet they shine beautifully. But those are finished diamonds. Not how they look in nature. When they're first mined, they're called roughs. They look like pieces of stone. It takes a diamond cutter to cut the rough so it turns into a beautiful diamond. That's what your grandmother did."

"Huh," I said. "Like with a hammer?"

Smith smiled. "Actually, we have more precise tools than that. But the idea is the same. You take away the bad parts and leave what shines." She stood up and I thought she was going to tell us to leave, but instead she said, "Wait here." Then she went back inside.

Nike and I waited.

"What do you think she's doing?" he asked.

"Calling the cops."

He sighed. "You're killing me."

A few moments later, Smith was back with an envelope in her hand. "Come here, boys, right up to the coffee table." She opened the envelope and pulled out a folded piece of paper. Carefully she opened it so we could see what was inside. There were three mud-colored stones, each the size of my thumbnail. "Do you know what these are?"

I stared at them a second. "Roughs," I said.

She nodded. "Good job."

I couldn't believe it. They looked like something you'd find in a gravel lot.

"Are you sure?" Nike didn't believe it either. "These are million-dollar diamonds?"

Smith looked amused. "Well, not quite. They're heavily included. That means, they have flaws inside them that would make them hard to sell. But these roughs still give you an idea of what your grandmother did. She took stones that look like these, and made them into the kind of jewelry you see at Tiffany's."

"Wow." I was impressed.

"Here." She picked one up and gave it to me.

I held it to the light but I didn't see anything inside. I didn't have the gift my grandmother did. But I was appreciating the work. I gave it back to Smith.

"Then these aren't worth much," Nike said. "Like with the includings."

"Inclusions," Smith corrected. "No, not worth much at all."

"So we could take them home, right, like souvenirs." He winked.

She gave a little laugh. "No, I'm sorry, they're still worth something to us here. Sometimes we practice on them. Though we've really gotten good at what we do, if I say so myself."

She put them back in the envelope. "And now I do have to get back to work, boys. I'm glad you stopped by, kind of nice to remember Rose before all that crazy stuff happened." Her voice trailed off. "You know, we were worried when she disappeared. Then we heard the news about her car. That must have been very difficult, Peter."

"Yeah," I said. "Well, it happened."

She looked at me gently. "Rose was extraordinary. Not too many female diamond cutters in the business, even now. She was one of them. You're looking at the other."

After she left, the guard stopped us on the way out. "Did Ms. Smith remember Rose?"

Nike shrugged. "A little bit."

"You never know who remembers what." His pudgy hands

rested on a shoebox in front of him. "Now, this isn't much, just a box I keep in my drawer with odds and ends. But there is one thing I have from Rose." He pulled out a folded-up map. I looked at the words at the top: *The Old Croton Aqueduct Trail.*

"Aqueduct?" I said. "What's that?"

"The old waterworks system," said the security guard. "It runs to the city from Westchester County. Rose loved to walk on it. She was always telling me to go, she even brought me this map, but I never did." He gave it to me. "It's not much, but I thought you'd like to have it."

I looked at the folded paper. "This all you have?"

"I'm afraid so."

Nike said, "Thanks, Mister."

Outside Rosen & Smith, we began walking again.

"So, Petey, what do you think?" Nike asked.

"Grandma Rose was a lover of the Aqua Guard. Whoopee."

"Aqueduct," Nike corrected. "Maybe it's important. You never know."

"Oh, I know all right. That big old guard isn't ever setting foot on a trail. Neither am I."

"Well, he was all gaga to see you, Petey Boy."

"Stop calling me that."

"Bet he was crushing on your grannie all these years."

I gave him a shove.

"But that lady was cool," Nike said.

"Yeah," I said, surprised because he was right. I'd liked how she trusted us to hold those roughs. Was it because I was Rose's grandson? Or because she was decent?

"You heard what she said. She's one of the few ladies around, she and your grandma."

"Yeah, I heard."

Nike nodded in approval. "Your grandma, she owned it, that's what."

The sun was dipping down in the sky when we got back to the gym.

"If I knew you were coming, I'd ask you to get me more spray paint," I said. "I left Skinny's number at home. It sucks I can't buy myself."

"Next time, bro," Nike said.

"Want to come with Tops and me tonight?"

Nike shook his head. "Sorry, dude. Have to get back. I'm working at the church now."

"What about Music Land?"

"Bunch of losers coming in there all the time. No peace, know what I mean?"

I saw his point. Nobody had peace these days, it seemed. At least Nike was searching.

After he left, I was about to open the gym door, when I was dragged back by my shirt.

"Hold on, Mr. Wilson." Jimmy the Fencer shoved me against the outside brick wall of the building. "We want to hear *all* about your trip to Rosen & Smith." Tyson stood on the other side of him as Jimmy held me up by the front of my neck.

Not choking me but enough that it was hard to talk. Plus I was trying not to hyperventilate.

"Nothing happened, man," I said between breaths. "If you followed me, you know that."

"What happened inside?" He pushed harder so it felt like my windpipe was caving in.

"Nothing," I wheezed. "The diamond cutter didn't know anything."

He pressed even harder and I thought I'd be sick, except there was nowhere for the sick to go. I shook my head until he stopped, but he didn't let go. "So we went to CVS and I thought you'd like to see what we got developed there. Show him, Tyson."

From his pocket, Tyson took out a photo.

"It's your *Om* at 125th," Jimmy said. "There's a message below it. Read it to him, Tyson."

Tyson made a show of clearing his throat. "It says 'Find me in Dobbs Ferry—PW.'"

My mouth went dry. I knew where this was going. I tried to wriggle away, but Jimmy's grip on me tightened. "That made me curious," Jimmy said. "You got your face in the newspaper for tagging Dobbs. Then there's this message from PW. Now, who's PW?"

"It's not him," I whispered. "It's somebody else."

"Oh, I don't think so."

"They don't know anything," I whispered.

"Which is why we're going after you. Uncle Bern thinks asking gets results. But Bern is like an anaconda. You know those snakes, they squeeze their prey *slowly* to death. That's Bern, squeezing Tops nice and slow."

"What's he got on Tops?" I wheezed.

"Wouldn't you like to know?" Jimmy said. "But listen, if Uncle Bern is an anaconda, then I'm a barracuda. I'm the fish that likes to cut, and I cut quickly."

Then lucky for me, while he was flapping his trap, Jimmy's grip loosened and I took off. I tore as fast as my fakes could take me. First I crossed Madison Avenue. Then Park Avenue. I kept thinking I'd lose them, that they'd get tired of chasing me. But they kept dogging after me.

Should I turn? Run inside a building? Then I saw it ahead, the Central Park wall on the other side of Fifth. I'd never done a vault without Tops spotting me. But here was my chance to put my practice to action. Of course, I didn't know what was on the other side. I'd have to take my chances. But if I got over, I'd lose Jimmy and Tyson for sure. The light changed just as I got to the crosswalk, with them still on my heels. So I pulled ahead with the last energy I had. My hands went down on top of the stone wall, and I felt my feet pushing me forward. Over the wall I went. And I was flying.

40 PETER

I WALKED OVER TO WHERE CHEETAH WAS STANDING at the top of the stairs, and grabbed the black book from him. “Thanks. But wasn’t it stolen from Myla’s room?”

Cheetah swallowed. “It was. Just not by the person you thought.” He looked miserably from Myla to me. “I’m sorry, Peter. I didn’t want to take the book. But I heard what Kai said to Myla. She said the black book was the only way to keep Myla safe. When you came to our house, I didn’t want you to take it away. Myla wouldn’t steal your book unless she had a good reason. But this afternoon she said you were a good guy and that’s why you’re friends.”

Myla looked mortified. “You can shut up any time, Cheet,” she muttered.

“Seems like somebody from your family is always taking the black book,” I observed. “Maybe your dad will be next. He’ll be all, sorry, Peter, guess I needed it for a math problem.”

“I’m sorry, Peter!” Myla exclaimed, flushed with embarrassment. “I know I suck.”

“Please don’t be mad,” Cheetah said to me. “This time it’s my fault, not hers.”

“What about the necklace?” Myla demanded from him. “Did you take that, too?”

Cheetah shook his head. “Why would I steal that from you?”

I sighed. "What is up with your family? You're like a bunch of messed-up do-gooders. I bet you give each other Band-Aids for Christmas."

"Actually, we're Hindu so we don't celebrate Christmas," Cheetah said, all earnest-like, and got a shove from Myla. I knew that shove. I had a permanent bruise on my shoulder from Randall.

"It means Craggy still took the necklace," she said. "But at least we're down to only one thing stolen, thanks to my brother coming clean." Then she and Cheetah chattered like squirrels, Myla scolding him and all.

Meanwhile, I looked through the black book. It seemed the same, and all the pages were there, including the one tucked in at the back with Skinny's number on it.

"I have to go," Cheetah said. "My dad and I are going to the library to get a book for spelling club. No hard feelings, right, Peter?"

"We're cool, bro," I told him. Then it's weird, but the way he smiled back lightened me up.

After Cheetah left, Myla was very quiet, and I knew she was still feeling bad about her part in the black book's disappearance. "Look, no hard feelings with you either, okay?" I told her.

She gave me a grateful smile. And I guess that lightened me up some more.

"Come on," I said. "I have some other stuff to show you."

I took her to my room and pulled out the duffel bag. At first I felt a pang. What would Randall say if he knew I was showing the bag to someone else? Would he say I was betraying the family and Pop and our brotherhood? But then I went ahead. It was too late to worry what Randall thought now.

Myla looked at each item carefully. She noticed things I hadn't—like most of the clasps looked brand-new, but the ropes were old, and the pulleys were worn like they'd been used a lot.

I leaned back on my bed. "That's it," I said. "I've shown you everything. Now what?"

"Let's go back to the necklaces," Myla said. "Mine says 'keeper.' But that's what half the other necklaces say in the box upstairs. Yours is different. We should focus on that. 'Shouse.' Is that a name? A place? A swear word?"

I didn't know. I was feeling frustrated. "Meanwhile, everybody's out there searching."

"You really think your brother won't come back ever?"

I looked down at my fake Jordans, my last tie to Randall. He always seemed to hate these shoes. Sure, we knew they were fakes, but that didn't mean other people on the street did. And even if everyone did, something about seeing the Jumpman on my feet sent a thrill through me. I'd imagine that Jumpman could be Randall. "Randall's selfish. He's always been a little like that. Now he's a lot like that."

"But you still want him to come home," Myla said.

"I just want him . . . around. He's the older one. It's wrong to leave a little brother behind."

Myla wrinkled her nose. "Well, it's not easy being the older one, either. With Cheetah . . ." She paused. "I can't even explain. He's around too much."

"But Randall isn't. Unless we find the diamonds."

"You think that's all he cares about? Doesn't he want to see you and your mom?"

I looked away. I didn't know how to answer that.

"Okay, then we have to find a way to stop everyone else," she said. "From looking, that is."

When she said that, I suddenly remembered MOST14. MOST had a hand style that would chill anybody. He could make his tag pop so you saw it across a busy street. Randall said he'd make space on a wall any day for that dude. Even the Points agreed MOST14 would be king someday. Until MaxD came along. I don't know what his beef was with MOST, who'd done nothing to him. Maybe it was pure jealousy. At any rate, MaxD decided he would destroy MOST14. Not with his fists, but with his spray cans. When I remembered what he did, I jumped up. "That's it!"

"What? What?" Myla stared at me.

The idea shone down at me as bright as one of Randall's tags.

"I know what to do," I told her. "I know what will stop everybody from finding that *Om*."

41 MYLA

DINNER WAS CAULIFLOWER-AND-POTATO CURRY with rotis, my favorite Indian meal, even if it was from a place downtown. But all I could think about was the evening Peter and I had planned, and if it would go well or we'd get caught. I'd never been caught doing something illegal. Then again, I'd never done anything illegal. Tonight was a first, and even though I was scared, I was excited. All my life, all the words I had written down in my journal, and on scraps of paper attached to The Wall, seemed like training for this night.

Mom tore off a soft piece of roti and wrapped it around a piece of cauliflower and ate it slowly, watching me. She wasn't stupid. She could sense something was up. She just didn't know what, so she figured it had to be the bed.

"Myla, maybe you can read for a while before going to sleep," she said. "There's that new one from the bookstore you haven't read yet that's still on the couch."

"Hmm," I said.

"You like the new bed?" Dad asked. "Kind of nice to come home from school and find it all set up and ready to go."

"Mom thinks she's still scared," Cheetah said.

"No, I don't," Mom said.

I ate my roti quietly. The bed wouldn't be a problem. Because I wouldn't be there to sleep in it.

"Dad, have you seen the Rock of Gibraltar?" Cheetah asked.

Dad pushed up his glasses. "To what do I owe this question?"

"Gibraltar, it's a spelling word," Cheetah said.

"I thought there weren't proper nouns in spelling contests," Mom said.

"It's a common noun, too," Cheetah said. "It means 'an impregnable stronghold.'"

"Whoa," Dad said. "Is 'impregnable' a spelling word, too?"

"Yes," said Cheetah. "But have you been there?"

Questions like this—because of their randomness and complete lack of relevance to our lives—usually annoyed the daylights out of me. But today I was grateful, because while my parents and Cheetah were talking about the Rock of Where Ever and whether it was more *impregnable* than the Palisades, it gave me a chance to go over in my mind what Peter and I had decided.

Of course, at first he said no, he was totally not letting me join.

"You need someone to help," I said. "Like, don't you guys cover for each other, look for cops, be on the down low?"

Peter crossed his arms. "First of all, that's not even right slang. Second, you're scared of heights." He held up a finger when I tried to protest. "Don't even try to lie about that. Third, you don't have a clue how to hold a spray can. You'd probably spray-paint your face."

I bristled. "If I'm so scared of heights, who climbed down her window and warned your brother at the station? And who spray-painted her own bed? I got the paint from my garage, and there's more of that stuff where it came from."

Peter wasn't listening to any of it. "It's too dangerous," he said. Then he called somebody named Skinny for help, and it was Skinny who said no.

"You're eighteen. Come on man, I can't get the paint without you," Peter pleaded over the phone in his kitchen, while I listened. But Skinny kept saying no. Peter finally hung up, but not before saying he was going ahead anyway, and besides he already had plenty of spray paint. That's when he turned to me.

"Plenty of spray paint?" I repeated. "I have maybe two cans."

He sighed. "Well, it's a start."

I crossed my arms. "You're not getting them unless I'm helping." And that's how I got in on the plan, whether Peter liked it or not.

"What difference does it make?" Mom was saying now. "The Palisades is probably just as old as the Rock of Gibraltar. So it isn't as famous. They've both lasted."

"What lasts, lasts," Dad said.

"Who said that?" Cheetah asked.

"Me," Dad said.

After dinner, Cheetah and I cleared the table while Dad made a pot of chai on the stove.

"What does Om mean, Dad?" Cheetah asked. "You never really said."

Dad was measuring out tea leaves into the boiling water. "Om is a sound," he explained, "that means everything, that's all-encompassing. When you say it the right way, your mouth makes all the sounds there are to make. And in yoga, saying Om creates a vibration, a kind of movement inside you." He added milk and sugar to the pot until the tea turned a rich golden color.

"Can I have some?" I asked as I handed Cheetah a plate.

"Can I?" asked Cheetah.

"There's enough for everyone. But not too much. Or you'll be up half the night." Dad poured a steaming cup for himself.

"In other words, Om lasts," Cheetah said.

Dad smiled. "But not like Gibraltar. There is a beginning and end to Om." He carried his cup out of the kitchen to the study.

Cheetah and I continued cleaning up, the dishes clattering in the cupboards as we put them away. "It's cool there's an *Om* at the station," he said suddenly. "Like it's about us for a change."

"What do you mean?" I asked nervously. Was this another case of Cheetah guessing what Peter and I planned to do tonight?

"Om. An Indian symbol. Us."

"We're not Om. Hate to break it to you."

"We come from it," Cheetah said. "So many kids were talking to me yesterday at school because they wanted to know about Om."

I glanced at him as I cleaned the counter. This was a part of Cheetah I didn't know. Like, I knew who his two best friends were: Manny and Jaden. They were spelling geeks like him, and they got together at each other's houses to play video games or to quiz each other on spelling words. But I didn't know who his other friends were, if he was noticed in school, or if he was invisible like me. Had this *Om* tag elevated his status? I still felt like no one saw me at all. No one but Ana. And now Peter. "I thought you said you don't care if you're noticed," I said.

He shrugged. "I don't care if people notice me. But at least they're noticing Om."

After we were done in the kitchen, I went to the family room to get my book.

Outside, the sun was setting and I could see the Palisades fading into the darkening sky. I thought of Cheetah's Rock of Gibraltar, and what Dad said. What lasts, lasts. The Palisades had been there as long as I could remember. That was a kind of lasting, wasn't it? Remembering. I'd have to tell that to Cheetah.

42 RANDALL

WE STARTED FROM THE LOWER EAST SIDE, WORKing our way slowly until we got to Midtown. Then we went to a courtyard that Tops said was important, where Pop used to go because the concrete benches and wall were great for doing vaults. I stalled, letting Tops go first.

"You'll never find his tag if you stay on the ground," Tops said. "He wasn't stupid enough to leave a tag in plain sight. Climb up this wall when you're ready. You'll see something different."

Truth was, concrete was a whole different ball game from the cushioned playground. But I did what he told me. I jumped onto one bench, then another, and did a cat onto the wall, and hoisted myself to the top. I didn't stand on it like a crazy person, but I was able to see, and Tops was right. There was all of East Fortieth Street ahead of me. I could see the streetlight, and taxicabs, and the corner of Second Ave. But no *Om*. So I took out my Sharpie and added my own.

We continued through Midtown, along more courtyards and walkways between buildings. I'd had all these grand plans to outstep Tops, to PK past him on our quest to find any clues my pop had left behind. But the honest truth was that by Fiftieth Street, I was dog tired. "How many tags you think he did?" I asked as we crossed the street to the other side. "Cause I haven't seen one."

"A lot of them are gone. The city went and cleaned them up. But there are still a few in the Sixties. And there's one on the FDR, but it's not a place to hide anything."

"Maybe Pop didn't hide them at all. Maybe we're searching for something that doesn't exist."

"Oh, yeah?" Tops asked. "What makes you say that?"

"Running the past few hours with you. Partaking in the craziness."

"Maybe he said something to you, Mighty. Think. Did he give you any kind of clue?"

I shook my head. There were stars dancing inside my head, I was that tired.

"What about his black book? Maybe there was a clue there."

I saw him watching me intently. I was so tired, I could barely think. Maybe this was his plan all along—to wear me out until I told him everything I knew. Why else go from jump to jump like a madman? Wouldn't he have done these runs already? Wouldn't he have scoured the territory when he had a chance? It was the black book he was after. I could see it in his stinking face. So I said, "I don't think he had one."

"Mighty, we both know he did. If we could find it, it might answer a whole lot of questions."

The black book. I had looked through it night after night, while Petey was asleep in his bed. And I could say with my life betted on, and Petey's too, there was nothing in there. For sure, the black book wasn't something Pop had on him when he died. That thought stopped me. "Wait. We're here."

"Where?"

My tired feet picked up. "We just passed it. Fiftieth Street. I have to go back and see it."

"Whoa, hang on." He jogged behind me as I hurried to Fiftieth Street and turned. I didn't know where the building was exactly, only the address: 303 East Fiftieth Street.

After a block or so, Tops called, "I think it's a mistake. You don't want to go there and . . ."

We stopped.

We were standing in front of it: *Crestwood Residential Tower.* I peered up and felt dizzy. Maybe he'd landed where I stood. I pressed my eyes with my palms. "I have to go in," I said.

"Mighty, you can't," Tops said. "They won't let you."

"It's the place he died. Somebody's got to let me in. It's the decent thing."

"No, it isn't. This isn't a place of visitation. It's a place of residence."

"Maybe," I said slowly, "but I can try." Before he could say more, I ran to the front doors.

"Randall, wait!" he shouted, and I almost stopped in my tracks at the sound of my real name, the one I'd never told Tops. But I kept going because that was the only way in.

Inside, the air was cold and dry. A doorman stood there blocking my way. He was maybe only a few years older than me. His face was cold like the air. "Who you want to see?" he asked me.

I didn't know what to say. So I said, "Someone on the fortieth floor."

He gave a laugh. "That's impossible. This building only goes up to thirty."

"But that's wrong. I know, because my po—my father helped build this place."

He shrugged. "Yeah, well, unless you know somebody here, I can't buzz you in."

I glanced at the elevator behind him, at the numbers at the top. He was right. I could see there was no number 40. Instead 30 was lit, as if to say, that's how far anybody can go.

Outside the building, Tops was waiting. "You okay?" he asked when he saw me.

We got as far as the end of the street and then just like that, I sat down on the sidewalk. My arms and legs throbbed, and I could feel a vein pulsing in my throat.

"Come on, Mighty," he said. "Get up. You can't sit here."

"I give up. This is the end of the road. My pop isn't here. His tags are gone. He's gone!"

A few people glanced at me as they walked past us on the sidewalk.

"Mighty, calm down." Tops bent down so he was at my level. "You have to keep going." He saw my face. "And not for anybody else. You look for the diamonds because they belong to you."

"Really? They belong to me?"

Tops stood up. "As much as anybody." He helped me up.

I stared a moment longer at my shoes, the way they stood over a crack in the sidewalk. When I was young, I'd imagine myself a giant, walking over cracks like they were the Grand Canyon, and across sticks like they were the George Washington Bridge. I started shaking. But I don't know if it was from fatigue, or from the idea I just got. I was no giant, but could my feet take me there?

"What are you thinking, M?" asked Tops.

"There's one place we haven't tried," I said slowly. "It's the place my pop still lives on."

43 RANDALL

I LIED WHEN I TOLD TOPS I'D NEVER BEEN TO THE city with my pop. There was one place he did take me. I was almost nine years old, when we got on a bus at St. Vincent Ave because he said there was something he wanted to show me.

It was cold and bright inside the bus, the air-conditioning humming like a bee. I sat next to Pop, and I could see our reflection in the window. Everybody said I looked like him, and here I could see it. The same sharp nose, the same shoulders round at the top, the same lanky arms hanging on both sides. We spent the whole time chilling, listening to Pop's music on his phone. He brought earplugs, one in his ear, one in mine, and we listened to "Little Wing" by Jimi Hendrix, which Pop said was his favorite song in the world, which is why I can't listen to it even now.

When we got to West 176th, it was dark with streetlights cutting through the night air. Pop and me walked along the sidewalk until we got to the park. It was a disaster, garbage everywhere, weirdos hanging around giving us dirty looks. But I was with Pop, and I wasn't afraid. We kept walking until we got to a lookout where we could see a bridge stretched across the Harlem River.

Pop pointed. He told me how the bridge went all the way to the Bronx, how when he was little, he and Grandma Rose walked across it during the summers to go swimming in Highbridge Pool. But now the bridge wasn't open. It was broken down and nobody walked on it anymore.

From his knapsack, Pop pulled out binoculars. What I saw through the lenses made me suck in my breath. How, what, where? All these questions stuck in my throat. It occurred to me then that my father really was a superman. There was no other explanation for how he'd landmarked an *Om* where no human could reach. *Remember that one*, he told me. *Remember because nobody's washing it away.*

"We should have started here," Tops kept murmuring. "It's his masterpiece."

"You don't need to tell me that," I said. It was getting so I hated it when he told me stuff about Pop now. In the big picture, who was he anyway, except some chump my pop ran with?

We walked through the park until we got to High Bridge. It was open to the public now. Ma and Petey didn't want to go, so I went by myself during the summer without telling them. There was a ceremony—you know the kind, where some bozo cuts a ribbon and everyone cheers and walks through. I was one of the people walking through, and I made a beeline for the other side, where I knew it would be. And it was. And damn, there was nothing better than the satisfaction of knowing the *Om* survived. It *survived.* I didn't go back again after that. Not until now.

The bridge was closed at night. There was a fence with a lock, so Tops and I did our thing, him with his chalk, me with his hands as my foothold. On the other side of the fence, we walked across the bridge carefully and quickly. Finally we got to the other side, yards away from the Bronx. We looked down at what we knew was there, a few feet below us on the curve of the last arch.

"Still here after all these years," Tops said.

Most tags are block or bubble letters, but not my pop's. His *Om* always had a face inside the "O." Sometimes I wondered if it was his own face he painted. The straight line of the nose, the round lips that were his and mine, and not Petey's. But the eyes were always two horizontal lines—they were closed. When I asked him why he painted them that way, he told me, that's how you show thinking. His was a thinking tag.

Tops was searching. "Where would he hide them? Everything's so open. Look at the masonry."

My heart started pounding. I pictured my pop traversing below, one foothold at a time. "You've got it all wrong. The *Om* isn't where we are. It's down there."

Tops stopped. He stared slowly over the railing. "You think it's . . . *there*?" He looked back at me, his face round as the moon. "But . . . that's impossible. I don't even know how your dad did it. That's not parkour. I don't know what it is."

"I've seen videos of people climbing bridges. Sometimes with ropes. It's done."

Tops shook his head. "Don't get me wrong. It's brilliant. No ordinary person would dare to look for the diamonds there." He paused, measuring his words. "At least not me. I'm too big, too heavy. One gust of wind would knock me over."

While he spoke, I scanned the area. For the first time I wished I had the duffel bag. Pop used a harness and ropes and pulleys to get himself over. I didn't have those. I could go back and buy some equipment. There was a 24-hour hardware store on Broadway. But that would mean leaving, and chances were Tops would find a way to stop me from coming back. And then come later without me. It was now or never, with this fool Tops assisting.

"Look," I said. "Here's what we do. I'll get over the two fences and climb down. When I get to the bottom of the outside fence, you hold me by my hand through the opening. You brace me until I reach that ledge down there. Once I'm on it, I'm safe."

Tops went over what I said, peering between the spires to an outcrop jutting from under the bridge support. "You think you can reach that ledge if I hang you?" he asked.

"If you're man enough to spot me." There, I'd said it. There was no turning back.

Tops paused. "All right, Mighty. Go for it," he said, his voice low.

I turned to the two fences. The inner one was shorter. Tops made the foothold I'd grown accustomed to using. All the while, I made myself focus. I thought how Pop and I had the same narrow, long feet. I pictured him climbing the fence now, not me, one foot in front of the other. He had his harness and rope. I didn't have those. But I could still pretend I was him. It was a matter of using those fences and holding on. And just a few feet away was the *Om*.

The sound of traffic faded away into a distant hum. The only sound I heard was my heart, so loud it was in my ears and throat and behind my eyes. Time slowed down to a halt as I imagined myself climbing with Pop's feet and hands, up and down the fences. On the other side was victory, I told myself. On the other side was a whole new life, where we wouldn't live day to day but year to year, planning big. Like Petey going to college. My ma taking a trip to India. And me painting canvasses like a professional bad-ass.

Tops's voice was part of the distant hum of everything else ... *lean in, keep your body pressed to the fence* . . . But it was easier to ignore him. *Think of Pop's feet*, I said to myself. *One foot in front of the other*.

It was his feet that climbed the first fence. It was his feet that climbed the second one. It was his superman feet that were going to get me to the arch. The air was blowing in my ears on both sides. I was hanging, maybe flying, with Pop's feet as I inched slowly down the length of the second fence. I was near the bottom when I looked up and saw Tops's hand through the spires. It was out ready to brace me, ready for me to hang from. The hand was worn and callused and squat. It was the hand of life or death. I didn't know which.

As he waited, I made the mistake of looking down, not at the river, but at my own foot to see where to place it. Then something strange happened—even though I had Pop's feet locked squarely inside my mind, I saw the fake Jordans. And it was Petey's feet I imagined instead. Petey who couldn't tie his own shoelace years after Pop was gone. Petey who couldn't do a jump to save his life. Thank god he wasn't on the tracks with me that night the train came. His feet were curiously big, almost the same size as mine, and on him, they made him look like a clown.

My arms were cramping, and I heard Tops calling to me. But I couldn't stop looking at my feet. At the fake Jordans that Petey was so happy to get. "I'm hanging like Jordan!" he yelled, leaping in the air and doing the most pitiful slam dunk imitation I'd ever seen. Like you wanted him off the court where nobody would see him and his fakes. But that was Petey, happy to have fakes.

"Pop," I whispered. He was a superman all right. But he had fallen, and he had left us. I don't know what he was doing in that building that night. I don't know if the Fencers got to him there or not. I wasn't sure I would ever really know. But he had put one foot in front of the other, and just doing that had taken him away from Petey and me and our mother. The wind under the bridge howled and I floundered, half on the fence, half not.

I could feel myself swimming, the water in my eyes blurring the fake Jordans and everything. But not enough that I couldn't go up, one foot in front of the other. Then again, and again. Pop had chosen High Bridge, and the way of the night. But whatever he left behind, whatever promise finding those diamonds would fulfill, they weren't what I wanted. Because the fact was, more than anything else, I wanted life. I chose life. I went back up the second fence, and down the first one. Each step was easier than the one before it. When I got back, I threw myself on the brick walkway.

Tops stood without moving. "You couldn't do it," he said, a statement of fact. His voice dripped with the sadness of it all. It was enough to make me want to finally punch him. But there was a sound that stopped me right at that moment. The ringing of his phone inside his pocket. He answered. Then, "It's for you."

Nike's voice was loud and strong in my ear. "You got to come now. I just heard from Skinny. He says Petey is in for a whole lot of trouble. He wanted Skinny to buy him a load of paint so he could bomb Dobbs. Think MOST14."

"Okay," I said. "Give me an hour."

"No, Mighty. We need you here *now*."

"I have to go to Dobbs Ferry," I said to Tops, "because of my brother." But when he kept looking at me with that dead expression in his eyes, I knew what had to be done. I said what he'd been hoping to hear ever since he met me. "And because we have to get Pop's black book."

"I'll take you now," said Tops. "I got my car a few blocks away."

44 MYLA

IT'S FUNNY HOW CLIMBING OUT OF YOUR WINDOW gets easier with practice. The scariest part was looking down, so I stopped doing that. I let my feet find their way. They knew where to go, and when they touched the soft ground, I was ready for anything.

I felt my head to see if my cap was on right. I was wearing everything Peter told me to: a dark cap to cover my hair, a dark gray hoodie, and jeans. Nothing black—Peter said that was the worst color to wear if you're trying not to look conspicuous. I remembered that from the videos, too, how black made you stand out even in the shadows.

I heard a sound, like a twig crunching underfoot. I turned around, thinking it was Peter.

"Cheetah!" I sputtered.

He ran up to me. "I'm going with you," he whispered. "I don't care what you say."

"How did you know I was here? Did you climb out the window, too?"

He shook his head. "I just waited until Mom and Dad were in the kitchen making more tea, and then I snuck out the front door."

I groaned. How did Cheetah manage to walk out the door

when here I was, climbing out of my two-story bedroom window? "Just turn around and go back, Cheet. You can't follow me."

But he didn't budge. "It has to do with the diamonds. And you almost got arrested!"

"No, I didn't!" I let out my breath. "And I'm helping Peter find his brother."

"Who are you talking to?" whispered a voice behind me. It was Peter. He had on the same blue hoodie he wore every day.

"Nobody," I whispered back. "Just Cheetah. And he's going back inside, right?"

My brother shook his head no.

Then I had an idea. "Cheetah, I need your help."

"You do?" he asked.

"Yeah, you have to go back and do lookout. Like if you see Mom and Dad coming up to check on me, you have to stop them. Make up something, but just don't let them see I'm gone."

"I'd rather come with you," Cheetah said.

"No kidding," Peter said, smirking. "Trust me, I know what lookout is."

I gave Peter a sharp glance and said, "Cheetah, I'm serious. Will you do it for me?"

At first he didn't want to, but I was able to change his mind.

"After two hours, I get worried," he warned. I nodded, and he went back inside.

"What took you so long?" I asked Peter.

He pulled out a piece of paper. "We finally got our computer and printer hooked up so I was printing out a map of Dobbs."

"You don't need a map. I know where everything is."

"Well, this has the places I think we should target." He showed them to me: the library, the Historical Society, the horse trough, the Masters School, the Cedar Street Café.

"All those places?" I squeaked.

"You can still back out. I don't need help. Or maybe you can do *lookout* with your brother."

"Very funny."

"Plus I got you this." He took something out of his pocket and gave it to me. "There were so many in the attic, I thought you'd like to have one again. The hard part was figuring out which one to give you."

I turned the necklace over. "It says 'keeper' like the old one."

He nodded. "I thought about you and your wall with all the papers on it. Then I decided you had the right one all along. If anybody's a keeper, that's you, Myla."

I swallowed. It was weird how happy it made me that he'd thought about it, and who I was. "Thanks," I said softly. I put the necklace on. This time I wouldn't lose it.

I knelt down and took out the spray cans I had stashed under a bush. We had a total of three. Peter's hoodie was bigger, so he carried two, and I carried one. Then we set off down Cherry Street, trying to walk casually as if we weren't about to spray-paint Dobbs Ferry.

"Tell me again about MOST14," I whispered. I wasn't sure if we were supposed to talk about tagging just before doing it, but I was getting nervous, and maybe it would be good for Peter to talk about something else, too.

"He was maybe fourteen or fifteen years old when it happened." It was surprising how clear Peter's voice was even when he whispered. "I don't know if 'beautiful' is the word to describe a tag, but his was. Randall uses orange, right? MOST14 used pink. Not exactly manly—but along with black, *MOST14* stood out from all the other tired-looking tags. You'd be on the other side of the street, or in a bus going somewhere, but soon as you saw one of his tags, you'd go *Damn*. Because MOST was king for getting noticed."

I sighed. "If I was going to tag on the street, that's what I'd want."

"To be MOST?"

"To be noticed. To have people say 'damn' about me." I blushed because I'd never sworn in front of someone and I sounded stupid, not down like Peter. But somehow I didn't care. I knew he'd understand what I meant, because Peter understood about tags.

But then he gave me this look like I was from another planet. "You're talking like my brother and his crew," he said. "And most of the time they're talking crap."

"What?" I asked, surprised.

"Tagging isn't what gets you noticed. Like, I notice you plenty."

"You do?" I blinked. "Because in school . . ." But I wasn't

sure I could explain the years of feeling short and small and in the shadows. Not without feeling something else I hated: tears in my eyes.

"I notice you helping me," Peter offered.

I sniffed. But hopefully he didn't notice *that.* "So what happened to MOST14?" I asked.

"Well, here's the thing. You talk about being noticed. And some people think it's all about how much you tag. The more the better. But MOST14's trick was that he was *limited.* You didn't see a lot of his tags. One here, one there, but that's what made you keep looking. If one popped up on the Bronx River Parkway, you'd be sure to notice it every time you went by. It was ironic, him being MOST, when what he did was the least."

A car passed by at the end of the street, and we both paused until we saw it keep going.

I glanced up. We had stopped in front of Ana's house. All the lights were off downstairs, but Ana's room was lit. "You know who lives here, right?" I asked.

Peter gave a half smile. "Yeah. I know."

I suddenly wanted to tell him it was okay if he liked Ana, and if he thought she was pretty. And that it was okay if she liked him back. I wanted to tell him, but somehow I think he knew. Or maybe it wasn't anything I had to say out loud. So I just said, "Okay, just checking."

We continued walking.

After a while I asked, "So then what happened to MOST?"

Peter nodded. Maybe he was relieved we weren't delving into girl talk. "MaxD understood that MOST's tag stood out because it was rare," he went on. "So that's why he bombed *MOST14* everywhere. And MaxD did a lousy job. Even with the right colors, it looked trash. After a while, the bad copy of MOST's tag was everywhere—all the gas stations and the A&P, and even on a church. Not only that, there were so many *MOST14* tags, now the cops noticed. Then MOST got caught. He got fined for every single tag, including all the ones he didn't do. It was so much, I hear he's all-out broke, and stopped tagging, period. And that fool MaxD won."

"That's terrible! Is that what we're doing by painting all these *Om* tags?"

"Nah. We're not trying to get rid of the tag. We just want to confuse everybody else."

I nodded. "Yeah, more *Om*s, and people won't know which is the real one."

"Exactly."

Peter fell silent as we turned onto Walnut. I had so many other questions—like how long did it take to paint a tag, or what happened if the word didn't show exactly right? But most of all, was he scared like me? And if we got caught, what would we do? He'd told me to throw down the paint and run as fast as I could if a cop came. But that didn't cover the part about actually getting nailed.

I could feel the adrenaline flowing in my blood, like every single cell was opening up inside me. I glanced at Peter and I could tell he felt the same way. At the end of Walnut, there would be fewer trees, less cover, and we'd be half a street away from our first stop, the Historical Society. It was a beautiful house, and it was about to become less beautiful in a few minutes.

"Peter," I whispered. I was about to tell him what I was feeling, the misgivings inside me. But just then a car pulled around the corner, and this time it came down our street. Peter reached out to stop me with his hand. We stood there, not knowing what to do. It wasn't a cop car, was it? Like one of those undercover ones?

The car came slowly, and it seemed it was coming toward us. I felt a sudden panic. I hadn't counted on this—a cop, maybe, but not a stranger in a strange car approaching us. Automatically Peter and I stepped backward, off the sidewalk, onto the grass, although there was nothing there to hide us. Peter pulled at my arm, signaling for us to turn around and run, but then the car came to a stop about twenty feet from us, and the front passenger door opened.

Peter froze, staring at the guy who was on the sidewalk, then walking toward us. I had been at the train station, I had seen the newspaper, so I knew who it was. Even then, I couldn't believe my eyes, that he was here before we'd even sprayed the first drop of paint.

He stopped in front of us, and glanced at me. Then he spoke. "Nike told me what you planned to do, Petey. It doesn't make any sense. Just go on home and we'll forget about this."

Peter was breathing in and out hard. Then I saw something

that surprised me. His hands balling up into fists. Wasn't he happy to see Randall?

"You're here to stop me?" he asked quietly.

Randall broke into a grin. "Sure I am. You'll get caught faster than you can say jackass. I know you, Petey. This isn't your thing."

I barely had time to look at Randall's face—that easy smile that reminded me of his tag, bright and sunny and superconfident. But that smile quickly turned to shock as Peter lunged forward and shoved his brother to the ground.

45 PETER

I NEVER FELT SO MUCH RAGE COURSING through my body. Something about Randall's smart-aleck grin made me want to punch him in the nose. And I'd never punched anyone in my life. "Who do you think you are, telling me what I can't do!" I hollered as he scrambled off the sidewalk and stood on his feet, gawking at me.

"Petey," he said, "man, you're really losing it." Behind him for the first time I noticed Nike was there, too. He'd been riding in the car, and he was standing right behind Randall. There was also somebody else, a man I hadn't seen. He was the one driving the car, and he stood outside, leaning against the driver's door. I ignored them both and turned to Randall.

"All this time, I've been busting myself trying to get you back. I've been telling myself, us brothers got to stick together. But you know what, Randall? You're right. I don't need to be tagging on your behalf. I don't need to be doing anything on your behalf. You can move to Timbuktu, all I care." I turned around, ready to walk away from my brother, his stupid dreams about the diamonds, and every other crazy thing he'd ever thought was more important than me or Ma.

Then I heard Nike's voice. "You sure know how to say the wrong thing, Mighty."

"Petey." Randall's voice was different now, softer, and cracking in the middle. Then I felt him pulling me back, tugging on my arm. I turned to glare at him. But something strange had happened. It was like he was somebody else, somebody smaller, a deflated balloon.

"Petey, I'm—I'm sorry." He tried to stand taller, look like he always did, but the truth was it was hard for my brother to say sorry to anybody.

"That's not enough," Nike said. "Tell him you love him." For this, Nike got a shove from Randall. Behind them, the strange man was getting restless.

"You guys sorted through everything?" he asked.

Meanwhile, where was Myla? I looked around, then saw her halfway up the street. She was standing in front of the old house that Uncle Richard was working on, reading a sign in front. From a distance she didn't even look like herself, with her curly hair stuck under that cap. She looked like a small girl, lost inside a hoodie, and it reminded me of the way I felt wearing Randall's. But that was going to change. Soon as I got home, I was tossing my brother's hoodie away.

"Give us a minute, Tops," said Randall.

I jerked my head up. *This* was the legendary Tops? The guy with a belly? I looked at him carefully and saw the restlessness in him, the tight way he was holding himself. Something else was going on. I took a step back.

"Just why did you come back here?" I asked quietly. "Are you fooling with me?"

Randall made a face. "No, Petey, you got it wrong. Don't

you see? I was on High Bridge, and I swear to you, something changed. Something changed in me."

"You look about the same."

"I don't mean how I look. I mean, I had a revelation, know what I mean? Like a moment."

But I wasn't ready for Randall's moment, whatever it was. I searched for a bone of contention. "Then why is he here?" I pointed with my face. "You're bringing more people in? Wasn't your crew bad enough?"

Randall glanced behind him. "Oh, that's Tops. He's cool." But something in his eyes told me he wasn't. "He brought me here."

He was about to say more when Myla came running back to us.

"Peter, you have to see this. It all adds up. We're on the Aqueduct Trail!"

"Aqueduct Trail?" Randall repeated. He and Nike looked at each other.

"Come over there. Here I thought it was just some old haunted house, but it's part of the Aqueduct. It was built in 1857, and that's where one of the Keepers of the Aqueduct lived. The house had many different names, but look what it was finally called. It must have been called that before your grandma Rose died."

"How does she know about Grandma Rose?" Randall asked.

"Come, see for yourself," Myla insisted. She dragged me up the street to the sign, and everybody else had no choice but to join us. "Look at the name now."

RESTORATION OF THE KEEPER'S HOUSE

The New York City water supply system is one of the great municipal water supply systems in the world. During the active days of the Aqueduct, Keepers were provided with houses on or near the section of the tunnel for which they were responsible in its maintenance. Here remains the last such house on the Aqueduct Trail. Known previously by different names, this Italianate-style home is now called the Keeper's House, and is a designated landmark.

"Okay," I said. "I don't get it. Why is it important?"

"Keeper's House," Myla said slowly. "Keeper . . . shouse. That's what the necklaces spell."

"Whoa," I said.

"And you say we're on the Aqueduct Trail?" Nike asked.

That's when I noticed a dirt path cutting past the Keeper's

House and continuing on the other side of the street. I'd never paid attention to it before.

Meanwhile, Randall was pulling something out of his pocket. "That's what my map is for," he said. He unfolded the sheets. "Anybody got a flashlight?"

Tops had a mini one on his key chain. He flashed it on top of the map. Shadows danced around, but we found everything: High Bridge, Croton Dam, and in between, the Keeper's House.

"I don't believe it," Randall said. "It was here all this time."

"It was in the black book, too," Myla said.

"What?" Randall asked, surprised.

Myla's eyes shifted to mine. "Well—that's what Peter told me," she finished uneasily.

"Look, who cares?" Nike asked. "Sounds like this place was what your grandma meant. It's now up to us to get inside and check it out." He turned to Randall and Tops. "And we can use our feet to get in."

They looked at each other, then at the second-floor ledge of the dilapidated house.

"The house could fall down," Tops said. "It looks pretty shaky."

"*We* might fall down," said Randall. "I don't know if I can make the height."

Nike shrugged. "The worst is we fail. Or break our legs. So what? You in?"

Tops thought a moment. "Yeah, I'm in."

Randall nodded. "If these fakes hold up."

I watched as they circled the house, three silhouettes against the crumbling walls. Seeing them, it was like some kind of mysterious, silent dance, where only they knew the moves. Part of me wanted in on it, while part of me was scared of what I was about to see. In the distance I heard a ferry horn as the three of them ran, one after the other, and leaped into the night.

46 MYLA

WOW WOW WOW! WHEN NIKE SAID THEY WOULD use their feet, I had no idea what that meant. Like maybe they were going to kick in the door? I was about to tell them to stop. Graffiti was one thing, but breaking private property was another. Plus somebody might hear us. But for once I decided to keep quiet.

Then I couldn't believe what I saw: first the middle-aged guy *ran* at the wall, and before I knew it, he'd climbed up and stood on the ledge. Then Nike followed, and finally Randall, though it took him a few tries, and for one scary moment I thought he'd fall and land on his head. But he finally got himself up. I'm still not sure how they did it. They ran and just kicked themselves up like acrobats. I stared at Peter in wonder.

He shrugged. "Parkour."

"You mean you've seen this before?" I asked, astonished. What else was I going to find out about Peter's family before the night was through? Meanwhile, the three of them were scaling the ledge around to the other side, where there was an open window, and one by one, they climbed in. "Come on," I told Peter. I went around the back of the house, seeing if there was another window on the first floor they could open to let me in.

The house was crumbling, but it was sturdier than I thought. All these years Cheetah and I had imagined it haunted, and we'd dared each other to go as near the house as we could. Once I came as far as the back window and peered in. It was dark, with rubble on the floor, and that was as much as I could see before I ran back to the street where Cheetah was waiting. Now I was here standing next to the same window, and I could hear voices inside that seemed to be coming down a staircase. I rapped on the window so they'd know I was there. I called softly, "Hey, guys, over here." I rapped some more until the window came up.

Nike's head poked out. "You don't like to be kept waiting, do you?"

I flushed. "Just wanted to help," I said.

"Well, it's not easy climbing up an ancient house without the ceiling giving on you," he said. "Maybe you can just wait outside some more?"

I stood there, not knowing what to say, but worried I'd somehow pissed off this guy.

"Cut it out, Nike," said Peter. "Let Myla in."

Nike broke into a big smile. "Can't take a joke, either of you."

I looked more closely at him as he helped me in through the window. His hair was a tight, wiry brown, and he was wearing a bandana wrapped around each wrist. His shirt had a picture of a shark fin on it, and he had long, sinewy legs. "Why is your name Nike?" I asked after we were in. "Like the shoe company?"

"Actually, no," said Nike. "I'm winged victory. Like in the Greek story."

I widened my eyes. "That's cool. But isn't Nike a girl?"

"Say what?" asked Nike.

Next to him, Randall burst out laughing.

"Ha-ha, that explains a lot," he said.

"Stuff it," Nike told him.

We started picking our way through the rubble in the dark. It was hard to see much of anything. Tops had that tiny flashlight, but that wasn't enough inside the house. Gradually my eyes got used to the darkness, and some of the streetlight came in through the uncovered windows. The floors were bare except for the rubble, and the walls were mostly peeled away, except for the front entrance where an old parlor mirror hung, probably the only remaining furniture in the whole house. But most surprising of all, the walls were covered with graffiti. Everywhere I saw words scrawled on the wall in marker and pen. There were words like *Hippie* and *World Peace*, different sets of initials—that kind of stuff.

"Mighty, looks like your kind of place," Tops said.

"I'll say," I murmured. I felt the spray can that was still inside my hoodie. But who was I kidding? I was in the company of a master graffiti artist. I didn't want Peter's brother laughing at me. It was hardly the time to try out my tagging skills.

"Anybody seen an *Om*?" asked Randall.

"Maybe it's on the second floor," I said. "I'm going up."

"I'll come with you," said Peter.

We made our way gingerly up the narrow steps.

"Be careful," Randall called out. "There's no light up there. Nike, you go up with them."

“We’re fine,” Peter said. “You don’t have to baby us.”

There was tension between Peter and his brother. I could see why. Randall was like a big-brother version of Peter, with the same hair and frame, but his face was cocky, and he had this way with him like he thought he was better than you. I could see Peter wanting to punch his brother down. Maybe Peter had been in Randall’s shadow his whole life, and now it was like, no more. For a moment I wondered if Cheetah felt the same way around me. Like if one day I was going to get a punch in the nose at the dining table.

By now, Peter and I had reached the upstairs and skirted along the walls. There were actually two rooms, and we started with the first one. “I don’t know what we’re going to find here without a flashlight,” Peter said grimly. “Plus I don’t even know what we’re looking for. Would Grandma Rose really hide the diamonds in this house? It’s a disaster.”

“Well, it’s a landmark, which means they can’t demolish the house, right? Maybe that’s why she chose it. But it’s got to be somewhere in here that won’t be renovated.”

“Right, like a permanent structure,” Peter said. “How about the fireplace over there?” We crossed the room, and felt the ground buckle under our feet. We quickly ran to the other side.

“The floor isn’t sound,” Peter said. “Don’t go in the middle.”

I nodded. We got on all fours, peering along the sides of the fireplace, and then inside, feeling with our fingers. As far as I could tell, there was nothing. Nothing etched in the brick or on the hearth. But we kept looking. The house had seemed small when we first saw it from the outside. But now that we were inside, the place had suddenly become vast. The *Om* could be anywhere. It could take days before we found anything. I wondered if that's what we would do. Come here night after night, climbing through the window, and getting down on our hands and knees.

From outside came a distant rattling. It grew louder, and it sounded like the gunning of a car engine. Peter groaned. "I know who that is. And he still hasn't changed that muffler."

"Who?" I asked.

"You stay here. I'll handle it." He stood up and made his way to the stairs. "And don't walk in the middle," he reminded me.

Meanwhile, I continued my search of the fireplace, now feeling with my hands along the mantel. It was actually a beautiful fireplace, the kind you read about in books. I wonder if the Keeper who lived here had sat by this fireplace with his family, warming their hands. Was it a hard job, looking after the Aqueduct? I imagined the tunnel underground where the Aqueduct Trail ran, ninety million gallons of water rushing though it every day.

By now, I heard a new voice downstairs, and it was loud. I could hear him say that someone from his work crew saw us breaking in, and he was here to check it out. Then a moment later the loud guy said, "Shazam! If that's true, then the best place to look is upstairs!"

Peter said, "Fine, Uncle Richard."

"That's where all the original parts are still intact," the uncle explained as he came up the stairs with Peter. He sure didn't try to be quiet for one second. He was like his car, loud and reverberating. Behind him I could hear Peter telling him to keep his voice down.

I crossed the room so I wouldn't startle them. His voice was strangely familiar, but I couldn't place it. Then Peter's uncle was standing at the door, saying something about the fireplace. When I saw his face, I let out a small shriek.

Even in the dark room, he could see me. "It's you," he said. Then he laughed like I was some joke he couldn't believe.

"Peter, it's him!" I shrieked, scrambling back.

"What? What?" Peter called out, looking back from him to me. "You know each other?"

"It's him." I couldn't stop screaming, even though I knew I was being a big baby. "*That's* Craggy." I stepped back as far as I could, and suddenly felt the ground give under me, as a century of plaster and wood crumbled under my feet and I crashed through the floor, falling and falling through the unlit air.

47 RANDALL

ONE MINUTE I WAS STANDING THERE WITH NIKE and Tops, the next minute the girl came crashing down like a meteor. Everywhere there was dust and plaster, and the girl was screaming. Nike, Tops, and I ran toward her, while everyone else came down the stairs.

"Myla, are you okay?" Peter cried out. We gathered around the girl.

"I'm all right, I'm all right," she said, coughing, as plaster shook from her hair. Then her face twisted in pain. "My ankle," she gasped.

Tops came forward and squatted down. "It looks injured. Let me see."

Then Uncle Richard, who was standing nearby, gave a low whistle. "Well, if it isn't Michael Biggs coming to save the day. I didn't smell you when I came in."

I turned to Tops, surprised. "You know him?" Even before I could get a good look at this uncle of mine, I find out they've got a connection?

Tops looked uneasy. "Yeah, but it was Omar I was friends with."

"And I know why you were friends with him," Uncle Richard said coolly.

I looked at Uncle Richard more closely as he stepped out of

the shadows, and for one gut-stopping moment, it was like Pop was in the house. Then a second look told me not. He was the same height, with the same features, but spaced out differently on his face. But I remembered him now. If not his face, then the idea of him coming to our place to chill with Pop.

By now, Tops was brushing rubble from the girl's leg. "Where is it hurting?"

"Over there, near my heel." She sucked in her breath while he felt the area with his fingers.

Tops turned to Nike. "Those bandanas on your wrists. I need them."

Nike paused, then took them off. I knew about his handkerchiefs. They were his lucky ones, what he wore when he didn't know where he would end up in the night. Then Tops made a knot at one end. "That will stop the swelling. But you need to see a doctor to make sure nothing's broken."

"Then you best get the lady home," Uncle Richard said. "That goes for everybody. Time to go, folks. Let's call it a wrap, ha-ha, get it?"

Tops stood up. "I was thinking maybe some of you can take her home, and the rest of us could stay back and check out the place more."

"Negative on that," Uncle Richard said. "I could lose my job letting you all stay, now with the ceiling caving in. Petey and Randall, move it. You too, Bandana Boy. And of course, I'm booting you out first, Mr. Tops."

Tops flinched at Uncle Richard's tone but he continued

calmly enough. "Richard, I've driven Mighty all the way from the city. He'd be disappointed if we didn't do one sweep of the place."

"Oh, right, poor Randall," Uncle Richard said, "when you're the rat."

"Actually, *you're* the rat," Myla spoke up from the floor. "You parkoured into my room and stole the necklace."

"Me parkour?" Uncle Richard exclaimed. "Don't make me laugh. Leave that stuff to Omar and Topsy-Turvy to break their necks."

"Hey, don't disrespect the sport," said Nike.

Uncle Richard looked at Myla. "Anybody can climb up to your room. They just need a good foothold. And let's get one thing clear, girlie. *You* took that necklace. I don't care if you paid money, my ma had no right selling something that was mine."

"So are we staying or going?" Nike interrupted. "Personally, I say we blow this place before the roof falls on our heads."

"Just an hour more," Tops said. "We're so close."

"So you can get the diamonds," Uncle Richard said.

"You're the one who's after them," Tops said. "Omar said he was sick of listening to you talk about them all the time. You think I don't see how you're using this girl as an excuse to get us out of here?"

"It's true," Myla butted in. "We're letting him get the place all to himself."

"I work here," Uncle Richard said. "None of you have a reason to be inside, and I could have you all arrested myself. I'd start with this here girl because she's the biggest pain, then I'd move to Tops, who's been looking for the stones before Omar's body was cold in the ground."

"Omar was my friend!" Tops shouted. "You have no idea what you're saying, or what his death did to me. Who do you think taught him PK in the first place? And he was really good—but that's the problem. When you're good you forget the risks you take every time you go out."

"That's what my pop did? He forgot what he was doing?" I demanded. All I could say was when I was on the wrong side of the fence on High Bridge, it was hard to forget the swirling river below. But what if you were inside a building? Did you forget the cost of falling down? I didn't understand how you could. Or how you could be jumping on the inside, and then land on the outside, dead on the pavement.

Tops's face softened. "Mighty, it could have been me who fell down those thirty floors. We all forget. Only now I try to do it less. I remember your dad every time I run. That's why I use the chalk. I never forget the chalk."

Uncle Richard folded his arms. "That's real sweet, Tops. We're all crying here."

Nike, who was at the window, suddenly cut in. "Listen everybody, there's somebody coming up the front. Oh God, he's at the front door."

Uncle Richard groaned. "I knew it. You dumb people."

Myla was struggling to her feet. We were all freaking out, but it didn't make any difference. The door opened and a body framed the entrance so he was like one big, solid wall of misfortune.

"Everybody freeze!" he shouted, just like in the movies.

What happened next went by so fast I didn't remember it all. First, the cop shone a flashlight on us, and we looked like ghosts with the plaster all over our faces. Then he informed us we were trespassing, and he'd have to bring us in, and nobody was going anywhere, so we shouldn't even bother trying. That's when Uncle Richard spoke up, and it was like *mumble-mumble-jumble* and him showing his contractor's card. But the gist was he'd come on behalf of the construction company because somebody called to say the roof was caving in. When he came, he found us kids out front, the ones who called him in the first place. Then, against his advice, we dumb-asses followed him inside where more plaster fell on us, explaining our freaky appearance.

That's when Tops cleared his throat. "Yeah, I'm his assistant."

Which was like the biggest joke, but still we all kept quiet.

Even so, the cop wasn't buying a single word. "That girl is injured," he said, pointing to Myla who was hobbling on one foot.

But when we looked at her, she wasn't hobbling but shaking with excitement. In the middle of the cop saying how we were all going to the station, she burst out, "Look, it's the *Om*!"

All conversation in the room stopped—that is, the cop shut his big trap. I waited for him to say, *What's an Om? What are you talking about, girl?* But he knew exactly what she meant. We all knew exactly what she meant.

"Myla, are you sure?" Petey said.

The cop cleared his throat. "You kids are looking for . . . the Om?" He looked at us for a moment and said, "You know I'll have to report all stolen property. And . . ." He paused. Then, like he could wait no more, he said, "So, where is it?"

With one finger, Myla pointed straight ahead of her to the front of the house, where an old mirror hung on the left side just before the staircase. We all looked hard, seeing nothing. Then I saw it—not paint, not marker, not anything I've ever seen used to tag before. "On the mirror," I cried out. "She scratched it."

Petey shook his head in wonder. "That's right. Diamonds scratch glass."

Everyone hurried to the wall except for Myla who stood there balanced on one foot.

"I didn't see it until the flashlight went over it," she explained.

The cop and Uncle Richard stood on either side and held on to the frame of the mirror.

"On the count of three, okay?" the cop asked. Uncle Richard nodded.

"One, two, three!"

With a heave, the two of them hoisted the mirror off the wall and set it carefully on the ground. There behind the mirror was a small shelf built into the wall. Perfect for hiding a secret.

"There's something in there!" called out Tops.

The cop shone his flashlight onto the shelf and we all hovered around.

"Is it the diamonds?" Myla yelled from behind, shorter than all of us, and on one foot.

Uncle Richard reached in and pulled it out. "Son of gun," he said in disbelief. But that was nothing compared to the shock on Tops's face. Or the way he looked at me, like he was sending a ball of fury my way. Honest, what was he getting mad at me for?

Meanwhile, I couldn't believe what Uncle Richard was holding in his hand. Seemed like I could hear Pop laughing his head off somewhere in heaven, just like that day I told him I thought his chalk was meant for drawing on the sidewalk.

It turns out it was good for something else. Because that's all we found filling up that space inside the shelf: a big, hulking piece of climbing chalk.

48 MYLA

ON THE TWO-MINUTE DRIVE HOME, OFFICER FILnik decided to lecture Randall, Peter, and me on the dangers of being outside after dark, unsupervised. "Plus you don't know who can be out there," Filnik said. "Just a couple of days ago, a youth was at the train station, defacing public property."

It took everything in me not to glance at Peter or Randall. I couldn't believe it was the same cop from the other night—Kai's dad! Did he really not know it was the three of us at the station? Also, I was still hyperventilating over the chalk. Think about it, a diamond, the hardest substance in the world, and chalk, the softest, except for talc. This was something we learned in fifth grade science. So it had to be a joke, the chalk behind that mirror. That, or another clue. But why chalk?

Meanwhile, Randall was all cool. "Graffiti is a disgrace," he announced. I stared at him, wondering where he found the nerve. For all we knew, Filnik could still put two and two together and come up with runaway graffiti artist.

"Graffiti is ugly," Peter said next.

I wasn't one to be left out. "Graffiti doesn't mean anything," I added.

Then we were all grinning like fools as Filnik pulled into my driveway. He turned off the engine and looked at us. "Graffiti is more trouble than you think," he said. I thought, he's onto us, this is when we get the book thrown at us, or whatever cops did to juveniles.

But all he said was, "You boys stay in the car," as he got out and helped me to the front door. I dreaded the thought of seeing my parents. I'd rather see Peter's mom and the look on her face when she saw Randall. She'd be the happiest mom in the world.

Not my mom. Her face turned ashen when she opened the door and saw me limping on one foot beside Dobbs Ferry's finest law enforcement officer.

"Myla!" she yelled. Well, not "yell" exactly, because my mom doesn't do that. But as close to yelling in a quiet way as possible.

Filnik explained the whole thing in excruciating detail while she listened, throwing me appalled looks every few seconds. I wondered where Dad was, but I didn't say anything. I just waited and waited through the whole explanation, wondering when Filnik would announce all the charges against me. Would he take my fingerprints here or at the station? Would there be a photograph taken, too? Would I be written up in the newspaper by his daughter?

But at the end of his spiel, Filnik said, "All right. Consider this a warning, young lady. I don't want to run into you again at night where you don't belong. Got it?"

I didn't want to run into him either. I didn't think we'd have any problems. He and Mom said goodnight, and the front door was closed.

Mom's face was a picture of fury. "You don't know how worried we were," she fumed.

"Where's Dad?" I asked.

She didn't answer. Instead she took out her cell phone. It began to dawn on me that my "lookout" had failed, and Mom and Dad had realized I was gone. But why wasn't Cheetah coming down the stairs, telling everybody stuff already?

"It's all right, she's here," Mom said into the phone. "You can come home."

"Dad was looking for me?" I squeaked.

"They both were. Cheetah was hysterical. Do you have any idea what you did to him?"

"Oh! I'm so sorry." I felt terrible. This was worse than being brought home by a cop.

We sat on the sofa without Mom uttering a word. Getting yelled at would have been so much better. Then at last the front door opened, and Dad and my brother came in. Cheetah raced into the living room, and when he saw me, he kind of shrieked and landed on the sofa, burying his face into a cushion.

"Cheet, I'm sorry," I whispered. I didn't know what else to say. I laid a hand awkwardly on his back. He didn't say a word, but I could tell he was crying, and it was my fault. He was my little brother, and I'd left him behind.

Meanwhile, Mom and Dad grilled me on everything. While they did, Cheetah stayed with his face in the sofa cushion, but I knew he was listening as I explained about the necklaces and Peter's uncle Richard, and Randall being gone because he was looking for the diamonds. It took a long time and Mom and Dad butted in with more questions, but mostly they let me talk.

"Margaret," Mom said at the end of it. "She engineered the whole thing."

"She gave me the key to her attic," I said. "Did she want me to find Rose's things?"

"Margaret's always had that way of bringing people together, hasn't she?" Dad mused. "She was the one who rented her house to Shanthi. It's like she wanted Myla and Peter to meet."

"Or Randall to be found," Cheetah mumbled.

Mom shook her head. "How could she expect these kids to solve so many problems?"

We all fell silent, speculating over what Margaret did or didn't intend by making Peter and me neighbors. Was she playing God? Or was it all a big coincidence?

"Well, one problem's solved," Dad said. "Can you believe Myla climbed down a window?"

Mom shuddered. "You could've had a lot worse happen tonight. Didn't you realize that?"

"I was too busy," I said. "I didn't have time to think about falling."

"I knew Myla wasn't scared of heights anymore," Cheetah mumbled again. He still wouldn't look at me from the pillows.

"Can Cheetah and I be alone?" I asked.

While Dad and Mom were in the kitchen, I turned to Cheetah. His back was to me, but he had lifted his head from the cushion. "Did you know Randall did the *Om*s? And he's Mighty, too?"

He wiped his nose with the back of his hand. "Really?" he asked.

I nodded. "I think he used to be a jerk. Like, Peter was really mad at him for running off. But they're okay now. I think Randall feels sorry."

"Like you?" Cheetah asked.

I sighed. "Yeah, Cheet. I shouldn't have left you to be lookout. It's just I didn't want you to get hurt. See, Peter and I had this idea." I told him our plan to paint *Om*s all over Dobbs to stop everyone from finding the real *Om*. "But I'm glad we didn't do it, that we found Randall first."

"You could paint your wall instead," Cheetah said. "If you get tired of paper."

I smiled. "I like paper."

"Sometimes I go to your room to look at your wall." He twirled the cushion tassels with his finger. "That's why I was jumping on your bed when I broke it. I thought if I jumped, I'd see more of your wall. I'd see more of you."

"Cheet!" I felt suddenly smaller than ever. "You see a lot." I put my arms around him, even though I knew he wouldn't like it. We weren't the kind that hugged. He just sat there stiffly, letting me hug him, but he didn't move away either.

Finally I let go and asked what he'd done while I was gone. So he described how he'd made up excuses like wanting a glass of water from downstairs to pretending to stub his toe—anything to keep Mom and Dad from my room. He also stuffed pillows under my sheets to make it look like I was sleeping in my bed.

"Wow!" I said incredulously.

"I read *Harry Potter* with a flashlight in your room. I figured

I'd wait for you. But then I forgot about *my* bed. Mom saw I was missing, then figured out you were the one gone, not me."

Cheetah had done a lot. He had looked out for me, more than I thought he could. He was just like Peter, who had been searching for his brother. Cheetah had been searching for me, too. Why hadn't I noticed it before?

"Tomorrow let's decorate your wall, Cheet," I said suddenly. I didn't know why, except it was something I liked to do, and maybe he would, too.

"Really?" Cheetah flashed the biggest smile.

"Yeah, but with your own words. Like 'sequester.'"

He made a face. "I like 'illuminate' better. And 'bravado.'"

"I think everyone should go to sleep," Mom said. As Dad helped me upstairs, I looked at the gray-and-black bandanas belonging to Nike around my ankle. I wasn't sure how I'd get them back to him, if I'd ever see him again. I was hoping I would, though. He had pretty eyes, if you can say that about a boy. I liked his nickname, too, and his hair that was frizzy like mine.

Dad helped me to the bathroom and waited outside. When I came out I said, "I was wondering, maybe you could start teaching me yoga." I hopped a little. "I mean, when I'm better."

He looked at me and smiled. "Okay," he said. He pointed to my ankle. "Maybe we'll start with tree pose. You only need one foot to stand on for that."

"Ha-ha," I said.

Then as Dad was guiding me to my new bed, I saw it. "Dad!" I shouted. "Look! Someone's breaking into Peter's house!"

49 PETER

THERE'S THAT MOMENT WHEN YOU'RE STANDING on the porch with your brother, and you both have on the same Jordans. Which means if you squint your eyes, you can imagine it's the same as it ever was, without a cop ringing your doorbell, summoning your ma at an unholy hour. Then the door opened and all bets were off. We were in trouble—with the law, and our mother.

"What's he done?" Ma asked. She was staring at Randall, so I suppose she meant him. What was I then, the invisible son?

"Ma'am, I'm Officer Filnik. I found these two at the new construction site of the Keeper's House on Walnut. No one was hurt, but I'm escorting them home. This is their residence?"

Ma nodded. "They're okay?" she asked fearfully.

Filnik said we were. "But make sure they stay away from there. It's closed to the public."

"Of course." She paused. "Thanks for bringing them home, Officer."

Filnik turned to us. "I believe we're all lucky when we're given a second chance. Stay out of mischief. We've got a moon again."

A few minutes later he was unbelievably gone. We weren't going to jail! He didn't even take down our names. It seemed impossible that this guy who chased after my brother two nights ago was dropping us off home like a free taxi service. But what was that comment about the moon? Did he know who we were the entire time? Was this his way of letting us off the hook?

The door closed, and then it was us and our ma. And I started having my doubts. So far she hadn't shown a speck of gladness Randall was home. Like, I didn't see the sun rise in her face, just a weakening of her shoulders, and a sigh so deep and long it was like air being let out of a balloon. Maybe she was going to ask Randall to leave. Maybe she was going to say he had his chance to be in our family, and now that chance was gone. So we stood waiting, nobody saying anything. It was all quiet and strange and painful. Then Ma started crying. She cried so it was like her crying filled up all the space around us. At last she hugged Randall hard, almost like she was choking him.

There's nothing better than sitting down together and telling it as it is. Which is what my family did after that crying session ended. Ma made a big pot of coffee and even let me have some.

"You should have seen Uncle Richard getting all bent out of shape when the cop showed up," Randall said. He did an imitation of Uncle Richard looking mad as hell, and we all laughed. "If I didn't remember him before, I sure remember him now!"

"So how come he stopped seeing us after Pop died?" I asked.

Ma's smile faded. "I made mistakes, Petey. I thought I could protect you two by cutting off all relations with Pop's family. I blamed Richard for egging on Omar to look for the diamonds, and for living a life of danger. It wasn't fair. Richard may be many things, but he loved your dad. Most of all, I was angry at Rose for all the trouble she caused."

"Smith said there weren't many women diamond cutters," Randall said. "She said Grandma Rose was extraordinary."

"Ms. Smith," Ma corrected. "And yes, that's true. Rose was special. She wanted to carve her own path. Pop was the same way. You couldn't stop them from doing what they wanted, from who they wanted to marry, and how they wanted to live their lives. It's what I loved about your father."

From her room Ma brought out a cardboard box and put it on the dining table. She pulled out a photo album and handed it to me. She handed another one to my brother.

Randall and I glanced at each other.

"It's been a while since I looked at them," she said.

For the next hour, that's all we did. We looked through old photos. Ma showed us the wedding album, and she named everyone she saw. "See, that's my parents. That's my aunt from Baltimore, the one I stayed with when I went to high school. And look at Grandma Rose. She's wearing pink!"

"What's wrong with pink?" I asked.

Ma turned the page of the album. "There's Richard."

"He's got a goatee!" Randall exclaimed. "He looks like a fool!"

"Oh, but he had a way with the ladies," Ma said, smiling. She turned the page. "And here's your pop and me. Look how handsome he is." Pop was wearing a blue tux. He had a crooked smile, his arms hanging in that way that looked like Randall. I swallowed hard, but I wasn't sad. I was grateful. For the first time I was glad Randall looked like our pop. It was like, any time I wanted to remember my father, I could look at Randall, and they were both there, my brother and him.

Then we looked at pictures of Ma and Pop in college. I recognized the background now—the waterfront, Cedar Street, and the Dobbs train station. They'd met at Mercy College right here in this same town. I'd known that, and I'd seen these pictures a long time ago. But there was something sweet about seeing everything now. Like for the first time I believed it all really happened.

At last we got to looking at baby pictures, and Randall and me laughed our heads off. We were ugly babies. I was scrawny and Randall just had more hair than was legal for a four-year-old. Ma said she couldn't bear to cut his beautiful hair.

At some point I dragged down Grandma Rose's suitcase from the attic. We sifted through all the items like the diamond-cutting tools, and the purple sweater that even Ma exclaimed over. Then I pulled out the postcards sent to Margaret.

"I think these are from Grandma Rose," I said. "Who else could they be from? Pop?"

Ma agreed. "That's not Pop's hand. The address looks like Rose's handwriting."

"But when did Grandma Rose die?"

"About eight years ago," Ma said. "Why, Petey?"

"Myla and I noticed something the first time we saw these cards. I wasn't sure then but now I am. These are all postmarked after Grandma Rose died. The last one is two years ago."

Randall and Ma stared at me.

"What are you saying?" Ma asked. "That would be impossible. I saw the car. No one could have survived that crash."

"Look at the postmarks," I said. "I'm not making it up."

"Maybe the postcards were like code Grandma Rose used to tell Margaret she was okay. That would make her one down grandma," Randall said approvingly.

Ma shook her head. "Not even coming for her son's funeral? I don't believe it. Those postcards can't be from her."

"What if the Fencers threatened her?" I asked. "And she had to go into hiding?" But as soon as I mentioned the F word, Ma's face darkened.

"Those are the people who need to be in prison, that's what," she said.

"Who are they, the Fencers?" asked Randall. "Other than being class A jerks?"

"They steal diamonds and sell them for money," I said. "Right, Ma?"

Randall nodded. "Now I get it. And that Fencer was lying to you, Ma. That night after Pop died. He got the wrong floor number."

"The fortieth floor," I said.

"But that's wrong," Randall said. "There aren't forty floors. There's only thirty."

Ma nodded. "I knew he was lying already. There's something else I didn't tell anyone, not even Uncle Richard." We waited as she got up to refill her mug, then sat back down at the table.

"Your father was found outside the building all right. But the coroner said his injuries didn't reflect a fall from a great height. More important, he didn't fall on the sidewalk. He fell someplace else. Somebody moved him."

"That's crazy," Randall said. "That means—"

"He was murdered," Ma said. "The coroner found a single hair on Omar's clothes that wasn't his. We never found a match for that hair."

"How come you never told us?" I asked.

"Why did you need to know? We moved, that was the best I could do to keep us safe." Her face pursed together. "And if what you boys are telling me is true, maybe Pop found those diamonds after all. What he chose to do with them after that, nobody knows. But I'm telling you right now, it doesn't matter. We don't need anybody's dirty money to keep us afloat. You hear me?"

Randall rolled his eyes but he said, "I hear you, Ma." And it was like an earthquake happened, not the kind with the ground shaking beneath our feet, but like two powerful forces uniting together at last. Randall and my ma were actually agreeing on things for once. That's when I knew something serious had changed in Randall.

After Ma went to bed, Randall came up and looked around our room. "The house isn't so bad," he said. Then, "You put up my posters." He eyed the New York City and Michael Jordan posters on the wall appreciatively.

Just a few hours ago I'd shoved my brother down on the

sidewalk. But now I felt a tide of warmth. "So you're staying?"

He nodded. It was the best brother moment we had in a while, but then suddenly there was a large swooshing sound to our right, of the window being yanked open.

Randall stood in front of me instinctively, his arms spread out. "What are you doing here?" he said to the figure at the window. "Haven't you heard of the front door?"

50 PETER

TOPS JUMPED DOWN FROM THE SILL, BRUSHING off imaginary dirt from his sleeves. "Your house is harder to climb than the Keeper's House. But it's got these fantastic footholds. Though Jimmy wouldn't agree." He glanced at the window, where another face appeared.

Randall saw him and stepped back. "You brought your thug with you."

Jimmy jumped down next, untying a harness and rope from his waist. "I'm never doing that again."

I watched the second guy with a wave of fear. I recognized him right away. He was the one with the rings. Now he was here with Tops, and I knew I wasn't getting off so easy this time.

Randall's eyes narrowed. "You dudes aren't here for the view. What gives?"

Tops walked slowly around us. "Well, it's that chalk, Mighty. It was vexing, wasn't it? So close, and yet so far. All these years, I wasn't sure if Omar had found the diamonds or not. That was always the big question. Then at the Keeper's House, it was finally answered."

"Oh, yeah?" Jimmy asked. "What was that answer?"

"I told you, Jimbo. Their dad found them all right. And he had them ever since. Which leads me to you, Mighty."

"They're not here," Randall said shortly.

"I'm not so sure," Tops said. "I've been more patient with you than anybody said I should. And now you've played me for a fool."

"Tops, you stay away," Randall said. "You and Jimmy go out the same way you came in, and nobody's messing with nobody. We'll forget we ever heard about the diamonds."

Tops gave a laugh. "Mighty, that doesn't sound like you."

Randall didn't say anything, he just stood there, staring at Tops.

I watched them talking, trying to size up both guys. Tops was in his forties, but his legs were two walls of muscle and his arms were battle-axes—he could crush us, one in each hand, and whistle a tune while he did. And Jimmy was the one with rings on his fingers that cut like glass. And now that I took a closer look, the middle one actually had a diamond on it. No wonder I bled the way I did. So we couldn't use our fists with these clowns. We'd have to use our brains to get them out of our house. "You've got chalk all over your hands," I said to Tops.

He smiled. "You're the nice brother, right? The one without the attitude."

"Tops always got the chalk," Randall said, sneering. "It's his thing, along with thievery."

Tops's smile faded. "Maybe your pop should have made chalk his thing, too," he retorted.

"Of course my pop used chalk," I said. "He had tons of it."

"Oh, he used it all right. Just not . . ." He stopped.

"I bet Pop would spit on you if he saw you now," Randall said.

"It's your pop who held out on me," Tops said.

A pulse started in my neck. "You mean the night he fell, don't you?"

"What?" Tops asked.

"When he didn't have chalk—it was the night he fell."

Tops paused. "Not sure what you're getting at."

Meanwhile, Jimmy grabbed me by my shirtfront. "What are you all up in Tops's face for?"

Randall sprang toward me. "Leave him alone!"

I gasped but pressed on, my shirt still in Jimmy's grip. "Tops, how did you know my pop didn't have chalk with him that night?"

"I never said that," Tops said.

Jimmy shoved me so hard I fell on the floor. "What's the big deal with chalk?"

Randall helped me up. "Lay off with the chalk," he said to me.

I knew I was going to get a diamond-ringed fist in my face any second, but I went on. "You just said it, he didn't have his chalk." I pointed at Tops. "It's because you were there. You were his PK buddy that night." I really didn't know for sure, but at that moment, it was the only thing that made sense.

A look of disbelief crossed Randall's face. "No flipping way, Petey."

"None of it's true!" Tops exclaimed.

"Then how did you know it was thirty floors?" I pressed on. "You made a slip at Keeper's House."

"Hey, junior, it was forty," Jimmy said. "We all knew what happened to your daddy."

"No, you guys made up that number forty when you called our ma. But Tops knew the right one because he was there."

"Lots of people knew the floor number," Tops said. "It was in the newspaper."

"It wasn't," Randall said. "Petey's right. I never told you the floor number. You didn't come inside the building with me today. But you knew."

"Don't you think I visited the building before you did?" Tops asked. "Don't you think I had the same questions, the same yearning to figure it all out? I must have realized it then."

Randall pointed at him. "You're lying. You were there. And you moved my pop's body."

There was a silence. Was it true? Were we looking at our pop's murderer? But what proof did we have? What if Randall had gone out on a limb and now that limb was about to snap in half?

Meanwhile, Jimmy was looking from one face to the other. "What's going on here? Tops, do we have a situation?"

But by now, Tops's composure had finally cracked. "It was an accident," he said hoarsely. "Omar said there was plenty of scaffolding inside that was perfect for PK. We went in thinking we were safe. But Omar didn't have his chalk that night. Lots of people don't use it, but Omar always did. So he was doing a jump, when he lost his grip and . . ." Tops ran his hand through his stringy hair. "My fingerprints were all over the place. I had a record. I freaked out and called Bernie."

Jimmy was furious. "Tops, are you nuts? Shut up already. Don't tell these punks anything."

"Bernie's the one who told you to move my pop outside," Randall said. "What a scumbag."

Jimmy said, "Listen, enough of this. We want those diamonds, Mighty. We know one of you has them. If you don't cough them up, fine. We'll ask your mother." He reached in his pocket and flicked his knife open.

Tops gave Randall a hard look. "Time's up, Mighty. Sorry, but my uncle's been holding the gym and other stuff over me for years. The diamonds are the only way to pay him off and get my life back."

"Stop explaining everything," Jimmy huffed. "I say we cut them up and search the house."

By now I was sweating bricks. Was this nightmare ever going to end? There was no way we could let this pyscho near Ma. But I didn't know how Randall and I were getting ourselves out of this one either. And then suddenly downstairs, there was a loud rapping.

"Who's that?" Jimmy demanded.

We saw flashing red lights shine through the window outside. Then we all knew who was at the door. Randall and I had the same idea. I dove for Jimmy's legs as my brother went for Tops's midsection. Together we had Tops and Jimmy on the floor. Neither of us was strong enough to last for more than a few seconds, but maybe that was all we needed. So long as I stayed away from Jimmy's rings and his switchblade. Twice I dodged his flailing arm.

Downstairs, we heard Ma cry out, "WHAT'S GOING ON?" as voices met her at the door.

"Up here!" I shouted. Tops tried desperately to free himself, kicking his powerful legs at Randall, but my brother held on. Then I heard footsteps on the stairs, at least two pairs this time.

"You don't have a thing on me," Tops hissed. "It's all hearsay. I won't admit a thing."

"I know we have burglars," I said.

At that moment, two police officers appeared at our bedroom door. This time, it wasn't Filnik, but a different guy and a lady.

"Officers," I told them shakily, "these guys were breaking into our room."

The woman cop stepped forward. "We know. The girl next door called it in," she said as she led Tops and Jimmy in handcuffs from our room. That was the last time Randall and I saw them.

51 PETER

FOR SEVERAL MINUTES THE NEXT MORNING, I lay in the sunlight, hardly daring to move. It seemed like a dream, Randall back where I could see him lying in his bed every time I looked. Outside I heard seagulls, and the sound of the early train our ma had just missed. My legs were getting cramped so I stretched, feeling the footboard with my feet. My legs had grown in the last month Randall was gone. Our shoulders were now coming to the same height.

"You awake?" came Randall's voice from the other side of the room.

"Yeah."

"I've been up for the last hour. Damn, this bed is soft. Like sleeping on a pile of feathers."

We went back and forth, whispering about stuff that had happened, and what was going down for Tops and the rest of the Fencers.

"Will Bernie get caught, too?" I asked.

"He should. He was blackmailing Tops. Then I guess Tops had enough. He figured he could pay his uncle off with those diamonds. But you know how these thugs work. No money will pay them off for good."

"What do you think Bernie had on Tops?" I wondered.

"Something bad. Something that forced Tops's hand."

"So maybe Tops was caught in a hard place. Maybe he didn't make Pop fall."

Randall sneered. "Tops is a bucket of slime. He had a chance to go clean. He was ready for you and me to get cut up tonight. That makes him jail material in my book."

Then Randall asked me what happened to the duffel bag, and I told him it was in the closet.

"Important we don't lose it," Randall said. "It's Pop's legacy. The last thing of his we own."

I told him I'd gone through the whole bag while he was gone. "Even Myla helped," I added cautiously. I wanted him to know she had seen the bag, too. But he didn't seem bugged at all.

"Myla, that girl with the foot," was all he said. "She sure does talk a lot."

"She's smart." I thought for a moment. "Actually, it's more than that. She saved you, Randall. She saved you and our family. And she doesn't talk a lot. Only when she's got something to say, and to somebody she likes." I tried to think of all the things I could tell him so he'd understand. But that was the best I could do. Sometimes there just aren't words. There's only what you know. It was like Myla and me being two letters in the same word. Maybe that was what friendship was.

"She's got guts," Randall said agreeably. "You both looked through the bag?"

"Every last inch. Well, everything but the box of chalk. And then we—"

Randall sat up like a jack-in-the-box. "Quick, Petey, get me that box of chalk."

I didn't understand. "Why?"

He jumped out of bed. "Just give me the box, Petey." He grabbed a piece of paper off my desk and laid it on the ground while I got the chalk box from the duffel bag.

"Right here," Randall said. "Empty it on this paper."

Out tumbled a jumble of different shaped white chalk, mostly big, chunky pieces, and some little ones, too, and a powdery mess across the paper. Randall sifted through and lifted a small round piece. "This," he said.

"It's chalk."

"No, it's heavier."

It was beginning to dawn on me. "Are you saying what I think you're saying?"

We got a cup of water from the bathroom and washed off all the smaller pieces of chalk. Only they weren't chalk. We sat back and looked at what we had: twelve dull, yellow pieces, each the size of my thumbnail. "Rocks?" I asked.

"Roughs," Randall said triumphantly. "If I didn't see them with my own eyes at Rosen & Smith, I wouldn't have known. Don't you get it, Petey? He covered them with chalk dust and hid them in this chalk box. *Pop had the diamonds all along.*"

I stared at the twelve yellow pieces. They didn't even look like diamonds, but stones you'd find outside in the grass. I thought about everything I knew to be true, that diamonds were the hardest element in the world, that they came fully formed from somewhere deep inside the earth, that people spent their prized money just to own them. And my pop had spent time looking for them, too, these pieces of money left like a trail from Scottie to my grandma to him, and now us.

Truth is, I was excited and I was scared. I didn't know what finding twelve diamonds in your pop's duffel bag meant. Was the world going to swallow us whole, take us back to where the stones came from in the first place? Or would we rise, would we fly on the wave of all the money these jewels would bring us? How would our lives ever be the same again?

For Randall, it was uncomplicated. "Holy mother of God!" he yelled. "We're the stuff, Petey. We solved the puzzle. Not Bernie, not Tops, not anyone but us." He did a victory dance, then he hurried down the stairs yelling for Ma.

We told her the news, and once we did, I finally got what Randall was feeling, and I was swept up by the excitement of it all. Even Ma had a scared giddiness cross her face. How could anyone in the company of twelve diamonds be any different? We stood with stars in our eyes, we thought of all the things the diamonds could buy for us.

"Petey can go to college!" shouted Randall.

"No more painting in the streets," Ma intoned. "You get yourself a high school degree and maybe art school for you, Randall."

"A gallery," I said. "That's how the real artists do it. They get themselves seen for money."

"I could get down with that," Randall said, smiling. "And Ma, you could take a trip to India and see the Taj Mahal!"

But then as the hour wore on, the stars began to fade from our eyes, as we remembered where the stones had come from. "It's okay to dream," Ma said. "So long as we understand reality."

Then each of us came down, little by little, till we were all sitting at the dining table, this time looking at each other with a kind of sadness, but with a kind of smartness we had been learning the last month. It was Randall who said it first. "We need our lives back. No money can do that."

We knew the stones could buy us a lot. But returning them would give us more. And if they were real, maybe they could even give us the protection we'd never had so far.

In Ma's room, Randall found an envelope. He carefully folded the stones inside a piece of paper and put it inside the envelope. "I know somebody who can help. She can tell us if they're real. And I guess she'll know what to do after that."

"Ms. Smith?" I asked. "Can I come with you?"

Ma started to freak out in her old way. Then she settled down. She looked at both of us. "The old me would have said no. I'd say let's move away again, some place the Fencers won't find us. But I'm tired of running. I'm tired of the Fencers. We need to get this resolved once and for all. And I'm taking the day off to come with you."

"You never do that," I said, surprised. "Not even the holidays."

"I believe other people's blood can wait for once." She looked at her watch. "You both have breakfast. I'm having a shower. And Randall, put on another pot of coffee for me, will you?"

Outside I heard a car. Was it the garbage truck? No, just Myla's family pulling out of their driveway. Hard to believe we were all awake. Wait till she heard what Randall and me found in our pop's duffel bag. She'd be all over herself wondering why we didn't think of the chalk box first.

On my way to the kitchen, I almost tripped over Randall's shoes. "Watch where you're leaving these things," I called out to him over the sound of the coffee brewing. Not that he could hear me one bit. I moved the fakes to the mud room. They'd covered a lot of ground this year, bending and giving with Randall's feet. The twin Jumpmans had held their own, with only a few cracks. Just like mine. There was a magic in them after all, the magic of lasting, and lasting some more. The way I saw it, soon we'd be putting on our fakes that were fakes no more, but legits that would carry us to the train, and the city beyond. Then we'd show the world, my brother and me, how we'd take what our Ma had given us, and just how far we'd go.

52 MYLA

IT TURNED OUT I HADN'T BROKEN ANY BONES. I'd just sprained my ankle from my fall in the Keeper's House. Which meant hobbling my way through September, with Ana and Peter carrying my books for me. After my ankle healed, I started learning yoga from my dad. At first I wondered, how will a short person like me do all those bends and stretches? But what I learned was height doesn't really matter. It's all about the strength of your body and mind. Dad and I did our sessions at night, and afterward, I would lie in my new bed, feeling floaty and loose.

Sometimes Cheetah would come after yoga, or when I was doing homework, and read on my bed. It was nice hearing the crinkle of pages turning while I did math. And at night I slept pretty well, even though there were a few nights I'd grab my pillow and blanket and sleep on the rug. From there I could see the stars through my window, like I did that night on top of the garage. All this time I'd wondered about being noticed, but here I was noticing things that had been around me all this time, things I'd never stopped to really see. Like the stars. And Cheetah.

Lots of things were settling down in our lives. too. Turns out the diamonds were with Peter's family all along. Ms. Smith confirmed their authenticity and turned them in to the state for evidence. With that and Peter's and Randall's testimony, the Fencers went to jail, including Bernie. Tops did, too, for armed robbery and manslaughter. A hair that was found on Omar's body matched Tops's DNA. And a surveillance video found with Bernie showed Tops moving Omar's body outside. Jimmy also did time for armed robbery, and the only person who got away was Tyson. But Kai tracked him down when she saw him in a stolen vehicle and looked up the license plates in her dad's database. Turns out she made a good cop. She says now she wants to go into law enforcement like her dad.

After Scottie Biggs got out of jail, sometimes I'd see him at the Cedar Street Café. One day I asked him for his autograph. He was eating a grilled cheese sandwich, and he looked surprised. "Nobody's ever asked me for that," he said. He glanced curiously at my necklace, but I didn't flinch.

"I'm Peter Wilson's friend. He lives next door to me in Margaret's old house." I wanted to see what he'd say. Did he know who everyone was?

He signed my napkin. Then he pointed at my necklace. "You know who made that?"

When I nodded, he leaned back in his chair. "Well, since you're such good friends with Peter, tell him this. With the Fencers in jail, I had my people do a look around for me. Seems they found somebody who's been making jewelry for years up north near the border. She's one hell of a jewelry maker. I know because I've seen her work. And her hair's still red."

I stared at him, my jaw wide open. "Sir?"

He waved me away. "Now take that napkin and let me finish my sandwich in peace."

You can imagine the state *that* put me in.

For Thanksgiving, we were invited to Peter's house. Ana came, and she and Peter smiled and blushed at each other, but now it didn't bother me so much. Nike came, too, and he had on a new pair of bandanas so he said I could keep his old ones. He even showed me how to tie them on my wrists, and I felt swoony and happy while he did.

"When's the exhibit going to be ready?" Dad asked.

Shanthi said December.

"They're giving me a ribbon-cutting ceremony," Randall said, grinning.

"And it's not an exhibit," I told Dad. "It's an *installation*." Because Randall helped solve a crime *and* lots of people liked his *Om* at the station, the village council voted to keep it. With Mom's recommendations, they've hired an artist to seal the tag and make it permanent.

"Aren't you a feisty young lady?" Richard said to me.

"Oh, hush," said his mother. "You're just sore because she figured out the necklace and you didn't. Selling it was the best thing I ever did."

"I never said she wasn't smart." Richard smiled, and then he didn't seem half as bad. But Mom's still mad at him for breaking into my room and defacing our front door. She only warmed up a little after he replaced our door for free. He still hasn't fixed his muffler.

Once, I told Peter my family's theory about how us being neighbors was no accident.

"Margaret made everything happen," I said. "Kind of like God."

Peter looked skeptical. "I barely remember her."

"Well, I'm not sure if I agree," I said. "But it does seem like she orchestrated it all."

"If you and me weren't neighbors, I wouldn't have found Randall, that's what," Peter said.

"Because of Margaret."

"Because of you. Nobody can take that credit but you, Myla. You got to own it."

I flushed under his praise. Finder and Keeper. That was us.

"There's a kind of magic that goes on in the universe, is what I say," Peter said. "If you want to call that God, or if you want to call that Margaret, all right."

It seemed that the universe was working in our favor. I knew it as soon as the doorbell rang. I grabbed Peter to come with me. This was a surprise for him, a month in the planning.

On our way past the dining table, I expected Cheetah to leap out of his chair and tag along. But he went on talking to Randall, asking him where he learned to do graffiti.

"You don't learn, bro," Randall was telling him. "You just do."

It was weird seeing them together. Peter heard them, too, and we smiled at each other. I guess some things with Cheetah will never change. Like I'll always be impatient, and I'll always want to do things without Cheetah trying to help. And he'll always try to spell out what I'm thinking, whether I like it or not. But what *has* changed is knowing all of it, and knowing that when you're in a family, you need to look over your shoulder. Because sometimes it's you up ahead, and sometimes it's you coming from behind.

At the front door I said to Peter, "You can't get mad. You can't say, why didn't you tell me before? These things have to happen suddenly, or they don't happen at all."

"Well, now you're just scaring me," Peter said. "Who's on the other side of the door?"

When we opened it, she was facing the other way. I suppose she was looking at the Palisades in the distance, those majestic cliffs that had lasted longer than any of us. When she turned our way, a gentle wind began to blow, picking up the ends of her copper hair.

One glance and I could tell she and Peter knew each other all over again.

Rose reached out to him, her weathered hands extending across the cement steps.

"Peter," she said.

FACTS AND FICTION

Finding Mighty is a modern mystery that brings diamonds, parkour, graffiti, yoga, and trivia about the old waterworks system of New York City all to the historic village of Dobbs Ferry, New York. Here's a list to separate some facts from fiction.

George Washington and his soldiers camped in Dobbs Ferry: **TRUE**
During July and August of 1781, General George Washington and his Continental Army troops really did camp in Dobbs Ferry and the neighboring area. From there, Washington and his soldiers would continue their revolutionary march to Virginia and victory.

The Keeper's House is real: **TRUE**
Built in 1845 in Dobbs Ferry, the Keeper's House was one of the houses provided for the Keepers of the Croton Aqueduct. Following renovations, today the Keeper's House is both a designated landmark and a visitors' center for the Friends of the Old Croton Aqueduct (FOCA).

The High Bridge is the oldest standing bridge in New York City: **TRUE**
The High Bridge was completed in 1847 and is older than the George Washington and Brooklyn bridges. After a period of disrepair, it was reopened to the public in 2015 following its restoration.

Parkour is only meant for doing dangerous stunts: **FALSE**
It's not all about jumping off buildings! Parkour is an urban sport used for flexibility and fitness training. Charles Moreland, a parkour trainer, explains in his TED talk that parkour is a sport suitable for all ages and abilities. He goes further to say that parkour is a way to overcome your obstacles, physical and mental, and learn how to move efficiently through your environment.

The Diamond District is a real place: **TRUE**

The Diamond District is located on West Forty-Seventh Street in Manhattan and is one of the world's largest shopping districts for the buying, selling, and cutting of diamonds.

St. Vincent Avenue is a real street in Yonkers: **FALSE**

Yonkers is the largest and one of the most culturally diverse cities in Westchester County, New York. But if you're looking, you won't find St. Vincent Avenue. The street is a fictional one where strange and mysterious events happen. Similarly, Cherry Street, where Myla and Peter live in Dobbs Ferry, is a made-up street where equally strange and mysterious events take place.

There is permanent art installed at the Dobbs Ferry Train Station: **TRUE**

At this station, you won't spot an *Om* tag that Randall painted one moonless night. Instead, you'll see on the wall the lovely floral mosaic: *Floating Auriculas*. This permanent public art was commissioned by the Metro Transit Authority Arts for Transit, and created by Nancy Blum in 2007.

Om is an important sound in yoga: **TRUE**

Om is a sacred syllable appearing at the beginning and end of Sanskrit prayers and texts. It is widely used in yoga as a way to attune your body and mind, and turn your attention inward.

You can find *Om* tags around New York City: **FALSE**

The *Om* tags painted by Omar, then later by his son Randall are fictional. But if you drive on the Hutchinson River Parkway in Westchester County, you *might* see *Omar* tags along the highway walls and on the backs of signs. I don't know the real story behind those tags. *Finding Mighty* is the one I imagine in its place.

ACKNOWLEDGMENTS

Just like the many elements running through the lives of Myla, Peter, and Randall, this book came into being by the love and immeasurable importance of so many people.

I thank my beloved family, Suresh, Keerthana, and Meera, for holding me up and leading me forward, for listening to all my absurd story lines, and most of all, for building me a room of my own. I thank my parents as always, for being the first to send me out into the world as a writer.

Thanks to my superman agent, Steven Malk, who saw the potential of this story in its earliest stages, and who helped me chisel away at this "rough" until I was left with a book that shines. This book could never have existed without him.

Many thanks to Courtney Code, Erica Finkel, Pamela Notarantonio, and the rest of the Abrams team for helping my book reach its final form; and especially to Susan Van Metre, my fearless editor, who is just like Myla: curious, bighearted, and the truest reader of words. One of my happiest book moments was spending an afternoon with Susan in Dobbs Ferry, talking about characters and ideas, and soaking up in person the world of my novel.

A huge thanks to R. Kikuo Johnson, who brilliantly conceived the world of my story on the jacket cover. If you look, you will see everything there. And thank you to my friend, Meena V., for being our brave and beautiful cover model.

A big thank-you to the Friends of the Croton Aqueduct (FOCA), Mavis Cain, its president, and the Dobbs Ferry Historical Society for all their valuable information, resources, and tours. And thank you to Springhurst Elementary School for inviting me to speak to your fourth graders. They gave me some of the best ideas about landmarks and interesting buildings in Dobbs Ferry!

I'm also grateful for the Museum of the City of New York's "City as a Canvas" exhibition on graffiti, the entertaining and meticulous YouTube tutorials on parkour by Jesse La Flair, and all the fascinating information I garnered on diamonds and roughs by Diamond Expert Person who wishes to remain unnamed.

Special thanks to Olugbemisola Rhuday-Perkovich for critiquing the manuscript when it was completed, and to Jacklyn Dolamore, April Henry, Anne Marie Pace, and Melodye Shore for reading earlier drafts.

And last but not least, I'd like to express my gratitude for my indomitable writing group: Sayantani DasGupta, Veera Hiranandani, and Heather Tomlinson. They read draft after draft after draft! Eternal thanks to them for reading and improving my work, month by month, year by year, and for keeping me on the path of writing.

FINDING MIGHTY READING GUIDE

DISCUSSION

Before You Begin

FINDING MIGHTY IS A MYSTERY ABOUT FINDING A missing brother. But it's also a story about finding family. Pay attention to the ways Myla and Peter learn to value their siblings and assume responsibility for one another. Myla and Peter also come from different backgrounds, which shape the ways they respond to friendship, family life, and even detective work. Understanding how they relate to the world and to their families will help you understand the mystery behind Peter's missing brother.

Questions

1. As you read *Finding Mighty*, use the Mystery Organizer to track clues and suspects. Will you discover where the diamonds are hidden before the characters do?

2. Setting plays a major role in this mystery. Identify the important locations, buildings, and landmarks in the text, and explain why they are significant to the story.

3. *Finding Mighty* is told through alternating points of view. How does switching between narrators affect the telling of the mystery? Do you appreciate hearing different voices? Why or why not?

4. What personality traits does Chari use to develop the central characters? Which characteristics and motivations stand out to you? Provide text evidence to support your ideas.

5. Discuss how the relationship between the two main characters and their siblings evolve throughout the story. Identify the events that change their relationships. Compare and contrast the two sets of relationships, using the Character Chart to support your thinking.

6. Chari skillfully embeds clues in the novel. Were you able to identify them before finishing the story? Go back and locate those hidden clues. Use the Mystery Organizer to record your thoughts and ideas.

7. The author teases readers with false clues (red herrings) to lead them astray. In what ways did the author distract you from solving the mystery?

8. Suspense is an element writers use to make readers feel uncertain about the outcome of a story. Recall when you began quickly turning pages to discover what would happen next. Explain how Chari creates suspense in *Finding Mighty*.

9. Select passages in the story that were funny, interesting, revealing, or striking in some way. Share your choices with a partner and discuss why the passages made you stop and think.

FINDING MIGHTY WORKSHEETS

MYSTERY ORGANIZER

Title	
Detectives	Suspects
Other Characters	
Where does the story take place?	

What is the mystery that needs to be solved?

Clues

★ Put a star next to the clue that solves the mystery!

Who found it?

CASE CLOSED! How was the mystery solved?

Red herrings are false clues to throw you off track. Name some that the author used.

CHARACTER CHART

Describe the relationship between the siblings at the beginning of the story.	
Peter & Randall	Myla & Cheeta
1.	1.
2.	2.
3.	3.

Describe the relationship between the siblings at the end of the story.	
Peter & Randall	Myla & Cheeta
1.	1.
2.	2.
3.	3.

Identify three events from the text that result in changes to the sibling relationships.	
Peter & Randall 1. 2. 3.	Myla & Cheeta 1. 2. 3.
Compare and contrast	
Peter & Randall	Myla & Cheeta

MORE ACTIVITIES

Background Information: Parkour

What is parkour? Watch Charles Moreland's Ted Talk to learn more about this growing discipline of physical expression: youtube.com/watch?v=3x-vqr3ZnZE.

The Big Debate: High Art or High Crime?

Myla and her mother have different ideas on the role of graffiti in city life. Myla thinks graffiti is a type of art but her mother, an urban planner, views graffiti as vandalism. Where does one draw the line? Research two views on graffiti: Graffiti as Art, or Graffiti as Vandalism. Whose arguments and evidence are more convincing and why?

The Writing on the Wall

Graffiti writers pride themselves on their "hand style" or way of writing letters to communicate with the world. Design a "tag" (a special name or symbol) that reflects your own identity and personality. Create a wall mural using markers, paint, or spray chalk using your tag.

Social Emotional Learning

In *Finding Mighty*, Myla and Peter express feelings of inadequacy and doubt. Recall a time when you felt excluded or made someone feel this way. Write about the experiences, including strategies you can use to support friends who are excluded, and what you can do yourself to change unkind behavior. Write a letter of advice to Myla or Peter, using the knowledge gained in the writing exercise.

Field Trip to Ossining, NY

An important landmark in *Finding Mighty* is the Old Croton Aqueduct, a waterworks system that includes High Bridge and underground tunnels, which was used to bring freshwater to New York City from 1842 until 1900. This system is no longer in use, but you can still visit the Aqueduct in Ossining, where you can step inside the actual 1842 brick water tunnel and learn about its history. To plan a trip, visit the Friends of the Old Croton Aqueduct website at aqueduct.org.

This discussion guide was developed by Jenice Mateo-Toledo, M.Ed, an English as a New Language educator in the Hastings-on-Hudson School District in Westchester, NY. She holds master's degrees in Literacy Education, Educational Leadership, and English as a New Language. She is currently a doctoral student in the Curriculum and Teaching Department at Teachers College, Columbia University. This guide can be downloaded from amuletbooks.com.

Check out these other great reads!